George Melville Baker

The Social Stage

Original Dramas, Comedies, Burlesques, and Entertainments...

George Melville Baker

The Social Stage
Original Dramas, Comedies, Burlesques, and Entertainments...

ISBN/EAN: 9783744768801

Printed in Europe, USA, Canada, Australia, Japan

Cover: Foto ©Andreas Hilbeck / pixelio.de

More available books at **www.hansebooks.com**

THE LAST LOAF.

THE SOCIAL STAGE
BOSTON: LEE AND SHEPARD.

THE

SOCIAL STAGE:

ORIGINAL

DRAMAS, COMEDIES, BURLESQUES, AND ENTERTAINMENTS

FOR

HOME RECREATION, SCHOOLS, AND PUBLIC EXHIBITIONS.

By GEORGE M. BAKER,

AUTHOR OF "AMATEUR DRAMAS," "THE MIMIC STAGE," "AN OLD MAN'S PRAYER," ETC.

BOSTON:
LEE & SHEPARD, PUBLISHERS.
NEW YORK:
LEE, SHEPARD, & DILLINGHAM.
1871.

Rand, Avery, & Frye, Printers, Boston.

TO

AN OLD FRIEND AND FELLOW-TRAVELLER,

HENRY C. BARNABEE, ESQ.,

NEVER

"TOO LATE FOR THE TRAIN"

WHEN HIS VALUABLE ASSISTANCE IS NEEDED IN A GOOD CAUSE,

This Book

IS FRATERNALLY INSCRIBED.

CONTENTS.

PAGE.

THE LAST LOAF 7

A GRECIAN BEND 43

TOO LATE FOR THE TRAIN 65

SNOW-BOUND 93

BONBONS 139

LIGHTHEART'S PILGRIMAGE 191

THE WAR OF THE ROSES 205

THIRTY MINUTES FOR REFRESHMENTS 219

"A LITTLE MORE CIDER" 241

"NEW BROOMS SWEEP CLEAN" 263

PREFACE.

The plays comprised in "The Social Stage," like those in "Amateur Dramas" and "The Mimic Stage," have been prepared for the special use of amateurs, with a view to "home production" and the school platform. Some of them have been written at the request of instructors in the public schools, committees of literary societies, and temperance organizations; and, having been performed with success under their direction, may be said to have received the stamp of public approval. The musical and dramatic entertainments, "Bonbons," "Snow-Bound," and "Too Late for the Train," have been publicly performed, and received with favor. "The Grecian Bend," "The War of the Roses," and "Lightheart's Pilgrimage" originally appeared in "Oliver Optic's Magazine;" while "The Last Loaf," "Thirty Minutes for Refreshments," and "A Little More Cider" are *débutantes*. All are specially commended to the wants of the social circle, where they can be produced at a very little expense, and where they will at least afford amusement, if not instruction, for the long winter nights. The author takes this opportunity to thank those individuals and associations who have forwarded to him programmes, photographs, and notices, where his pieces have been performed. Such remembrances are most kind, and will always be appreciated.

G. M. B.

207 West Springfield Street, Boston.

*** All the plays in this collection are published separately, and can be had of the publishers. "Snow-Bound," 25 cents; "Bonbons," 25 cents; others, 15 cents each.

THE LAST LOAF.

A DRAMA IN TWO ACTS.

CHARACTERS.

Mark Ashton, a Silversmith (thirty-eight years of age).
Caleb Hanson, a Baker (forty years of age).
Harry Hanson, his son (eighteen years of age).
Dick Bustle, a Journeyman Baker (twenty-five years of age).
Tom Chubbs, a Butcher (twenty-five years of age).
Kate Ashton, Mark's wife (thirty-six years of age).
Lilly Ashton, their daughter (sixteen years of age).
Patty Jones, a Yankee girl (twenty-two years of age).

COSTUMES.

Mark Ashton. Act 1, Neat modern dress, with breakfast-jacket. Act 2, Rusty-black suit and black necktie, without collar; general seedy appearance.

Caleb Hanson. Act 1, Blue coat, brass buttons, white vest, light pants. Act 2, Brown coat, plaid vest and pants.

Harry Hanson. Modern suits.

Dick Bustle. Act 1, Short light pants, white stockings, shoes, plaid vest, green jacket, paper cap. Act 2, Blue sailor-rig, — pants, shirt, and jacket, — with paper cap as in first act.

Tom Chubbs. Act 1, Butcher's frock — white — and cap. Act 2, Butcher's frock — blue — and tall hat.

KATE ASHTON. Act 1, Handsome evening dress. Act 2, Black dress, white collar and cuffs.

LILLY ASHTON. Act 1, Pretty evening dress, flowing curls. Act 2, Plain black dress white apron, collar, and cuffs.

PATTY JONES. Act 1, Brown dress, white apron, collar, and cuffs, cap. Act 2, Plaid dress.

A period of five years supposed to elapse between the acts.

ACT 1. SCENE.—*Apartment in* MARK ASHTON'S *house. Table,* C., *at which sits* MARK ASHTON, L., *reading a newspaper.* KATE ASHTON, R., *sewing. Lounge,* R. *Piano,* L., *at which sits* LILLY, *playing "Home, sweet Home," as the curtain rises* (should it be inconvenient to have a piano on the stage, let LILLY sit L., engaged with some fancy needle-work, and sing, if she can, "Home, sweet Home"). *Flowers, little knick-knacks, any thing to make the room look cosy, should be displayed about the stage.*

Mark. "Home, sweet Home." Ah, Kate! blest is the man who can say that, conscious he is the possessor of such a treasure. Now here am I, Mark Ashton, once a gay, thoughtless dog, throwing my money away as fast as earned, never taking heed of the morrow,—easy-going Mark Ashton, always ready for a lark. But across my path steps a neat, pretty maid,—don't blush Kate,—and, presto, change! before I know it, up springs a dear home, with a loving wife to adorn it, and a sweet little daughter — I declare, the girl is listening!

Kate. Of course she is; astonished to find her sedate father so far forget himself as to indulge in such absurd panegyrics.

Lilly. Why, mother, where did you find that stupendous word?

Mark. Ha, ha! Kate, you astonished her more than I did. Lilly, my dear, it strikes me that you and Harry Hanson are very intimate.

Lilly. Why, pa! I haven't seen Harry for ever and ever so long.

Mark. No, not since twelve o'clock, when I saw him beauing you home from school.

Lilly. But I can't help it if he happens to come along when school is out, and is coming straight home, can I?

Mark. Oh! certainly not; nor can you help taking the longest route, and managing to get home after dinner is cold.

Kate. Now, Mark, don't hector Lilly about Harry Hanson. If they like each other's company, there's no harm in it.

Mark. Well, I don't know about that. Caleb Hanson is a queer fish, and, since he has made money, a little inclined to be proud. He might object to this intimacy; and, as he is my oldest friend, I should not like to quarrel with him to humor a little girl who —

Lilly. You love very dearly, and to whom you never refuse any thing. If Mr. Hanson don't like it, send him to me. I could just twist him round my fingers —

Mark. As you do everybody else. Well, I won't meddle; but be careful, child, for matrimony is a terrible thing to contemplate.

Kate. Matrimony! I believe, Mark, you are losing your senses, to talk so to a girl only sixteen.

Mark. Only sixteen! 'Tis a dangerous age. I

remember the time when a young lady only sixteen entrapped me into a confession —

Kate. Lilly, you had better go up stairs: your father is quite ill.

Mark. No, no: don't send her away. I'll behave myself, indeed I will: I only wished to caution —

Lilly. Shall I go, mother?

Mark. No, don't. I'm dumb: give me "Home, sweet Home" again, and I will be very quiet.

Harry. (*Outside*, L.) Thank you, Patty. Don't trouble yourself. I'll find the way.

Lilly. Why, that's Harry! Now, what sent him here?

Mark. How innocent, — and only sixteen!

Enter HARRY HANSON, L., *with a bouquet.*

Harry. Ah! all here? Good-evening, Mrs. Ashton. Good-evening, Mr. Ashton.

Kate. Good-evening, Harry.

Mark. Come right in, Harry: glad to see you; always glad to see you.

Harry. Thank you. You are very kind. I brought a few flowers for Lilly (*presenting bouquet*).

Lilly. Oh! thank you, Harry. Ar'n't they beautiful, mother? Oh, I'm so much obliged to you for thinking of me!

Harry. Oh! it's no consequence. I happened to see them in a store on my way home, and they looked so pretty I thought I would buy them. After I had bought them, I did not know what to do with them, and so I — I — you'll excuse my bringing them to you, won't you?

Lilly. Why, Harry, I shall prize them very much because you did bring them; and I shall love — that is — I — shall like you all the better.

Mark. Kate, don't you think the young people could get along with their *eyes* a little better if we retired?

Kate. I think so, Mark. Lilly, you must entertain Harry till I return. I must give directions to Patty about breakfast. (*Exit*, L.)

Mark. By George! I forgot all about that letter of Smith's. Make yourself at home, Harry. I'll be back soon. (*Exit*, R.)

Lilly. O Harry! it was so kind of you to bring me those flowers, so fresh and sweet (*sits on lounge*).

Harry (*sits beside her*). I'm so glad you like them. After I left you to-day, I thought what a long time it would be before I saw you again to-morrow; and I tried to think of some excuse to come to-night, when these flowers attracted my attention, and away I went after them. Wasn't it a jolly good excuse?

Lilly. Harry, you need not find excuses to bring you here: we're always glad to see you. I'm sure father and mother are always glad to see you; and you cannot doubt that I am.

Harry. No, indeed, Lilly; of you I am sure. But to come here, where you are all so happy, seems like an intrusion. It's such a change from our old gloomy home! Since mother died, that place has been like a prison to me. Father never did take much notice of me, and now he absolutely shuns me. I can't stand it much longer. Some dark night I shall tie my clothes up in a bundle, creep out of the house, and wander off in search of fortune.

Lilly. What! run away? You don't mean it?

Harry. Ay, but I do. You know Capt. Bangs?

Lilly. Of course I do; and like him too: he's such a splendid sailor! I do like sailors. If I was a man, I'd be one, and climb up the main hatches and the jib-booms, and heave-ho with the best of 'em.

Harry. Now heave to, as the captain says. I've been talking with him. He's off to-morrow morning, bright and early, for China; and he wants me to go with him.

Lilly. What! you, Harry?

Harry. Yes: he says that it only takes five years to make a fortune in China. Wouldn't it be grand to come back in five years, rich, respected, and able to snap my fingers at the best of 'em?

Lilly. Yes; and with your head shaved, and a long queue dangling behind. Oh! I shouldn't like that.

Harry. What would you do if I should accede to the captain's proposal?

Lilly. Cry my eyes out. Oh, you mustn't go, Harry!

Harry. Well, I haven't gone yet; and, if I don't make up my mind to-night, my chance is lost. But come, Lilly; put on your hat, and go take a walk. It's a beautiful moonlight night.

Lilly. Oh, that will be splendid! Wait till I get my hat. (*Runs off*, R.)

Harry. She's a dear little girl. She'll make some fellow very happy one of these days. Heighho! I wonder if it will be me. Precious little chance I have of ever winning her. Father is evidently disposed to keep me under his thumb, and bring me up to a life of idleness.

When I propose to seek some occupation by which to earn my own living, he laughs at me, and tells me the place for boys is at home. Boy, indeed! He will yet find the boy can think and act for himself. Why should I stay here, to be the plaything of his changing humors, when Capt. Bangs offers me such a chance to make my fortune? why wait?

Lilly. (*Outside*, R.) One minute, Harry, and I'll be with you.

Harry. Ah! there's the answer. The old, old story. How can I leave her?

Enter LILLY, R.

Lilly. Come, Harry, tie my hat, and I am ready.

Harry (*tying the hat*). Certainly. What a pretty hat!

Lilly. Do you like it? I'm glad of that.

Harry. The hat is pretty, and the face —

Lilly. Now, Harry Hanson, don't be foolish. Why, how long you are tying it!

Harry. I'm not used to it, Lilly.

Lilly. Well, you needn't get so near it.

Harry. Something bothers me.

Lilly. What is it?

Harry. Your lips. (*Kisses her.*)

Enter DICK BUSTLE, L., *with a small account-book in his hand.*

Dick. Ahem! Now, then, what is it, white or brown?

LILLY *gives a little scream, and steps back*, R. HARRY *starts to* L. DICK, C.

Harry. Dick Bustle, what sent you here?

Dick. Business, Master Harry, business. I'm on my rounds, taking orders for the morning bread. What is it, Miss Lilly, — white or brown? Either, both, or neither? Square, brick, family, twists, rolls, or muffins?

Lilly. I'm sure I don't know. You must ask Patty Jones.

Dick. But I can't find her. She's not in the domain of pots and kettles; and, if she has retired to her domicile beneath the eaves, you surely would not expect me to ascend to that hallowed and sacred retreat, would you?

Harry. Nonsense, Dick. Your language is altogether too fine for a baker.

Dick. Well, I suppose it is. 'Tis the fruit of my early edication. I was born for a higher sphere; but Fortune, the fickle goddess, frowned upon my tender youth, and left me, like the lilies of the field, to toil and spin.

Lilly. What an idea! The lilies of the field — "they toil not, neither do they spin."

Dick. Don't they? Well, I knew 'twas one or t'other. It's this confounded business bothers me. Mixing so much dough with my hands rather mixes things in my head, and makes me —

Harry. A regular dough-head. I see.

Dick. Yes, exactly. No, — no, — I don't mean that.

Harry. But I do. Dick, you're the best fellow in the world; but you do muddle things dreadfully. Let books alone, and stick to your business.

Dick. Never! I'm determined to rise in the world.

Harry. Then stick to your business. You'll find plenty of opportunities to *rise* in that.

Dick. No, Master Harry: I'm not in my true *spear.* Fate has something better in store for me. I'm determined to be a philosopher, or an inventor, or a discoverer. I'll be a second Christopher Columbus, and discover a new world. By-the-by, how about that little China scheme. Made up your mind to go?

Harry. No: I've given it up.

Dick. Given it up! You don't mean it! Why, there never was such a chance. Fame, fortune, every thing, awaiting you in the great empire of pigtails and Schushong. You don't mean it!

Harry. Yes, I do, Dick. There are ties that bind me here, that I haven't the heart to break. Come, Lilly, are you ready?

Lilly. Quite, Harry. Good-by, Dick — I mean Mr. Bustle, philosopher, discoverer, inventor, baker. Ha, ha!

Harry. Stick to your dough, Dick. (*Exeunt* LILLY *and* HARRY, L.)

Dick. Stick to my dough! Not if I knows myself. Now, there's a youth, with Fortune a-winkin' at him with both eyes, turnin' away and goin' straight to destruction with a pretty girl a-hangin' on his arm. Ties that bind him! Nothin' on airth but that gal's apron-string. Jest let old Hanson find out what's goin' on, and he'd snap that air tie shorter than pie-crust. Another slip-up, Dick. Buttered side down, agin, Bustle. I did hope Harry would have taken up with Capt. Bangs's offer; and then with me to protect his gentle youth, how we would hev made them air Chinamen howl! But it's no use. In the poetic language of Smith, Jones, or some great poet, —

> I never had a piece of bread
> *Particularly* long and wide,
> But what it fell upon the floor,
> And always on the buttered side.

What is to be, won't, on this particular occasion, the prophets and so forth to the contrary notwithstandin'.

Enter PATTY JONES, R.

Patty. Law, Mr. Bustle, is that you?

Dick (*pulling out his account-book*). Exactly. White or brown? either, both, or neither? Brick, family, twist, square, rolls, or muffins?

Patty. Law, Mr. Bustle, I don't know. You must ask Mrs. Ashton.

Dick. And will you be kind enough, Miss Patty, and obliging enough, Miss Jones, to seek Mrs. Ashton, and propound to her the necessary questions, whereby I may obtain the knowledge of her requirements in the way of bread, Miss Jones?

Patty. Law, Mr. Bustle, in what a highly edifying, romantic, and elegant style you do talk! Been at the dictionary agin, hey?

Dick. Dictionary! 'tis my pocket companion; the pillow on which this weary head reposes when night falls upon the tired earth, and — and — the what — what you may call 'ems — fold — their — things —

Patty. Ha, ha! Dick, it's no use: you'll never be a

scholar. So drop the big words, and sit down and let's have a real good old-fashioned gossip.

Dick. With all my heart, Patty Jones. I'll lay aside my learning, and be, like you, a common clod.

Patty. Clod! and pray what do you mean by that? A common clod, indeed! Mr. Bustle, there's the door.

Dick. Now, don't get mad, Patty: 'twas only a *lapsus linguæ.*

Patty. Oh! was that all? Well, Dick, I'll forgive you. Do you know I've got something nice to tell you? I'm going somewhere.

Dick. Well, that is a piece of information highly conducive —

Patty. Mr. Bustle, there's the door.

Dick. Now, don't get mad, Patty. I must let off these big words once in a while.

Patty. Very well, Mr. Bustle: when you feel inclined to do so, just waste them on the desert air, not on me.

Dick. You are going somewhere?

Patty. Oh, yes! I'm going to singing-school to-morrow night with Tom Chubbs.

Dick. What! you, Patty Jones, — a high-toned damsel, — thus to demean yourself by accepting the attentions of such an insignificant, ignoble —

Patty. Mr. Bustle, there's the door.

Dick. Let it stay there. Tom Chubbs, indeed! — a man who cuts up hogs, slices steaks, dissects calves. Confound him, he's nothing but a calf himself!

Patty. He's clever, polite, and don't use big words. Why shouldn't I go with him?

Dick. He's nothing but a butcher.

Patty. And you nothing but a baker.

Dick. Don't go with him, Patty.

Patty. Why not? He's dying for me.

Dick. And so am I. O Patty Jones! you little know the heart that beats within this tender breast. Turn from this bloody butcher, and smile upon the high-toned baker.

Patty. Dick Bustle, you're a donkey. Your head, never too steady on your shoulders, has been completely turned by your trying to fill it with scraps of wisdom, tumbled in like old iron in a junk-shop. High-toned baker, indeed! I wouldn't have you if there wa'n't another man in creation.

Dick. Buttered side down agin, Bustle! Patty Jones, farewell. How I have loved you! I — you — that is, both of us — confound it, I'm going off to the far antipodes, where woman's smile can never reach me more. I'm a broken-hearted man, from this time henceforth and forever more.

Patty. Save the pieces, Dick. They may come handy some time.

Dick. And can you jest at such a time?

Patty. Of course I can. (*Sings.*)

"For I care for nobody, — no, not I,
And nobody cares for me,"

except Tom Chubbs the butcher.

Dick. Oh! that's the last camel that broke the — no — no — that's the last straw —

Hanson. (*Outside*, L.) Doors wide open, and nobody at home!

Patty. Gracious! why, that's Mr. Hanson! (*Exit*, L.)

Dick. O Lord! Old Hanson! Buttered side down agin, Bustle! Now, what's to be done? He'll find me here, and won't there be a breeze! This comes of neglecting business for pleasure. I wish I was well out of this. He's coming this way, and I can't get out of it. He won't stop long; so I'll make a merit of necessity, and crawl under that lounge. (*Crawls under lounge, face towards audience.*)

Enter PATTY *and* MR. HANSON, L.

Hanson. You're sure he is at home, Patty?

Patty. Oh, yes, sir! he's up stairs with Mrs. Ashton. Sit down, sir, and I'll run and tell him you are here. Why, where can Dick have gone? (*Exit*, R.)

Hanson. Snug quarters here. Mark is doing well, and that wife of his is a jewel. Well, we both started fair in the world; but fate has dealt kindly with him, while upon me she has showered her hardest blows. How comfortable every thing looks here! Mark can't have laid by much money: that's where I have the advantage of him; but I'd give it all for the happiness he must enjoy in this little nest.

Enter MARK, R.

Mark. Why, Cleb, old boy, I'm glad to see you!

Hanson. Ah, Mark! thank you, thank you.

Mark. Sit down, and make yourself at home. We don't see half enough of each other. (*They sit* R. *and* L. *of table.*)

Hanson. That's true, Mark. One would scarce believe

that you and I were once such cronies. Why, twenty years ago we were inseparable.

Mark. Yes, always together; gay, happy, thoughtless boys, up to all manner of mischief, and ever ready for a gay time. Ah! those days, those good old days! O Cleb, would I were a boy again!

Hanson. What! do you not enjoy this happy wedded life, this peaceful home?

Mark. To be sure I do. Why, Cleb, there's not a happier man in this city than I. But you know there's sometimes a wish in a man's heart to go back on life's journey, to smooth some rough spot where he stumbled.

Hanson. I scarcely understand you.

Mark. You know, Cleb, in those days I was a little wild; and the recollection of that sometimes saddens my thoughtful hours.

Hanson. Yes, I know; but why regret it? You have settled down into a quiet, happy man of family. There are no shadows now in your life, no rough places in the road you travel. Life has been all bright with you; but with me —

Mark. Ah, Cleb! you have tasted sorrow. No dear wife to cheer your home! How lonely it must be!

Hanson. It is, indeed, Mark. That it is lonely, desolate, is the reason of my being here to-night.

Mark. Well, I'm glad you came. Come often, Cleb. Make yourself at home with us: we'll try to cheer you. I'll call Kate down, and we'll have a pleasant evening together.

Hanson. One moment, Mark. I have a proposition to make to you.

Mark. Ah, indeed! Well, go ahead: if there's any thing I can do for you, you've only to say the words.

Hanson. My home is indeed desolate; and you can aid me in attempting to make it more cheerful. You have a daughter, Mark.

Mark. (*Aside.*) O Lord! he's found out Harry and Lilly are intimate. (*Aloud.*) Yes, a dear girl.

Hanson. She is indeed, — one who could make a home bright and happy.

Mark. (*Aside.*) Now, does he suppose I'm going to lose that little girl, and only sixteen? (*Aloud.*) That she could, and can in a few years.

Hanson. In a few years? She's quite old enough to marry.

Mark. Yes, in a few years.

Hanson. I want you to let her come to my house, — a bright, happy influence, to charm away the gloom which now shadows it.

Mark. Well, Cleb, I'm sure I don't know what to say. I've seen this thing growing, but hardly expected it would so soon blossom. They are very fond of each other.

Hanson. They! To whom do you refer?

Mark. Why, my Lilly and your Harry.

Hanson. My Harry?

Mark. Certainly. Ain't that what you are driving at? You want Harry and Lilly to make a match of it.

Hanson. Never.

Mark. Hallo! What do you want, then?

Hanson. I want your daughter Lilly in my house as — my wife.

Mark. The d—euce, you do!

Dick. The old catamarau!

Hanson. I have seen her often, admired her sweet and gentle disposition, and believe that in her I could find a solace for all my bitter hours.

Dick. 'Twould be a bitter pill for her!

Mark. Cleb, you must be jesting. You're old enough to be her father.

Hanson. And not too old to be her loving husband. I am in earnest, Mark. Give her to me. I will love and cherish her.

Mark. But she is so young.

Hanson. I will wait till she grows older: only promise she shall one day be mine.

Mark. I cannot do that. Her wishes must be consulted. She may not fancy you. I don't mean that. Hang me if I know what I do mean. You have taken me by surprise. The idea of your wanting to marry my daughter!

Hanson. If I should succeed in making her love me, would you then give your consent?

Mark. Well, — hang it, Cleb, I won't have any thing to do with this business. You must talk to Kate: she'll let you know what we'll do. I'll call her down, and leave you together. I've got an errand at John Fisher's store. I'll run down there, and you just drop in and let me know the upshot of this affair. (*Aside.*) Kate'll settle him: leave her alone for that. (*Exit,* R.)

Hanson. The same old easy Mark, — shifting the responsibility upon his wife. She's a harder customer to deal with; but I think I know a way by which even she can be made to consent. The girl is lovely, bewitching, and I am determined to have her.

Enter MARK, *with hat and coat, and* KATE, R.

Mark (speaking as he enters). I won't be gone long. Here's an old friend wants a little private conversation with you.

Kate. Ah! Mr. Hanson, I'm glad to see you.

Hanson. Mrs. Ashton, this is indeed a pleasure. I declare, you are looking finely.

Mark. Isn't she, Cleb? She's a woman that always looks lovely; and her sweet, winning disposition — oh, my!

Kate. Mark, you're a giddy, good-for-nothing —

Mark. I know it; and you're a — But I can't stop to tell you: 'twould take too long. I'll be back soon. I won't apologize for running away, Cleb, for I know that's just what you want me to do. Kate will entertain you far better than I could (*aside*), and crush your hopes too, or I'm mistaken. (*Exit*, L.)

Dick. Old Hanson's got a batch that won't knead so easy, I reckon.

Kate. You see, Mr. Hanson, Mark is still the gay, lively soul you have always found him, in spite of the lapse of years.

Hanson. Yes, yes: as gay and lively as when he and I both fell in love with the same pretty girl, — Kate Stewart.

Kate. Ah, you still remember that?

Hanson. I shall never forget it. He, lucky dog, carried off the prize; while I —

Kate. Found a far richer prize to strive for, in the heart of Annie Clare. You won her heart; and no better, truer wife ever blessed a man than she.

Hanson. She was a faithful wife; but all her virtues could never efface the recollection of the love I bore you, Kate.

Kate. Mr. Hanson!

Hanson. Kate Ashton, you little know how great a sacrifice I made when I gave you up to Mark Ashton. Ay, gave you up; for I had such influence over him, that, had I but spoken the word, you would never have been his wife. But I saw you loved him; and, rather than have you suffer, I sacrificed my love, and gave you up. Kate, this happy home, this loving heart you prize so highly, is all my gift. May I not ask some return?

Kate. Mr. Hanson, without acknowledging the gift you profess to have bestowed upon me, believing that the heart of Mark Ashton was all mine from the time we first met, beyond the power of any living man to wrest from me, may I inquire what return you covet?

Hanson. Your daughter Lilly, growing up into the image of her I once so deeply loved. Give her to me. I ask you, Kate, to let her be my wife.

Kate. Caleb Hanson, are you mad?

Hanson. As some atonement for what I suffered in losing you, I beg you give her to me. I will love her, cherish her; her slightest wish shall command me. All that money can purchase shall be hers.

Kate. Caleb Hanson, no more of this. Lilly is but a child, too young to think of marriage, especially with a man of your age. When she is old enough to decide for herself, her choice will be mine.

Hanson. Oh! I will wait: ouly use your influence, and she may be led to look upon me as her future husband. That is all I ask.

Kate. You ask too much. If ever my influence is exerted, 'twill be to make her the wife of your sou Harry. She can never be yours.

Dick. Buttered side down, Hanson!

Hanson. My son Harry! Do you mean to tell me that boy presumes —

Kate. He loves Lilly; of that I am sure. A mother's eyes are sharp. The young people are attached; and the best thing you cau do, Caleb Hanson, is to laugh at your silly passion, and help me to make them happy.

Hanson. Never! I'll turn that insolent puppy into the street: he shall never have a penny of my mouey. He marry! The idle vagabond!

Kate. And who's to blame if he is idle? Have a care, Caleb: he's ambitious; he'll slip away from you before you know it; aud what he attempts he has energy to pursue. You are making a boy of him, wheu his true heart is panting to do a man's work in the world. Ay, and he'll do it yet.

Hanson. So I've found a rival in my own son! and you — you sneer at me, and take his part. Have a care, Kate! I'm called a hard man. I never undertook any thing but what I succeeded; and I'll not fail in this. I will have that girl for my wife.

Kate. Not with my consent.

Hanson. Without it, then. Mark Ashton has one weakness that you dream not of. I know him better than you. Upon this I will work. You shall find yourself neglected, your idol crumbling to dust, your pretty nest scattered to the winds, want staring you in the face; and, when you are brought to your last loaf, perhaps my silly passion may find some recognition in your misery. We shall meet again. (*Exit*, L.)

Kate. Can this be Caleb Hanson, — the quiet, gentle Caleb Hanson? What can he mean? One weakness I dream not of? But he sha'n't have Lilly. What slumbering demon have I awakened? Lilly his wife! — better neglect, want. Merciful Heavens! what terrible blow is about to fall upon us? He *is* a hard man, — relentless, implacable. He has some horrible purpose in his black heart. Let him do his worst. My child shall find a champion here, watchful and wary, to guard and protect her. His wife! While a mother can battle for her child — never! (*Exit*, R.)

Dick (*crawling from under the lounge*). Well, I've heard of the pursuit of knowledge under difficulties, but I had no idea so much knowledge could be found under a lounge. What an infernal scoundrel my respected master is, to be sure! The very in—in—in—carceration of diabolical wickedness. Marry Lilly Ashton! I'd like to see him attempt it. Harry will have a word to say about that. So the old man will turn Harry out of doors! I've no doubt of that; but he shall find a friend in Dick Bustle, or I'm no scholar. Lord, what a muddle this world is, anyhow! The old man's got the money, but we've got the brains; and it's Bustle's opinion that money in this heat will find itself buttered side down.

Tom. (*Outside.*) Now, P-P-P-atty, d-d-d-on't.

Patty. (*Outside.*) It's no use talking, Tom Chubbs: I'm determined.

Dick. Hallo! Here's Chubbs, arter Patty. The darned stuttering donkey! I'd like to hear their conversation; and, as this lounge appears to be a safe hiding-place, I'll try it again. (*Crawls under lounge.*)

Enter PATTY, *followed by* TOM CHUBBS, L.

Tom. P-P-P-atty J-J-J-ones, l-l-l-isten to the v-v-v-oice of af-f-f-ection that b-b-b-ubbles in this b-b-b-osom.

Dick. Bubbles! Sputters, I should say.

Tom. My t-t-t-ongue is we-we-we-ak; I ca-ca-ca-n't sp-p-p-eak my l-l-l-ove.

Dick. Then whistle it, my boy.

Patty. Oh, do go away, Tom Chubbs! Between the butcher and the baker, I'm heartily sick of this nonsense. If you've got any thing to say, speak up like a man.

Tom. D-d-d-idn't you p-p-p-romise to g-g-g-o with me to s-s-s-inging sc-sc-sc-hool?

Patty. Of course I did; and I'm ready to keep my promise.

Tom. D-d-d-idn't you p-p-p-romise to make me the ha-ha-ha-ppiest of me-me-me-n?

Patty. If going to singing-school is going to make you the happiest of men, I did.

Tom. Then s-s-s-ay you l-l-l-ove me.

Patty. I sha'n't say any thing of the sort. Can't I go to singing-school with you without loving you?

Tom. N-n-n-o. I c-c-c-an't spend my m-m-m-oney without s-s-s-ome return, c-c-c-an I?

Patty. You mercenary butcher! Is not my company reward enough?

Tom. N-n-n-o, not quite. I want you to m-m-m-arry

m-m-m-e some time; and, if you wo-wo-wo-on't m-m-m-arry m-m-m-e some time, w-w-w-hat's the use of s-s-s-pending m-m-m-oney, s-s-s-ay?

Dick. Chubbs ain't such a fool as I took him to be. Philosophy in a butcher's frock! A sage of modern Greece!

Patty. Tom Chubbs!

Tom. M-m-m-am.

Patty. There's the door.

Tom. Y-y-y-es, m-m-m-am.

Patty. The quicker you place yourself on the other side of it, the better. You're a low, mean, greedy wretch; and I'll never speak to you again as long as I live.

Dick. Buttered side down, Chubbs!

Patty. For the future, you'll leave your beef, mutton, poultry, and lard at the kitchen-door, and depart in silence.

Tom. Y-y-y-es, m-m-m-am. I-I-I unders-s-s-tand you. It's all the w-w-w-ork of that D-D-D-ick B-B-B-ustle: he's g-g-g-ained your af-f-f-ections, and now you w-w-w-ant to wh-wh-whistle me off.

Patty. Dick Bustle, indeed! Do you think I would listen to that low baker?

Dick (*crawling out*). I think you will, Patty.

Patty. Dick Bustle, you here?

Dick. Accidentally, Patty. Quite accidentally.

Tom. C-c-c-onfound you, D-D-D-ick B-B-B-ustle! you've b-b-b-en l-l-l-istening.

Dick. Very attentively, Chubbs. And I must say, it's very cruel to slight so much love, when it is such an effort to express it. Chubbs, let us be friends. There's my hand. We are blighted beings. We have both showered our palpitating hearts upon the same object. Let us retire to some unfrequented spot, and there mingle our tears.

Patty. You're a couple of fools.

Dick. You hear that, Chubbs? Oh, how I loved that woman!

Chubbs. S-s-s-o did I.

Dick. The wealth of affection I lavished upon her!

Tom. S-s-s-o did I. T-t-t-wo d-d-d-ollars f-f-f-or singing sc-sc-sc-hool.

Dick. Come, Chubbs, let's go. Patty Jones, farewell. You will repent this cruelty to one who loved not wisely, but too well. There will come a time when the still, small voice of conscience will whisper to you —

Patty. Shut up, you donkey.

Tom. C-c-c-ruel P-P-P-atty, f-f-f-arewell: my h-h-h-eart is b-b-b-roken, my hopes are b-b-b—

Dick. Buttered side down! Come on. (*Exeunt* DICK *and* TOM, L.)

Patty. Well, I've lost them both! This comes of having two strings to a bow. I don't care: there's as good fish in the sea as ever was caught; and I'm not going to break my heart for either of them. Dick Bustle is worth the catching; but as for that Tom Chubbs, if he ever shows his face here again, I'll scald him. The mean, contemptible wretch!

Enter MRS. A., R.

Mrs. A. Patty, what's the matter? Who are you going to scald?

Patty. Only the cat, marm.

Mrs. A. And, pray, what has puss been doing now?

Patty. Upsetting every thing, as usual. Just let me catch him, that's all!

Mrs. A. Don't be angry, Patty. Poor thing, he knows no better.

Patty. I know that, marm; but I'll learn him better manners, or my name is not Patty Jones. The mercenary wretch! After I'd promised to go with him to singing-school too!

Mrs. A. The cat invite you to singing-school! Why, what are you talking about?

Patty. Indeed, marm, I don't know. It isn't the cat at all. It's Tom Chubbs.

Mrs. A. Oh! Tom Chubbs. Why, I thought Dick Bustle was the favorite.

Patty. So he was; but I changed my mind for Tom Chubbs: and now I've changed it again; and I won't have any thing to do with either of them. I'll scald Chubbs if he comes here again; and as for Dick Bustle —

Enter DICK, L.

Dick. White or brown, Mrs. Ashton? Square, brick, family, or twist?

Patty (*smiling*). Why, Dick! Back again?

Dick. Yes: I am back again. Business must be attended to; so, if you'll please give me the order for the morning bread, I'll be obliged to you, Mrs. Ashton.

Mrs. A. You know I always leave that to Patty, Mr. Bustle.

Patty. Come to the kitchen, Mr. Bustle, and I will give you the order.

Dick. Well, now, I don't know about that, Miss Jones. You've already kept me gallivantin' about this house for half an hour; and, if it's all the same to you, I'll stop here.

Patty. You're very fond of this room, ain't you? You like the furniture, the lounge, and the carpet under the lounge. Mrs. Ashton —

Dick. Patty, don't: let's go to the kitchen.

Patty. But I want to tell Mrs. Ashton where I found—

Dick. "The last rose of summer." Yes, I know; but come and give me the order for the bread. I'm in a dreadful hurry.

Patty. You always are. But come along, and we'll have a quiet chat in the kitchen. (*Exit,* L.)

Dick. Quiet chat! I don't like to trust myself alone with her, for she'll have me over ears in love with her again. But business must be attended to. (*Exit,* L.)

Mrs. A. I wonder where Mark can be. Caleb Hanson has made me very uneasy with his threats. Foolish threats; for I know that Mark is so noble and good, that he can have no power over him. But I wish he was safe at home.

Mark. (*Outside,* L.) 'Sno use talking, Cleb; I say you shall come in. We've had a jolly time, old boy, a jolly time; and we'll talk it over, and you sha'n't go — go home till morning, old boy, you sha'n't. Come along.

Enter MARK, *intoxicated, leaning heavily on* CALEB, *his dress disordered.*

Hallo, Kate! 'sthat you? This is Cleb Hanson! Glor'us fellow, Cleb Hanson. We've been having a little punch, — a little punch, — ain't we, Cleb? Glor'us punch, — capital punch! It's a glor'us jolly time. It's like the good old times before we was married, ain't it, Cleb? I say, Cleb, it's too much for me. My head's a spinning round and round and round; but it's glor'us punch. Where's something to sit down on? The chairs are all dancing round! Wait a minute, till a-catch that lounge (*falls heavily on to the lounge*).

Kate. Why, Mark, Mark! what is the matter?

Mark. Matter! I's al'ight, I tell you; I's al'ight. It's the punch, — ain't it, Cleb, — he knows, don't you, Cleb? We both knows; for we're all jolly good fellows, we're all jolly good fellows, — we're all jolly — good — fellows. (*Falls asleep.*)

Kate. Caleb Hanson, what is the meaning of this?

Caleb. Why, isn't it plain? Your noble husband has been indulging a little, and, as he says, it's all right.

Kate. Caleb Hanson, you have been tempting my husband to drink.

Caleb. Well, tempting is a pretty hard word, Mrs. Ashton. I did invite him to drink, — something I have not done for years; for, before you knew him, there was a time when a glass of liquor would excite him to such a degree, that his only safety was in totally abstaining from its use. He has shunned it as he would poison. But now he is older and wiser; and, knowing that our families were to be united before long, I thought it best to test him. I told you I had great influence with him; that, in the old days, I could lead him as I pleased. You see I still have the power.

Kate. O man, man! Is there not pity in your heart? Can you so basely betray his trusting nature?

Caleb. Kate, I must have Lilly. Say the word, and to-morrow shall find Mark Ashton the man he was yesterday. Refuse, and you know the consequences.

Kate. Do your worst. You shall not have her.

Caleb. As you please. There lies your husband, drunk, and

Enter LILLY *and* HARRY, L.

I put the glass to his lips.

Harry. You! You did this?

Lilly (*crossing to lounge*) O father, father! What ails you, father?

Hanson. Boy, go home: you are not wanted here. Do you hear? Home, at once.

Harry. Just one word, before I obey you. Did you speak the truth when you said you put the glass to Mark Ashton's lips!

Hanson. What's that to you? Am I to be lectured by my own son?

Kate. O Harry! It is true! It is true!

Harry. Then to your home I go no more. I am no longer son of yours. I have borne insults from you that no father ever put upon the son he loved. I have been brought up in idleness, and made to feel the power of your will. I have been taunted with my dependence; but, from this time, I will depend upon my brains and hands alone to make a way in the world. You have cruelly wronged those who love me. You have placed the poisonous cup to the lips of a weak man, who trusted you. You have disgraced the name I bear; but, with heaven's help, I will clear the name you have so foully disgraced.

Hanson. Bah! Boyish sentiment. Go: beg, starve in the street, for that will be your end. Never look to me for aid, for I've done with you. You are no longer son of mine.

Enter BUSTLE, L.

Bustle (to Harry). Capt. Bangs is looking for you. It's to hear your answer. "No," I suppose.

Harry. You're wrong. It is "Yes:" I will go.

Bustle. You don't say so! Well, Bustle, you're not buttered side down this time. I'm with you! Hurrah for China!

Kate. China!

Harry. Yes, Mrs. Ashton: I am about to accompany Capt. Bangs to China. It is the best, the only course I can pursue. He is my friend: he will care for me; and, with his help, I shall prosper. Bustle, you go with me?

Bustle. To be sure I do!

Lilly. O Harry! You're not going to leave us?

Harry. Lilly, I must go. Mrs. Ashton, let me say what my heart prompts. I love your daughter dearly, truly. It is a boy's love, which a man's heart shall cement. I know she loves me. May I not hope some day to return, and claim her for my wife?

Kate. O Harry! my heart is heavy with a new trouble. I know not how it may end; but, believe me, I love you with a mother's love. Go your way, make for yourself a name, as I know you will, and remember, that, rich or poor, when you ask it, Lilly Ashton shall be your wife.

Harry. Oh, heaven bless you!

Hanson. Kate Ashton, do you dare?

Kate. Dare, Caleb Hanson! I know you now. Bold, cunning, as you are, you have not conquered yet. A wife's love shall battle for the husband; a mother's love for the child. Scheme, work, tempt: do your worst. I feel my power, and Heaven's justice is always certain.

TABLEAU.

MARK *on lounge, asleep. extreme L.*, HARRY *kneels at* LILLY'S *feet*, R., *kissing her hand*. KATE, C., *with finger pointed at* HANSON, *who stands* L., *holding his hat in both hands, and looking fiercely at* KATE. DICK *extreme* L. *Slow curtain.*

ACT SECOND.

SCENE. — *Room in* MARK ASHTON'S *house. Plain table,* C. *Plain chairs,* R. *and* L. *Lounge,* R. *Furniture all of the cheapest kind.* MARK *asleep on lounge.* KATE *sits on a low stool at his side, watching him.*

Kate. Another long weary night has gone; another bright, beautiful morning comes to make glad happy homes and hopeful hearts, but brings no joy to our blasted life. O Mark, Mark! would I had stood beside your grave, mourning the loss of my early love, years ago, ere I had lived to see you such a wreck. Five years, five bitter years, have passed since that fatal night when Caleb Hanson marked you for his victim. Heaven knows I warned you, that I strove to keep you from his influence; but you laughed at what you called my foolish fears; still clung to him who led you, step by step, along the path of ruin. He spoke truly: first neglect, then poverty, — and such bitter poverty. No roof we can call our own, our little savings squandered, piece by piece our furniture sold to obtain bread, or, worse yet, the poison that has made the once noble father and husband a miserable drunkard. O Heaven be merciful to the wretched victims of a villain!

Enter LILLY, L., *in hat and shawl;* KATE *rises.*

Lilly. O mother! such a cruel disappointment; and I had planned such a surprise for you.

Kate. A surprise, my child?

Lilly. Yes, mother. Watching you growing feeble and careworn, working hard to keep the wolf from our door, — how wretchedly poor we are, — I felt it was time for me to try and do something for our support. So, three weeks ago, I called upon Mrs. Clarence, whose husband bought our dear old house, and asked her to assist me by allowing me to give her daughter instruction on the piano. She was very kind to me, and at once accepted my proposal. I was to have commenced this morning, she to pay the first quarter in advance. Judge of my disappointment, when I went there, to find that Mr. Clarence had become bankrupt, that the house had been sold yesterday to a gentleman recently returned from China. It was a cruel blow to my hopes, for I wanted to surprise you by placing in your hands my first earnings.

Kate. Lilly, darling, your thoughtful consideration is a source of pleasure to me.

Lilly. O mother! I do wish I could do something to help you.

Kate. Of that you have given proof. Who did you say had bought our old home?

Lilly. A gentleman from China. I didn't hear his name. O mother! perhaps he can give us some tidings of Harry.

Kate. I fear not, Lilly. Harry's long silence — not a line from him since his departure — is ominous of evil. He loved you so dearly that nothing but death could have so sealed his lips.

Lilly. Oh, don't say that, mother! The thought of his return is the only bright spot in the future to me.

Kate. We will hope for the best, my child. What is hidden in the sealed future, time alone can disclose. Its mysteries may be all the brighter when we reach them, because now enveloped in darkness, as the sun never seems to shine so gloriously as when bursting through the clouds that have obscured it.

Enter PATTY, R.

Patty. Mrs. Ashton, what am I to do for breakfast? There's neither bread nor butter, coffee nor tea, sugar nor molasses; the cat has drunk up all the milk, and the mice absconded with the last remnants of cheese. The grocer will not trust me, and the butcher declares we shall have nothing until his bill is paid.

Kate. Indeed, Patty, I don't know what to do.

Patty. We must have something to eat. Gracious, goodness! there'll be nothing but skeletons left here, if we don't look out.

Kate. Patty, we have reached the end of our means. 'Tis useless for you to stay here any longer: you must know we cannot pay you.

Patty. Fiddlesticks! What do I care for pay?

Kate. You see we have nothing, not even food. It's your duty to look out for yourself.

Patty. What do I care for food? I can go without just as long as you can. It's my duty to care for those who have cared for me, who nursed me when I was sick, who gave me a good home, and made my life pleasant and happy, and forgot all about my being a hired girl. I was brought up in the woods of Maine. I'm nothing but a plain Yankee girl, but I know what's right. Misfortune came upon you when I was sharing your prosperity, and I'm not going to desert you now. If there's nothing in the house to eat, it's my duty to find something, and I'm going to do it. (*Going*, L.)

Kate. Stop, stop, Patty! My purse is not quite empty. Here's a dime; that will at least buy a loaf of bread.

Patty. H'm! A dry breakfast that'll make; but it's better than none. So with the last dime I'll get a loaf of bread. Gracious! I hope it won't be the last loaf.

(*Exit*, L.)

Kate. (*Aside.*) The last loaf! Has it come to that? Caleb Hanson said we should be brought to it; and then — Ah! let him come, let him come, to find his wicked arts have failed to loose from their embrace a mother's guarding arms.

Lilly. O mother, mother! what will become of us?

Kate (*folding* LILLY *in her arms*). Fear not, my child. Heaven guards us ever. Trust on.

"The darkest day,
Live till to-morrow, will have passed away."

(*Exit*, R.)

Mark (*muttering*). Fill up! Fill up! Bumpers, boys, bumpers! (*Moves, and opens his eyes.*) Hallo! Where am I? Home! I thought I was at the head of the table, at Fowler's. Home! Cold as a barn. (*Sits up and looks round.*) But who made it, Mark Ashton? Who transposed a beautiful home to this den? Who dragged a trusting wife down — down — to such a miserable hole? Who blasted a daughter's happiness? You, Mark Ashton! You, curse you! Oh! is there no oblivion? Can I never drown remorse? Drink deep as I will, there always comes this terrible awakening, with Kate's care-worn face, and Lilly's downcast eyes, to tell me of my shame. O Death! will you never come to slay this Gorgon appetite, to hide this mockery of God's image away from the sight of man forever? (*Jumps up.*) Oh, I shall go mad! mad! mad! I cannot bear to look upon them; to read in their eyes my disgrace; to hear their sweet voices, that never reproach, speak loving words that scorch my wicked soul. I will away, ere they return. O wife, daughter! wronged, betrayed, neglected! pray, if you can, for the unhappy wretch who blasts and withers all your fondest hopes. Heaven knows he needs it, when his unhallowed thirst seeks to drown conscience with its greedy cry for drink, — drink, — drink! (*Rushes out*, L.)

Enter PATTY, L., *with a loaf of bread.*

Patty. What sends Mr. Ashton tearing off in that style, at this early hour? After his morning dram, I s'pose. Well, let him go: a small loaf won't go a great ways in a large family, and one mouth the less to feed is a great saving. (*Puts loaf on the table.*) Heigho! what's to become of us? Nothing to do, and no friends to look to for help. What a miserable little loaf of bread. It's not at all like Dick Bustle's. Oh, dear! I wonder what's become of him. I s'pose he's made his fortune in China, and settled down with some little pigeon-toed China girl to keep house for him. Well, there's as good fish in the sea as ever was caught; but they don't nibble here, that's certain. (*Knock at door*, L.) Who's that? Come in.

Enter TOM CHUBBS, L.

Mercy sakes! It's Tom Chubbs!

Tom. P-p-p-atty J-j-j-ones, as I'm a s-s-s-inner!

Patty. Where in the world did you come from?

Tom. F-f-f-rom the c-c-c-orner. I've j-j-j-est o-o-o-pened a p-p-p-rovision s-s-s-tore.

Patty. Indeed! and want our custom, I s'pose.

Tom. Well, I d-d-d-o'no' b-b-b-out that. Mr. A-a-a-shton's p-p-p-oor p-p-p-ay, ain't he?

Patty. What's that to you? He don't owe you any thing, does he?

Tom. P-p-p-atty J-j-j-ones, don't be so p-p-p-eppery. He's p-p-p-oor, ain't he?

Patty. Poor! O Tom! the family are suffering. They want help.

Tom. D-d-d-o they? Well, P-p-p-atty J-j-j-ones, I'm j-j-j-ust the m-m-m-an to h-h-h-elp, and I'll d-d-d-o it.

Patty. You will! Oh, thank you! You are indeed a friend.

Tom. Y-y-y-es, they shall have every th-th-th-ing they want.

Patty. O you dear Tom Chubbs! If you're not careful, I shall hug you.

Tom. D-d-d-o, P-p-p-atty. I'll be a w-w-w-illing v-v-v-ictim. L-l-l-isten to me. I'm in l-l-l-ove.

Patty. What, again?

Tom. N-n-n-o: it's the same o-o-o-ld l-l-l-ove, — as f-f-f-resh as n-n-n-ew l-l-l-aid eggs, as t-t-t-ender as sp-sp-sp-ring ch-ch-ch-ickens, and as st-r-r-ong as—as—as—

Patty. (*Aside.*) Old cheese, and green as your own cabbages. (*Aloud.*) And, pray, who is the object of this tender passion?

Tom. C-c-c-an you ask me? It's you, P-p-p-atty J-j-j-ones, d-d-d-ivine ch-ch-ch-armer.

Patty. Is it possible? Why, I thought I put an extinguisher on your ardent flame five years ago.

Tom. You did sm-sm-sm-other it a bit; b-b-b-ut it's b-b-b-urst out again. B-b-b-e my w-w-w-ife, P-p-p-atty J-j-j-ones. I've got a n-n-n-ice house, a n-n-n-ice l-l-l-ittle b-b-b-usiness, and a n-n-n-ice l-l-l-ittle s-s-s-um in the b-b-b-ank, and now I want a n-n-n-ice l-l-l-ittle w-w-w-ife.

Patty. Well, I'll think about it, Tom. In the mean time, as we've got nothing for breakfast, a good juicy steak would be very acceptable.

Tom. P-p-patty J-j-jones, y-y-you m-m-must s-s-s-ay y-y-y-es or n-n-n-o b-b-b-efore I do any thing f-f-f-or the f-f-family.

Patty. What?

Tom. Only s-s-s-ay you'll have m-m-m-e, and I'll p-p-p-rovide f-f-f-or the f-f-family —

Patty. You will?

Tom. Yes: they shall have every th-th-th-ing — at the l-l-l-owest w-w-w-holes-s-s-ale p-p-p-rice, for c-c-c-ash.

Patty. Tom Chubbs!

Tom. Y-y-y-es: I'll b-b-b-e g-g-g-enerous, t-t-t-oo. Take m-m-m-e, and I'll g-g-g-ive you a h-h-h-og.

Patty. I've no doubt you will, if I take *you.* Is this your boasted help?

Tom. It's h-h-h-ard t-t-t-imes, P-p-p-atty; m-m-m-ust l-l-l-ook out f-f-f-or m-m-m-yself.

Patty. Then look out for yourself now, or you'll find harder times. There's the door; if you're not out of it in a second, I'll smash your soft pate with that loaf of bread. (*Takes loaf from table.*)

Tom. B-b-b-ut, P-p-p-atty —

Patty. Clear out, you mean, miserable skinflint. Clear, I say! (*Throws loaf at him as he runs off,* L.) Was there ever such a — (TOM *enters,* L., *with the loaf.*)

Tom. You've d-d-d-ropped s-s-s-omething, P-p-p-atty. (PATTY *rushes at him, he drops loaf and exits,* L.)

Patty. You jest show yourself here again, Tom Chubbs, — that's all. What hateful things men are, any way. I'd just like to have one of them try to make love to me again, — that's all. I never want to see a man again as long as I live, or hear the sound of his voice.

Dick. (*Outside*, L.) Now, then, what is it? White or brown? Either, both, or neither? (*Enters*, L., *with a basket on his arm.*) Brick, square, family, twist, rolls, or muffins?

Patty. Why, it's Dick Bustle! O you dear old Dick! (*Runs into his arms, and clasps him about the neck.*)

Dick. It is that distinguished individual, sure enough.

Patty. Where did you come from? Where have you been? Where's Harry Hanson?

Dick. To your first interrogatory, Patty, I reply,—China. To your second, my answer is,—China. To your third,—China. So you see for your *where* you've a full set of China.

Patty. I'm so glad to see you. But why haven't you written?

Dick. Oh! I left all that to Harry.

Patty. But we haven't heard a word from either of you since you left.

Dick. Is that so? Well, it's evident that my late respected employer has been sticking his fingers into other people's dough.

Patty. What do you mean, Dick?

Dick. No matter now: tell me, how are all the folks? It strikes me that this is rather a cheap place for a man of so fine a taste as Mark Ashton.

Patty. Why, Dick, haven't you heard? Mr. Ashton is a confirmed sot. He has squandered all his property, and the family are now —

Dick. As I used to say, buttered side down. Well, I'm sorry, for Mark was a good fellow.

Patty. You'd scarce believe it, Dick; but, at this moment, every bit of food we have in the house is that single loaf of bread.

Dick. Well, that's a dreadful mean-looking loaf. It looks scared, don't it? Quite a curiosity. Give that to me, Patty: or rather let me exchange it for one of mine. I should like to preserve that. (*Takes loaf from his basket.*) Now, there's an article worth looking at. You'll find there's no short weight about it when it's cut. (*Exchanges loaves.*) So you say the family are real poor?

Patty. Indeed, indeed they are!

Dick. Well, how about you, Patty? Married yet?

Patty. No, indeed.

Dick. Well, I suppose not, from the garroting you gave me when I came in. Engaged?

Patty. Indeed, I'm not.

Dick. You'll excuse my speaking of it; but I met Tom Chubbs out here, flying away, and I didn't know but what it was "upon the wings of love" that are spoken of occasionally.

Patty. No, indeed! He's opened a provision store round the corner, and dropped in to acquaint us with the fact.

Dick. Well, then, I shall have the pleasure of giving our old friend Tom an order for as much of his stock as I can conveniently bring here in that basket.

Patty. O Dick! That is so like you, — ever thoughtful of those in distress.

Dick. Patty, I've been knocked about the world considerable since I left you, five years ago. I haven't made much headway in becoming a scholar; but I've found that a warm heart and a willing hand are worth all the learning in creation, and that the world has more need of philanthropists than philosophers. No friends of mine shall want while I have a penny in my pocket. I'm going to set up a provisional government here. You shall be chief cook, and I'll be chief butler.

Patty. O Dick! I'm proud of you.

Dick. That's comforting, Patty; for I've come back brim-full of love for you, and I want you to marry me.

Patty. O Dick! you're so abrupt.

Dick. Well, I always was; but this won't do. I must go and fill up the basket.

Patty. Let me go with you?

Dick. Delighted to have your company.

Patty. Let me run and tell Mrs. Ashton and Lilly that you have come: they'll be so glad to see you, and hear something from Harry. Why, Dick, you haven't told me a word about him.

Dick. And I don't mean to, just now. Now, you come with me. Don't say any thing to Mrs. Ashton at present. I have my reasons.

Patty. If you don't tell me something about him, we shall quarrel.

Dick. No, Patty, we mustn't quarrel; that is, — until after we are married.

Patty. And do you flatter yourself I'm going to marry you?

Dick. Well, we can't tell what may happen. Do

you remember what you said when I went away? That you wouldn't marry me if there wasn't another man in the world.

Patty. Did I? But, Dick, that was five years ago; and, besides, I've changed my mind.

Dick. O Patty Jones, Patty Jones! Come to my arms and fill my soul — No: business before pleasure, — let's go and fill the basket. (*Exit*, L.)

Enter MARK ASHTON, L.

Mark. Not a drop, — not a drop! Morgan has shut down! No more credit, — no money, no liquor. Have I fallen so low that I am refused a drop of liquor to quench the thirst that is strangling me? I must have it! My pockets are empty, — emptied into Morgan's till. There's nothing here worth pawning. I must have it, — at least one glass. Perhaps Kate has a shawl, or Lilly a bonnet. O wretch, wretch! Would you rob your own wife and daughter of their poor clothing? I must have something. What's this? bread, — bread, — to mock my thirst. I'll throw it into the street. No, no, no! there's money in it. Morgan will give me a glass for that. He can't refuse, for he robs the poor of their bread every day. Lucky thought. I'll try it. (*Takes loaf, and goes towards door*, L.) Who's this? Caleb Hanson! I can't meet him with this under my arm. He's coming this way. I'll wait till he is gone. (*Throws himself upon lounge.*) Oh, this maddening thirst!

Enter KATE, *followed by* LILLY, R.

Kate. I thought I heard your father moving; but he still sleeps.

Lilly. O mother! when and how will this end?

Kate. With his life, my child. See what a wreck your once noble father has become. Wretched as we are, his life is a thousand times more miserable. Oh, if he could be made to realize his condition! If one spark of his once noble manhood could be kindled, there would be hope for him.

Lilly. Mother, he must see how you are suffering: he must know that we are without means to live. 'Tis too hard for you, brought up with every comfort about you, to be reduced to this poverty, with but a single loaf of bread in the house, and no means to get another.

Kate. We will eat that contentedly, and not repine at the ways of Providence. He was the best of fathers, the best of husbands, in prosperity; and even in our wretchedness not one unkind word has passed his lips.

Lilly (*kissing* MARK *on the forehead*). Dear, dear father: if you only knew how dearly we love you!

Kate (*sits at* R. *of table*). Heaven send us some help in our sore distress.

Mark (*mutters as if in sleep*). And I would have robbed them of their last morsel. O wretch, accursed wretch!

Lilly (*putting her arm about* KATE'S *neck*). Poor mother! At last you sink beneath the burden. (*Knock,* L.) Come in.

Enter CALEB HANSON, L.

Caleb. Ah! Good-morning, ladies. I trust I see you well, Mrs. Ashton, — and Lilly, too; how charming you are looking!

Kate. (*Starts up.*) Caleb Hanson, leave my house.

Caleb. Your house! I beg your pardon; I was not aware that Mark Ashton or his wife were owners of real estate. This house is mine: I bought it yesterday.

Kate. Still hunting your victims.

Caleb. No: looking after my friends, that's all. I bought the house yesterday, and with it a bill for a month's rent now due. I called in to collect it.

Kate. We have not a penny we can call our own.

Caleb. I am glad of that.

Kate. I suppose you are.

Caleb. Just sitting down to breakfast too? Perhaps to your last loaf?

Kate. It is our last loaf. You are glad of that too.

Caleb. I am; for now I am nearing the consummation of my wishes. Now you will let me be your friend.

Kate. Friend! You?

Caleb. Yes, friend. You have seen how strong a foe I can be. I was a true prophet five years ago, — was I not? It's all turned out just as I said. I told you my influence could make Mark a drunkard, — could beggar you, — could bring you to your last crust.

Kate. You have performed all you promised. What next?

Caleb. 'Tis time you had a change. All this was brought about because you refused to give me your daughter. Give her to me now, and I will rebuild all I have destroyed. To-morrow you shall go to your old home; comforts shall spring up about you; every wish shall be gratified; your husband shall be reclaimed, and all made bright and happy.

Kate. And you could do all this?

Caleb. Do you doubt it?

Kate. No! I know the power of an inflexible will. I know the power of money at a strong man's command; but I tell you, Caleb Hanson, if you could do all this, — if you could give me the dearest wish of my heart, — my husband restored to manhood again, — the price to be my daughter's hand, my answer would still be, Never, — never!

Caleb. Still stubborn? I must go farther, then, — drive you into the street, homeless and houseless.

Lilly. O mother, mother!

Kate. Still, with my protecting arms about my child, I would defy you.

Caleb. Farther yet: Mark Ashton is now a drivelling drunkard. I'll drive him into crime. He shall be a hunted felon.

Kate. O Heaven, be merciful!

Caleb. I have the power.

Mark (*springs from sofa, takes centre of stage, with finger pointed at Caleb*). Caleb Hanson, you lie!

Kate. } (*Together.*) Mark!
Lilly. } Father!
Caleb. } Ashton!

Mark. Your power is gone, never to return. I know you now, smooth-tongued hypocrite.

Caleb. Mark, you're drunk.

Mark. False again, Caleb. I haven't been so sober for five years. To-day I cannot get a drop.

Caleb. Oh, I see! your nerves are unstrung, Mark. (*Takes out money.*) Here, — here's money. Go get something. You really need it. Get something, quick.

Mark. Too late, Caleb. Put up your money. Tempter, your power is gone. A few moments ago I was creeping out of this house with a loaf of bread under my arm, going to sell it for a glass of liquor, — the last loaf my poor wife and child had to keep them from starving. Stealing the bread from their mouths to feed my unholy appetite. The last loaf, Caleb, — don't it make you shudder? I saw you coming; and, ashamed to meet my friend, — my friend, Caleb, — I slunk back, back here. I heard my wife's sweet voice; I felt my daughter's kiss; I heard a tale of villany from your lips. I wouldn't believe my own wife, when she told me; but you, my friend, I must believe.

Caleb. Well, and what are you going to do about it?

Mark. Protect my child.

Caleb. Ah, indeed! fit protector you, — a broken-down drunkard.

Mark. Caleb Hanson, I believe there is a time in every weak man's life, when the hand of Providence is put forth, when a warning voice comes, "Thus far shalt thou go, and no farther." I believe that time has come to me, — the time to break my chains, and free myself. Heaven aid me! I will heed the warning. You, you, who have made me what I am, hear the vow, — Never, never shall the accursed poison touch my lips again!

Kate. O Mark, Mark! my own Mark again.

Lilly. Father, dear, dear father!

Mark (*folding them in his arms*). Now, Caleb Hanson, come and take my daughter.

Caleb. You will take your daughter and your wife out of my house at once. I'll drive you from town as a vagabond and a drunkard.

Mark. Have a care, Hanson, — have a care. It's as much as I can do to keep my fingers from your throat. We'll leave your house, — never fear; but, before I go, you, who so delight in noble acts, witness our morning meal. (*Takes loaf from table.*) 'Tis the last remnant of my life of shame, — our last loaf, of which I would have robbed these dear ones. But now I can share it with them; and, with the vow of repentance upon my lips, Heaven will bless it. (*Breaks the loaf, and pieces of gold fall upon floor.*)* What magic's here? (*Snatching up pieces, and letting them fall through his fingers.*) Gold, — gold, — gold!

Caleb. Confusion! Who has dared to interfere with my plans?

Enter DICK BUSTLE, *with basket,* L., *followed by* PATTY.

Dick. Dick Bustle, I expect: it's just like him.

Mark. What, Dick! Dick Bustle? (*Shakes hands.*)

Kate. Old friend, welcome home! (*Shakes hands.*)

Lilly. O Dick, Dick, how glad I am to see you!

Caleb. Confound the blunderhead!

Dick (*placing basket on table*). Thank you. Thank you all.

Mark. Explain this mystery, Dick.

Dick. Mystery! Why, that's a good loaf of bread, ain't it?

* To prepare the loaf, cut in two, perpendicularly, a round loaf; remove enough of the inside to hold the "gold"; then fasten the two halves, by passing around it horizontally an elastic band.

Mark. Yes; but the contents.

Dick. Oh! the stuffin'? Well, it's a pretty long story; and, as Mr. Hanson seems to be in a hurry, perhaps I'd better —

Patty. No, no, Dick: we're dying to hear it.

Dick. Well, then, five years ago two individuals went off to China.

Lilly. Yes! You and my Harry.

Dick. Exactly, Lilly: your Harry. Mr. Hanson, I beg you to take notice that the young lady says her Harry.

Patty. Do go on, Dick.

Dick. Well, this Harry was a driver, I tell you. No sooner had we landed, than he was snapped up by an English house, and given an important position. Wasn't he smart? Why, there wasn't his equal there, — such a hand at bargains, and such luck, — every thing he took hold of turned to gold; but the first money he made was enclosed in a neat envelope, and sent home, directed to Mrs. Kate Ashton.

Kate. I have never received it.

Dick. You haven't! I beg you to take notice, Mr. Hanson, that she says she never received it.

Hanson. What's this to do with me?

Dick. You'll find out, my late respected employer. This envelope was followed by many more.

Kate. Which were never received.

Dick. I suppose not. You see a friend of this Harry was one day forced to take refuge under a lounge, where he overheard a conversation between certain parties concerning certain other parties; and he and Harry made up their minds the money would be welcome.

Patty. That was you who hid under the lounge, Dick.

Dick. Exactly; but, as you know, the money never came to hand. I beg you to take notice, Mr. Hanson —

Patty. O Dick, do go on!

Dick. I have little more to say. A year ago, Harry was taken into the English house as a partner. Hearing nothing from his dispatches, he commanded me, his inseparable companion, to look them up. I am here for that purpose. The loaf was a little invention of mine, to block my late respected employer's game. I made the loaf, but another party supplied the stuffin'.

Lilly. O Dick, Dick! and that other party —

Enter HARRY HANSON, L.

Harry. Will answer for himself. Lilly, Lilly, my darling!

Lilly. O Harry! Dear, dear Harry! (*Rushes into his arms.*)

Kate. My dear, dear boy, welcome home!

Mark. Harry, my boy, God bless you!

Harry. Thanks for your kind greeting. This is indeed a happy moment.

Dick. Harry, there's your father.

Harry (*turning to* HANSON). Father! that man is not my father. His hands are steeped in crime. He has dragged his dearest friend to ruin. He has forfeited all right to the child he drove from his doors. Repentance alone can wash the stains from that man's soul.

Hanson (to himself, with feeling). The boy speaks plain. I have done all this. I have planned and plotted ruin. I have stepped between him and his love. I have committed felony in intercepting his letters. I could have borne it all, — all its penalties, — but to see my own son turn coldly from his father — I thought I hated him; but now I would give all my wealth to feel the clasp of his hand, to look into his face, and read there some token of love. Ah, well, — as we sow, so must we reap. Foiled everywhere, what is there left for me? (*Turns and slowly goes out,* L.; *the others stand watching him as he goes.*)

Harry. My own father! Oh, this is hard to bear!

Kate. Cheer up, my boy. Though he who should be your best friend has deserted you, there are warm hearts here.

Harry. I know it, Mrs. Ashton. You told me you would be my mother, — that Lilly should be my wife.

Kate. No, Harry, — that her choice should be mine.

Harry. Ah! then it is useless for me to ask any more questions, for I read her answer in her eyes. Do I not, Lilly?

Lilly. O Harry! you have the most truthful eyes I ever looked into.

Harry. Dick, old friend, you found my remittances had been appropriated by another party.

Dick. Yes, Harry; by my late respected employer. He must be made to fork over.

Harry. In good time, Dick. But now I have other matters to occupy my attention.

Dick. And so have I. Patty Jones is very anxious to change her name.

Harry. And you are anxious to have her. Well, Patty, you can't do better.

Patty. Thank you, Master Harry. I'm exactly of your opinion, — ain't I, Dick?

Dick. If you're not, then I'm buttered side down.

Mark. Harry, there is no need of my telling you our past experience. You read it in my altered looks, — in the wreck of a once proud man.

Harry. Mr. Ashton, say no more. I know every thing. "Let the dead past bury its dead." Your old home is waiting for you. Every thing is just as it was when you left it.

Lilly. Our old home! Then you are —

Dick. The gentleman from China, Lilly.

Mark. Our old home again? I feel like a new man, wife. Heaven has dealt kindly with me, to give me these kind friends after my wasted life.

Kate. Ah, Mark, you have suffered deeply. Let us hope there are better times in store for us.

Mark. I trust there are, Kate. My reformation cannot be accomplished in an hour. I must suffer from that accursed appetite, — must struggle to overcome it: be ever near me, lest I should fall.

Kate. Fear not, Mark: we will surround you in our dear old home with such loving hearts that temptation shall have no power to harm you.

Mark. Ay, gather about me close, — wife, daughter, son. In the hours of darkness, when temptation assails me, let me lean upon your true hearts to gather courage; for there are no trustier guards than loving hearts, — no stronger citadel than "Home, sweet Home."

TABLEAU.

MARK, C., *with his left arm around* KATE'S *waist, his right hand over* HARRY *and* LILLY, *who kneel,* R. DICK *and* PATTY, *arm in arm,* L. *Music, "Home, sweet Home," as the curtain slowly falls.*

TOO LATE FOR THE TRAIN.

A DUOLOGUE FOR TWO GENTLEMEN.

SOCK, a manager.
BUSKIN, an eccentric comedian in search of an engagement.

SCENE. — *Waiting-room in a depot. Placards on wall: Time-table; "Look out for Pickpockets;" "No Smoking Allowed."* *Trunk,* R.; *chair, table,* C.; *chair,* L. *At rising of curtain, a train is heard leaving.*

(*Enter* BUSKIN, L., *with carpet-bag, umbrella, and several packages, shouting*), Stop that train! stop that train. (*Exit* R., *outside.*) Conductor! engineer! brakeman! small boy, there! stop that train! (*Re-enter,* R.) It's no use. Too late again. Always too late. I'm an unfortunate, victimized, undone individual. Convulsively have I struggled with fate, always to be thrown like a short-winded bruiser: grappled with misfortune, only to get a blacked eye or a broken nose. Talk about your tides in the affairs of man, which, taken at the flood, lead on to fortune! I don't see it, — nary a tide. Don't

I take them, and don't I get taken in and taken under? Look at me! Somebody oblige me by taking a careful survey of the multitudinous crowfeet which straggle adown my once blooming physiognomy. Cast an oblique glance at this emaciated frame, once adorned with the plumpness and fulness of an alderman. It's all the effect of plunging into those selfsame flood-tides, and here's the effect of my last plunge: two minutes too late for a train which should be bearing me on to fortune in the shape of a fat salary as eccentric comedian of the Eden Varieties. And here I am, stuck fast in this out-of-the-way station, ten miles away from any habitation. I'm certainly in a very bad way. Is there anybody here? Hallo! ticket-office, porter, anybody! Hallo! It is *hollow* with a vengeance. Guess this railroad runs itself. What's to be done? I can't go back: it's getting dark, and I should lose my way. When's the next train due? (*Goes to time-table*, R. C.) "Trains for Eden, 7½ P.M., 9½ P.M." Half-past nine! two mortal hours! I can never stand that! Half-past nine! why that's the hour appointed for meeting the manager of the Varieties! Two hours to Eden! — 'twill be half-past eleven before I get there; and the manager will, no doubt, be snoring in bed. Well, it's no use to worry. Here I am, and here I must stay; so I'll make myself comfortable. Confound the train! *Just my luck!* (*Takes up paper, and sits*, L.) "Horrible murder!" Well, that's comfortable. What a dismal hole this is! I wish I was well out of it! (*Takes up paper again.*) "Highway robbery!" Good gracious! what comfortable arrangements they do have in this depot! Wonder if there's a gallows anywhere about the premises to complete the pleasing picture. I shall have the horrors! (*Reads the paper.*)

SOCK *saunters in*, L.

Sock. Well, I am in luck, decidedly. Here before the train. There's nothing gives one such pleasure as being on time, especially where trains are concerned; for trains, like time, wait for no man, except he be a general, when I believe they do grant a little delay. This place seems as lonesome as a graveyard, — deadly lively. Hallo! a stranger. Queer-looking customer.

Buskin. (*Reading.*) "One of our most influential citizens, while seated in the quietude of his chamber, was interrupted by a ferocious-looking burglar, who, in the most unceremonious manner, walked into his apartment, and, tapping him on the shoulder — "

Sock. (*Tapping him on the shoulder.*) Good evening, stranger!

Buskin. (*Starting up.*) Keep off! keep off! I'll sell my life dearly! Keep off! keep off!

Sock. My dear sir, don't alarm yourself.

Buskin. What do you mean by entering a gentleman's apartment in that manner?

Sock. Well, come, you are a rich one. Apartment!

Buskin. No: I ain't a rich one. I'm a decidedly poor one. What do you mean by tapping me on the shoulder in that manner?

Sock. I beg your pardon, sir: I merely wished to ask —

Buskin. Yes, I know, "Your money or your life." But you can't come it here. I haven't any money, and my life's insured.

Sock. Don't alarm yourself: I am not in that line.

Buskin. I wish you was on a line, with all my heart.

Sock. I merely wish to ask a simple question, such as one traveller would ask another. When is the train due?

Buskin. What train?

Sock. The train for Eden.

Buskin. You're too late: it's gone. (*Seats himself, and takes up paper.*)

Sock. Gone! is it possible? My watch must be slow. When does the next train come up?

Buskin. Sir, is there any thing in my appearance that would lead you to take me for a railroad-guide? There's the time-table: look for yourself.

Sock. A decidedly crossgrained customer. (*Goes to time-table.*) "Trains for Eden, 7½, 9½." Well, that's pleasant. Two hours to wait! How the deuce can I pass the time? I'll talk to my pugnacious friend. (*Comes down, and seats himself on table. Takes up* BUSKIN'S *umbrella.*) Going up or down, sir?

Buskin. (*Takes umbrella from his hand.*) What's that to you?

Sock. Oh! nothing. Going to Eden perhaps?

Buskin. Perhaps.

Sock. Business there? (*Takes up bundle.*)

Buskin. (*Taking bundle.*) Possibly.

Sock. (*Lifting carpet-bag.*) What is it?

Buskin. Minding my own business. (*Takes carpet-bag.*)

Sock. Very little conversation to be got out of him. I'll leave him alone. (*Goes* L., *and takes book from his pocket.*)

Buskin. Thought that would settle him. I do hate busybodies. Wonder who he is? (*Pause.*) Here! Going to Eden?

Sock. Hey? Oh! — possibly.

Buskin. Live there perhaps?

Sock. Perhaps.

Buskin. Might I inquire your name?

Sock. Certainly you might.

Buskin. Well?

Sock. Well, what?

Buskin. I asked your name.

Sock. No, you didn't: you asked if you might inquire.

Buskin. Oh, pshaw! What is your name?

Sock. The same as my father's.

Buskin. Well, what's his?

Sock. The same as mine.

Buskin. Well, what's both your names?

Sock. Both alike.

Buskin. Oh, humbug! Do you call that the way to answer a civil question?

Sock. You began it; but I will be frank with you, for I am in danger, and need a confidant. There is something in your calm, placid face, that tells me I can trust you. I can feel that the milk of human kindness bubbles in your bosom —

Buskin. Well, let it bubble. Go on with your story.

Sock. I will: be seated. Let me take care of your umbrella. (*Attempts to take it.*)

Buskin. No, I thank you.

Sock. Do. It's so handy in case of a shower.

Buskin. What kind of a shower do you expect here?

Sock. A shower of applause. They're very prevalent here. But, to my story. You were just reading the account of a horrid murder?

Buskin. Oh, horrors! You are the murderer? (*Jumps up.*)

Sock. Sit down. Not a bit of it. Should you think I had just escaped from a lunatic asylum?

Buskin. Oh, murder! A lunatic! (*Jumps up.*)

Sock. Sit down. Not a bit of it.

Buskin. Who the deuce are you, anyhow? Why don't you disclose yourself, and have done with this tomfoolery? You've got me into a perspiration with your infernal nonsense.

Sock. I will begin at the beginning.

Buskin. What! going back to the creation?

Sock. Well, then, in the first place, what have you in that bag?

Buskin. What's that to you? Go ahead with your history.

Sock. Well, then, first my name. It's Brown: singular name, isn't it?

Buskin. What, Brown? Nothing very singular about that.

Sock. Not in Brown? Why it's an uncommon name.

Buskin. Well, well, go on.

Sock. Well, as I said before, my name is Dunn.

Buskin. Brown!

Sock. Well, my dear sir, if you know my history better than I do, you had better tell it yourself.

Buskin. No! no! go on.

Sock. My name is Dunn —

Buskin. Brown.

Sock. Exactly! Dunn Brown.

Buskin. Oh, yes! I see it. Dunn Brown.

Sock. Well, as you see, it's Dunn Brown on both sides.

Buskin. (*Sepulchral laugh.*) Ha! ha! ha!

Sock. What's the matter?

Buskin. I was only laughing at your joke.

Sock. Do you call that a laugh? It sounds as though you were pulling up gravestones by the roots.

Buskin. Go on! Go on!

Sock. I am the son of poor but wealthy parents.

Buskin. Oh, pshaw! How can that be?

Sock. Pray, sir, are you acquainted with my parents?

Buskin. No, sir; never saw them; don't believe you ever had any. What kind of a way is that to tell a story? Listen to me. My name is Buskin. I am desirious of becoming the Eccentric Comedian of the Eden Varieties, and for that purpose had an appointment with the manager at Eden at half-past nine o'clock. Missed the train, and here I am with a madman or donkey — I don't know which. That's short and sweet.

Sock. Very. (*Aside.*) But long enough for my purpose. So this is the individual who has pestered me, the manager of the Eden Varieties. We've got two hours to stop here: he doesn't know me. A chance to combine business with pleasure. I'll find out his abilities. (*Aloud.*) By the way. Just now, when you were speaking of yourself, you mentioned the word "donkey." Can you tell me why a donkey prefers thistles to grass?

Buskin. No: why does he?

Sock. Because he's a jackass, of course.

Buskin. Ha! ha! ha!

Sock. Go it, gravestones. But come; as you are desirous of becoming a comedian, show me some of your eccentricities.

Buskin. No, I thank you. I keep them for appreciative audiences.

Sock. Well, try me. I'll make a capital audience. I'll drop in handsomely with the judicious applause.

Buskin. No, I thank you: drops won't do. We must have a shower.

Sock. Oh, come! that's a good fellow. I know your manager, and will speak a good word for you.

Buskin. Will you, though? That's clever.

Sock. And not only that, but I'll assist you. I do something in that way myself, as an amateur. I can give you a recitation or two.

Buskin. Well, agreed; and we'll divide the profits. You lead off.

Sock. I'll give you Macaulay's "Virginia."

Recitation. "*Virginia.*"—*Macaulay.* SOCK.

Buskin. Very affecting; but so sweet a maid should have died a sweeter death.

Sock. What do you call a sweet death?

Buskin. Well, choking to death with molasses candy: that's a sweet death.

Sock. Ha! ha! ha! I always liked that joke: but its your turn; proceed.

Buskin. I'll give you a forensic argument that has

acquired some repute, "The speech of Sergeant Buzfuz, counsel for the prosecution in the case of Bardwell *vs.* Pickwick."

Recitation. "*Sergeant Buzfuz.*" — *Dickens.*

Sock. No wonder Sam Weller, senior, cautions his son to "bevare of vidders." But come, let's have a song.

Buskin. Well, sing away.

Sock. No, I thank you. That's not in my line. You sing, you know.

Buskin. How do you know?

Sock. You said so in your letter.

Buskin. What letter?

Sock. (*Aside.*) Oh, pshaw! I've let the cat out of the bag. (*Aloud.*) Letter, did I say letter? I said you'd better.

Buskin. Oh, very well! here goes.

Song. BUSKIN.

Sock. By the by, you act, don't you?

Buskin. Yes, occasionally.

Sock. Let's have a scene from something. Let me see — what shall it be?

Buskin. What do you say to "Ion"?

Sock. It's too heavy.

Buskin. "Richard the Third." "A horse! my kingdom for a horse!"

Sock. No, I thank you: I don't ride.

Buskin. Something sensational? "East Lynne;" that's spirited.

Sock. I prefer "Saugus." There's more *sole* there. I have it. Let's have the scene so familiar in our school-days, — "Lochiel's Warning." That's a capital scene.

Buskin. Very well. I'll do "the wizard."

Sock. So will I.

Buskin. Oh, pshaw! we can't both have it.

Sock. Very well: let's toss up for it.

Buskin. Agreed. Here goes. (*Tosses up copper.*)

Sock. What is it?

Buskin. Heads.

Sock. You've lost — it's tails.

Buskin. Just my luck.

Scene. "*Lochiel's Warning.*" — *Campbell.*

Lochiel, — BUSKIN. *Wizard*, — SOCK.

END OF PART I.

PART II.

SCENE. — BUSKIN *discovered asleep*, L. SOCK *seated on trunk*, R.

Sock. My friend has taken advantage of my absence for the purpose of procuring a glass of water, to indulge in a *siesta.* How beautifully he sleeps! (BUSKIN *snores.*) How frightfully he snores! Once or twice, at the sound of his musical voice, I've rushed to the door, thinking the train had arrived. It's too bad. It's so deuced lonesome here I want some amusement, and I must have it. Hallo! what's this? Unclaimed baggage? "Lenville, Tragedian." Somebody's under the weather. Careless, leaving things in this manner. Some inquisitive fellow might be prying into it. (*Opens trunk.*)

Costumes for Hamlet complete, and lots of other things. Oh! now we'll have a show-piece. Hallo! Buskin! Buskin! I say, wake up: day's a breaking.

Buskin. Let it break. Don't owe me nothing.

Sock. Come, wake up! I've found a treasure. Share it with me.

Buskin. No, I never take shares: that's played out.

Sock. Wake up! wake up!

Buskin. What do you want now? Can't a man have any peace?

Sock. Yes; I want to give you piece,— a show-piece. Look here!

Buskin. Oh, pshaw! Let me sleep. "Rock me to sleep, mother, rock me to sleep." (*Snores.*)

Sock. Come, come, Buskin, this is not fair play. You know I'm to speak a good word for you, and I never should be able to do it unless you give me another song.

Buskin. (*Rising.*) There's no rest for the wicked, is there?

Sock. No, sir, — no rest for the wicked.

Buskin. You must be an awful tired man. What will you have?

Sock. Any thing you please.

Buskin. I'll sing you the remarkable history of "The Lost Heir."

Song. "*The Lost Heir.*" BUSKIN.

Sock. Very pathetic. Now, if you can manage to keep your eyes open, I'll give you a recitation.

Recitation. "*The Old Man's Prayer.*" — *Baker.* SOCK.

Buskin. That's a first-rate temperance argument, and,

strikes me, worth more than prohibitory law. By the by, speaking of laws, reminds me of a debating society. You've heard my story of "The Debating Society"?

Sock. Never did.

Buskin. Of course not: it's bran new.

Recitation. "*The Debating Society.*" BUSKIN.

Sock. Look here, Buskin: here's dresses for "Hamlet and The Ghost." Let's have a show-piece. (*Goes to trunk.*)

Buskin. Yes; but I don't know a line of Hamlet.

Sock. Neither do I. Let's guess at it. Come, get into these regimentals.

Buskin. What! Right here in the depot?

Sock. Of course: don't be modest. Here, I'll fix you. (*Drops curtain.*) There, dress away while our pianist plays the overture. (*Curtain drops.*)

Overture. Piano.

Curtain rises on "A Hamlet Fricassee." Enter SOCK, *as Hamlet,* C.; *costume, usual Hamlet dress.*

Hamlet. "To be or not to be!" oh! that's played out,
And gone with many a Hamlet up the spout.
The question now is not confined to slings,
To which state-constables have given wings;
Nor can we now take arms 'gainst seas of trouble,
Since Fenian caldrons cease to boil and bubble.
To die? — No! no! that Hamlet cannot tell
While we've a ——— * that can dye so well.
To sleep — to dream — ah! there's the rubber
Which in our snoring game may make us blubber;

* Local name.

For in that sleep, when we have muffled up our coils,
In soothing nightcaps, free from worldly toils,
What dreams may come — must give us pause
Ere we sup heartily on lobsters' claws,
Escalloped oysters! — fancy roast and stew,
Which all of human flesh are given to.
That's the respect makes fast-days come so fast;
For who would bear to hunger to the last?
To bear the pangs of clamorous appetite;
With watery mouths wage a perpetual fight;
But that the fear of troublesome digestion
Raises within the mind this weighty question;
But that the fear that on some dismal night,
Waked from a dream, and trembling with affright,
His burning eyes behold his mother's ghost,
Perched on the apex of a strong bed-post.

(*Enter* BUSKIN, *as "Ghost,"* L.; *costume, complete suit of white cotton "armor."*)

Talking of ghosts — *Police* defend us,
Prithee! no more such frightful spectres send us.
Be thou a spirit of air? or are you one of Hellas?
Spirit of Hartshorn? or some other fellow's?
Be thou the sphynx? or are you goblin stuffed
With laughing-gas, that's by our dentists puffed?
Be thy intents indifferent, good, or bad:
I'll speak to thee, thou lookest so like my dad.
In a trim grave so snugly wast thou lain:
Say, who the dickens dug you up again?
Ghost. I am thy father's spirit!
H. Hush! hush! I pray you speak more low
Of spirits: our state constable's below.
He'll seize on you.
G. Shut up your clam-shell, sonny;
Don't bother your poor dad, now, that's a honey.
Just hold your gab, for I must quickly go:
I'm pressed for time — we keep good hours below.

Soon I must go, and have another roast:
So pray attend to me.

H. Alas! poor ghost!

G. But that I am forbid to talk and chatter,
I could a tale unfold; but that's no matter.
If you would like to hear. List! list! oh, list!

H. (*Producing a long piece of list from his pocket.*)
Here 'tis, instanter; strong, upon my word.

G. Pshaw! I'm going to sing.

H. I see you want a chord. Mr. Pianist, oblige us with a chord.

(*Song*, GHOST. — Tune, "*Giles Scroggins' Ghost.*" *From J. F. Poole's* "*Hamlet Travestie.*")

Behold in me your father's sprite, — Ri tol tiddy lol de ray,
Doomed for a term to walk the night. — Tiddy, tiddy, &c.
You'll scarce believe me when I say
That I'm bound to fast in fires all day
Till my crimes are burnt and purged away. — Ri tol tiddy, &c.

But that I am forbid to blow, — Ri tol tiddy, &c.
The dreadful secrets which I know. — Tiddy, tiddy, &c.
I could such a dismal tale unfold,
As would make your precious blood run cold.
But, ah! those things must not be told. — Ri tol tiddy, &c.

Your father suddenly you missed, — Ri tol tiddy, &c.
I'll tell you how — List! List! Oh, list! — Tiddy, tiddy, &c.
'Twas given out to all the town
That a serpent pulled your father down.
But now that serpent wears his crown. — Ri tol tiddy, &c.

One afternoon, as was my use, — Ri tol tiddy, &c.
I went to my orchard to take a snooze, — Tiddy, tiddy, &c.
When your uncle into my ear did pour
A bottle of cursed hellebore.
How little did I think I should wake no more! — Ri tol tiddy, &c.

Doomed by a brother's hand was I, — Ri tol tiddy, &c.
To lose my crown, my wife, — to die. — Tiddy, tiddy, &c.

I should like to have settled my worldly affairs;
But the rascal came on so unawares,
That I hadn't even time to say my prayers. — Ri tol tiddy, &c.

Torment your uncle for my sake; — Ri tol tiddy, &c.
Let him never be at peace, asleep or awake. — Tiddy, tiddy, &c.
Your mother's plague let her conscience be:
But I must be off; for the daylight I see.
Adieu! adieu! adieu! Remember me! — Ri tol tiddy, &c.

H. My royal Nibbs, I'll read you a riddle short:
Oblige me with a tune on the pianoforte.
G. Oh, fiddle de dee! I can't play that, I own:
I'll give you a solo on the big trombone.
H. And yet you think on me that you can play,
Who can't handle this ere piano, any way.
Now, that's played out. Do you see that cloud up there?
G. Wait till I get my specs. I do, I'll swear!
H. Methinks it's like a waterfall.
G. 'Tis — to a hair.
H. Methinks it's like a whale. Pray, what think you?
G. A whale! no, no! Just whale me if it do.
H. And yet—

(*Bell rings, whistle sounds, outside.*)

Sock. What's that? The train! upon my word! Off with your togs! we shall be too late again. (*Both rush round, endeavoring to get off their dresses.*)

Buskin. Oh, murder! I can never get these togs off [in] time. What a pickle have you got me in now!

Sock. No matter: wear them. It's late: no one will see you. Come, get your togs.

Buskin. But what will the manager say to see me in this rig?

Sock. Say just what I do: it's all right. And you shall have the situation; for I am the manager.

Buskin. You? (*Gets his bag and umbrella.*)

Sock. Yes, I; and delighted to have so fiue an acquisition to my compauy. So let's be off.

Buskin. Yes; but we must say something here. (*To audience.*)

Sock. Of course we must; so you say it.

Buskin. What shall I say? Ladies and gentlemen, we are very much obliged for the kind and —

Sock. Come, come! hurry up!

Buskin. We have enjoyed ourselves waiting for the traiu; and, if you have been entertained, we should not regret being — being — (*Outside — "All aboard!"*)

Sock. Too Late for the Train.

CURTAIN.

Note. — Songs or recitations may be introduced in this piece to suit the taste and the ability of the performers.

A GRECIAN BEND.

A FARCE.

FOR FEMALE CHARACTERS ONLY.

CHARACTERS.

MRS. FIELD, a Matron of forty.
KITTY FIELD, eighteen, } Her Daughters.
BESSIE FIELD, twelve, }
SUSY FOLLEIGH, eighteen.
JENNY SANDS, seventeen.
AUNT DERBY DENT, sixty.
NORAH, the help.

COSTUMES. — Modern and appropriate.

SCENE. — MRS. FIELD'S *sitting-room. Table*, R., *with rocking-chair* L. *of it. Lounge*, R., *on which is reclining* SUSY FOLLEIGH, *reading a novel.* KITTY FIELDS *and* JENNY SANDS *seated*, C; KITTY *holding, and* JENNY *winding, a skein of worsted.*

Susy. (*Throwing down the book.*) "Bleeding hearts!" Nothing but "bleeding hearts!" Modern novels, with their sensational plots, are so stupid! Lovely young women rescued by interesting young men. Moonlight meetings in rustling groves. How very tiresome! I'd give the world for a glance at the last new fashion-plate, or one page of fashionable intelligence Why do not authors, by way of variety, pay more attention to descriptions of toilet, or sketches of fashionable society? I'm sure, nothing could be more interesting than to know how people are dressing. It would certainly astonish the dwellers in this desolate spot.

Jenny. Why, Susy, you are not very complimentary to Aunt Field's beautiful place. To be sure, it is not quite so elegant as your father's fashionable home in the city. But you know you came here for change, and you can scarcely expect the display of dress and fashion to which you have been accustomed.

Susy. Oh! I like it well enough. I'm only complaining of the stupid reading we are obliged to have here. I'm dying to know the latest fashion in dress, the last new style of hat; and there is positively nothing in this book to enlighten me, although it is called a modern fashionable novel.

Kitty. Why, Susy, would you have our authors taught the dressmaker's trade before they send their books into the world?

Jenny. Yes: Susy would have them learn to *clothe* their subjects in fashionable attire before they are introduced to good society.

Susy. (*Taking up a book.*) I'm sure they need teaching. How much more interesting it would be to read that "Stella Augusta, robed in white Cashmere, adorned with bugles, gored skirt, and flowing train, hair bedecked with japonicas and moss-rose buds, a white opera cape thrown over her shoulders, appeared upon the moonlit balcony, just as Alphonso, in his becoming shooting-jacket of black velvet, a resplendent diamond gleaming from his immaculate ruffled bosom, flowing collar and Magenta tie, lavender kids and Malacca cane, curly locks and raven mustache, advanced from the shadow of the trees!"

Jenny. Or "Stella Augusta, in her spotted gingham, brown Holland, or sixpenny print, with her hair tightly curled in the remnants of 'The Weekly Clarion.'" (*Laughing.*) Ha, ha, ha!

Kitty. And "Alphonso, in a butcher's frock, his shapely head shorn of its auburn locks, a brown 'wide-awake' shielding his lovely mustache from the sun, advancing from the grove, gayly whistling, 'Oh, dear! what can the matter be?'" Ha, ha, ha!

Susy. Girls, I am shocked at your want of delicacy. 'Tis the fault of your education. You have never moved in fashionable society, and can have little sympathy for the feelings of one who is out of her sphere when not moving in those circles whose boundaries guard the select.

Jenny. Oh, dear! what privations!

Kitty. My stars! what a martyr!

Enter MRS. FIELD, R.

Mrs. Field. Kitty, you must come into the kitchen and help me. I shall never get my washing out in the world. I've sent that Norah to Mr. Hanson's for soft soap. She's been gone an hour, and, for all I know, has tumbled into his barrel.

Kitty. I'll come, mother. I should like a good spell at the wash-tub.

Susy. The wash-tub! You don't mean to say that *you* wash and scrub!

Mrs. Field. To be sure she does; and a right smart washer and ironer she is too, if I do say it.

Susy. Why, it will spoil your figure, bending over a tub. I couldn't do it.

Kitty. I'm not a bit afraid of it.

Jenny. No, indeed: 'tis a wholesome exercise, and I'll go and help you.

Norah. (*Outside*, R.) Miss Faild, Miss Faild! I have the soap, mam.

Enter NORAH, R.

Mrs. Field. Why, Norah, where have you been?

Norah. Faith, mam, for the soap, jist. You niver towld me there was two Mr. Hansons; and I wint to the docthor's shop fust, but he had no soap; but he axed me, mam, were we well? and he towld me, mam, you should be very careful, for there's a terrible faver coome to the place, and it's breaking out iverywhere. Oh, it's myself wishes I was back in ould Ireland, sure.

Mrs. Field. A terrible fever?

Norah. Yis, mam. He called it "a Gracian Bind," that attacks the vitals, and binds one up like a jack-knife; and the pains are so orful that it lifts yer upon the tips of yer toes. Oh, musha! Oh, dear!

Kitty. Nonsense, Norah! 'Twas only a joke.

Norah. Joke, is it? Faith, it's no joke to catch the faver, sure.

Mrs. Field. Well, well; come to the kitchen at once.

We shall never get the washing out at this rate. Kitty, I can do without you now. Come, Norah. [*Exit*, R.

Norah. Yis, mam; I'm a cooming. O Miss Kitty! 'tis afraid of the faver I am. [*Exit*, R.

Kitty. "A Grecian Bend." That's what Norah would call a *quare* name for a *faver.*

Jenny. Oh! it's only a joke of Mr. Hanson's. (*Bell rings.*) Ah! visitors.

Kitty. On washing-day! Who can it be?

Susy. I must run to my room. I'm not dressed for callers.

Enter NORAH, *with a letter*, R.

Norah. If you plase, Miss Susy, here's a letther; and the expressman has brought a whacking big box; and he axed, had we it too?

Kitty. What do you mean by *it*, Norah?

Norah. The faver, Miss Kitty. "The Gracian Bind." Oh, musha! It's kilt we are intirely.

Susy. A letter for me. (*Opens it.*) From mother. (*Sits on lounge and reads it.*)

Kitty. Nonsense, Norah: there's no fever in the place.

Jenny. But I must say I have a great curiosity to know what this "Grecian Bend" is.

Norah. Curiosity, is it? Faith, I've none to see a faver.

Mrs. Field. (*Outside*, R.) Norah, Norah!

Norah. Coomin' coomin'! Oh, dear! I've got a chill and a hot flush; and I'm sure it's the faver coomin'! Oh, dear! What will I do? What will I do? [*Exit*, R.

Enter AUNT DEBBY, L.

Aunt Debby. Dear me! what have I done with my speticles? I declare, I'm always losin' somethin' or nother. (*Looks on table.*) They ain't here. My fust husband used to say, (*To* KITTY.) Ain't you settin' on 'em! (KITTY *rises.*) No, they ain't there. — My fust husband — Brass-bowed. — (*To* JENNY.) P'r'aps they're in your cheer. (JENNY *rises.*) No. Where could they have gone to? — My fust husband — Cost nine and six. — (*To* SUSY.) P'r'aps they're on the sofa. (SUSY *rises.*) No. I declare, where can they have gone to?

Kitty. Aunt Debby, what's that on your forehead?

Aunt Debby. (*Removes spectacles from her forehead.*) My speticles, I do declare! Well, well: my memory is ginnin out. My fust husband used to say — (*Goes to table.*) Anybody seen my scissors? (*To* JENNY.) — Won't you please git up; p'r'aps they're in your cheer. (JENNY *rises.*) No. My fust husband — him as was a Spooner, Hiram Spooner. — (*To* KITTY.) — Won't you please let me look in your cheer? (KITTY *rises.*) No: they ain't there. Spooner says, says he — Sharp-pinted — (*To* SUSY.) — Shall I trouble you ag'in? (SUSY *rises.*) No. Where on airth have them scissors got to?

Jenny. Aunt Debby, what's that hanging at your side?

Aunt Debby. Them plaguy scissors, as sure as I'm alive! Well, well: it does beat all natur! It's jest what my fust husband always said. Says he, Debby, you're so forgetful, you'll forget you've got a husband,

and be marryin' ag'in, some day. But I never did — as long as he lived, any way. (*Sits in rocking-chair and darns stockings.*)

Susy. Oh, isn't this splendid! A new sensation in fashionable circles. Mother has written me all about it.

Jenny. A new sensation! What is it?

Kitty. Something to do with "women's rights?"

Jenny. A new bonnet?

Kitty. Something good to eat?

Jenny. Or a new book?

Susy. Neither. 'Tis "the Grecian Bend."

Jenny and Kitty. "The Grecian Bend?"

Aunt Debby. Greasy Ben? Why, that must be John Hodgkins's son, that my second husband, him as was a Skinner, pulled out of the taller vat. They called him Greasy Ben ever arterwards. I want to know if you've got a letter from him?

Kitty. No, no, Aunt Debby: Susy has a letter from her mother, acquainting her with some new fashion.

Aunt Debby. Do tell! Are they wearin' bumbazines or ginghams mostly? And how's cotton — hey?

Jenny. The "Grecian Bend!" Why, that's Norah's *faver.*

Kitty. Oh, do tell us what it is!

Susy. No: I will give you an agreeable surprise. Mother has sent me every thing necessary for a display of the new fashion. When you next see me, you shall know all. Good-by. [*Exit*, L.

Jenny. Now, isn't this provoking!

Kitty. A proud, stuck-up thing!

Jenny. But a good heart, Kitty. I'm sure we both

love her dearly. Susy has been spoiled by over-indulgence. You know her parents are very fashionable people.

Kitty. I know they are; but that's no reason why she should come here and put on such airs. Her father and mine were nothing but travelling peddlers once. I think she might tell us about this new sensation, as she calls it.

Bessie. (*Outside*, R.) School's done. School's done. Oh, ain't I glad!

[*Enter* R., *throws her books into one corner, her hat in another, and her shawl on the table.*]

Hallo, Kitty! Hallo, Cousin Jenny! Oh, we've had such *splendid* fun to-day! Hallo, Aunt Debby! I've got home.

Aunt Debby. Well, you needn't have told on it. Sich a racket I never did hear!

Bessie. Oh! yes you have, Aunt Debby. Ain't you going to give me a kiss? (*Puts her arm around* AUNT DEBBY'S *neck, and kisses her.*)

Aunt Debby. Massy sakes! You've ruined my new cap!

Bessie. Well, it's too bad. But never mind; I'll iron it for you. Oh, such fun! I'll tell you all about it. Miss Jinks, our teacher, has got it.

Kitty. Got what?

Bessie. "The Grecian Bend."

Jenny. "The Grecian Bend" again.

Bessie. Yes: we were all in school, and having such

fun, throwing spit-balls, and making faces, and playing cat's-cradle, when the door opened, and in came Miss Jinks. My! such a figure! She looked, for all the world, like our speckled hen Fanny, when she waddles about hunting for crumbs, so — (*imitates*). She had a brand new black dress, with a trail, Oh! a mile long, I guess; and such high-heeled boots! She walked so — (*imitates*), and held her hands so — (*imitates*); and her nose was red, and her corkscrew curls stuck out, and — and — Oh, dear! I can't tell what she did look like! She was so funny! and the girls giggled, and the boys laughed right out! Tom Mason said she was sick; and Bobby Sawyer, he said she was in affliction! and Fred Jordan, he whispered to me she had "the Grecian Bend!" Oh, it was so funny!

Jenny. Kitty, we've a full description of it now.

Kitty. But I don't understand it.

Bessie. Well, here it is, exact. (*Produces a picture.*) Charlie Haddam gave it to me, and it looks just like Miss Jinks.

Kitty. (*Taking picture.*) Why, what a fright!

Bessie. Just like Miss Jinks!

Jenny. She looks as though she was going to fall.

Bessie. Just like Miss Jinks!

Kitty. It's black in the face!

Bessie. Just like Miss Jinks!

Aunt Debby. What Jinks is that? I used to know a Sally Jinks: she was a second cousin to my third husband, him as was a Moody.

Bessie. Oh! this ain't her, Aunt Debby. But where's mother? Where's Norah? I'm as hungry as a bear; and I want a piece of mince-pie and a pickle. Norah, Norah!

Norah. (*Outside*, R.) Coomin', coomin'!

Enter R.

Bessie. Hallo, Norah: I've got something for you.

Norah. What is it, honey?

Bessie. (*Gives her the picture.*) "The Grecian Bend."

Norah. (*Drops the picture.*) Oh, murder, murder! It's the faver. It's kilt I am intirely! [*Exit*, R.

Bessie. Ha, ha, ha! the *faver!* What does she mean by that?

Kitty. Some one has been telling her "the Grecian Bend" is a fever, and the poor girl really believes it.

Bessie. Does she? Oh, isn't that fun! Won't I plague her! But I'll have my mince-pie and pickle first. [*Exit*, R.

Jenny. We have discovered Susy's secret.

Kitty. Yes; and I propose to make a good use of it.

Jenny. How, pray?

Kitty. We know her silly passion for dress. Aunt Debby will be sure to remain here for the next hour. I am going to her room. You shall go with me; and I will describe a little plot I have in my mind, by which we may amuse ourselves, and perhaps give Susy a lesson.

Jenny. A little plot! So you have a secret, as well as Susy.

Kitty. Which I will tell you, for I shall need your assistance. So come with me.

[*Exeunt* KITTY *and* JENNY, L.

Aunt Debby. Now them gals are up to mischief. I never see two critters with their heads together so close, but what there's some kind of mischief brewin'.

[*Enter* SUSY, L., *in "Grecian Bend," rich dress, high-heeled boots, long train, pannier, &c., tottering slowly, endeavoring to keep her balance, and her hands in the position usually represented in the prints.*]

What on airth is that? Hosy said there was a caravan in town; and I do believe one of the *annemiles* has broken loose. It looks like a kangaroo. Shoo, shoo! Go away, go away, or I'll holler.

Susy. Oh, dear! I'm so tired. This waist is so tight, and this Bend is so painful! If it wasn't the fashion, I should say it was very ridiculous. (*Attempts to walk, and nearly falls.*) Dear me! I shall fall.

Aunt Debby. Shoo, shoo! Scat! Will you go away?

Susy. Why, Aunt Debby! don't you know me? It's Susy Folleigh.

Aunt Debby. Land sakes! You don't say so! Why, what's the matter? Got the rheumatics, or the sciatiky? or you going to faint — hey?

Susy. No, no.

Aunt Debby. Where's my camphire? (*Runs to table.*) Where on airth is my camphire! That's jest like me! Never can find nothin'. Here, Sarah! Sarah Jane! Norah! Water! Water! Quick!

Susy. Why, Aunt Debby, I'm quite well. (*Attempts to walk, and totters.*)

Aunt Debby. There you go.

[*Enter* NORAH, R., *with a glass of water on a tray, stumbles over the long train of* SUSY'S *dress, and drops tray.*]

Susy. You stupid thing! Couldn't you see my dress?

Aunt Debby. (*Leads* SUSY *to lounge.*) This poor child is sick.

Susy. I assure you nothing is the matter. I'm only practising "the Grecian Bend."

Norah. "The Gracian Bind," is it? Oh, musha! the faver's in the house, and we're all kilt intirely! Oh, murder! Will I run for the docthor?

Aunt Debby. (*Runs to table.*) Where's my fan? Massy sakes! where's my fan? Gone: that's jest like me!

Norah. Will I run to the docthor's for a *proscription?* She's doubled up! It's the symptims intirely!

Susy. Will you oblige me by stopping your meddling. I am quite well, and want none of your attentions.

Aunt Debby. Well, I'm glad of that. (*Goes back to table.*) I did think you had an attack of rheumatics; and I'm awful skeery about it, for my fourth husband, Deacon Higgins, —

Norah. Oh, dear! Oh, dear! The faver, the faver! I'll run for the docthor, sure! (*Starts for door, and meets* BESSIE, *who enters,* R.) — Oh, you poor, dear child! you mustn't come a-near the faver, or it's a poor lone orphan you'll be, sure.

Bessie. What's the matter, Norah?

Norah. It's the faver, — "the Gracian Bind." Miss Susy has it. Whist! Be quiet, darlin'! I'll run for the docthor.

Bessie. Oh, my! Susy's got a "Grecian Bend!" Oh, isn't this fun! Where are you going, Norah?

Norah. For a proscription to kill the faver.

Bessie. That isn't the fever, Norah; that's the new fashion. Everybody is going to adopt it. It will be raging.

Norah. It's catchin', and I've niver been vassinated.

Bessie. Yes: everybody, even the servants, must dress in that way. You must have one.

Norah. Must I? Will it keep off the faver?

Bessie. Yes. Oh, yes! it's a sure preventive.

Norah. But where will I get it?

Bessie. You come with me. I'll fix you all right.

Norah. Will I look like that? 'Twill break my back intirely.

Bessie. I'll fix you up so nice! Come along.

[*Exit*, R.

Norah. Yes, darling! Faith, she's a bright little thing to hilp a body in distress. [*Exit*, R.

Aunt Debby. Shan't I make you a little soothin' yarb tea?

Susy. No.

Aunt Debby. Some hot water for your feet.

Susy. No.

Aunt Debby. A little pennyrial —

Susy. No: I want nothing — but to be let alone.

Aunt Debby. Well, of all the kantagarus things that ever I did see! Why don't you lean back on the sofy?

Susy. (*Aside.*) I wish I could. *It* won't let me. I'd go back to my room, but I'm afraid to start, for fear I should tumble.

Enter NORAH.

Norah. Faix, here's another with it, mam, and she wants to see Miss Folleigh.

Susy. To see me? Show her up, Norah.

Norah. She's a coomin', ma'am. [*Exit* NORAH, R.

[*Enter* JENNY, *dressed in short red petticoat, with overskirt of brown, pinned up all around: a "pillow," high-heeled shoes, red stockings, small white shawl, roomy bonnet to hide her face: the dress of thirty years ago, in imitation of "the Grecian Bend."*

Susy. Whom have we here, I wonder.

Jenny. Miss Folleigh, I believe. (SUSY *bows.*) Glad to see you. I am Miss Rebecca Short, the leader of the *tun* in this place. I heerd there was a fashionable young lady here who had the "bend." You see, I have it too; and as I never had seen a real "bend," I thought I'd better give you a call. You must know I heerd of the bend from my brother Darius, who seed it in Saratogy. He told me what it was like, and I've fixed it up as well as I could, to git the start of that pesky Hannah Long, who's forever trying to get the start of me. How is it about the style? (*Struts round.*)

Susy. (*Aside.*) Mercy! what a fright!

Jenny. Now, speak right out: don't be mealy-mouthed: for of all things I detest a flatterer.

Susy. Well, then, Miss — Miss —

Jenny. Short: Rebecca Short.

Aunt Debby. Short? Becky Short? Be you any connection of the Shorts of Saccarap?

Jenny. Not the least in the world.

Aunt Debby. Oh! I thought p'r'aps you might be my fifth husband's —

Jenny. Miss Folleigh, won't you please stand up and step round a little, so I can see how you look?

Susy. (*Aside.*) Well, of all the impertinent people that ever I did see!

Kitty. (*Outside,* R.) Up stairs — hey? Now, don't trouble yourself. I'll find the way.

Jenny. That pesky Hannah Long, as sure as preaching! She's some to see the fashions too.

[*Enter* KITTY, *dressed similarly to* JENNY, *in old-fashioned style, made more ridiculous if possible.*]

Kitty. Miss Folleigh — Why, Becky Short! You here?

Jenny. To be sure I am: in the latest style too. I've got the start of you, Miss Long.

Kitty. Oh! have you? Well, I never did see such a ridiculous dress in all my life, never!

Jenny. Well, then, you'd better look in the glass, and you will.

Kitty. What do you mean by that? A pretty leader of the *tun* you are!

Jenny. Do you call that "the Grecian Bend?"

Susy. (*Aside.*) I do believe they will quarrel. Dear me! what a ridiculous situation! Ladies, I beg you'll be quiet: Aunt Debby there has a very bad headache.

Aunt Debby. Why, what a whopper? I never had sich a thing in all my life.

Jenny. Won't you please stand up, and let us see your "bend?"

Kitty. Do, Miss Folleigh: I'm dying to see you.

Susy. You're a couple of inquisitive females. Do you suppose I'm going to make an exhibition of myself for your benefit?

Jenny. Law! Now don't fly up. Congenial sperits, you know.

Kitty. Yes: twin worshippers at the shrine of Fashion.

Aunt Debby. Twins — did you say? Well, I declare! I thought you were twins, the minute I sot my eyes onto you.

Jenny. (*To* KITTY.) If you hadn't come here, I should have found out all about it.

Kitty. If it hadn't been for you I should have surprised the whole town.

Jenny. You're a meddler! (*Flout their parasols in each other's faces.*)

Kitty. You're a busybody!

Susy. Oh, dear! what a ridiculous situation! Ladies, ladies! what is the matter?

Kitty. It's Long.

Jenny. It's Short.

Aunt Debby. (*Who has been hanging round* JENNY

and KITTY, *carefully inspecting their dresses, with spectacles on her nose.*) They're a couple of thieves! That are is my bunnet. (*To* JENNY.) I knowd it the moment I sot my eyes onto it. My fifth husband, Jotham Snodgrass, bought it for four dollars and a half. And that's my petticoat, that I quilted the year afore I buried my fourth husband: bless his poor departed soul! It was yaller then; and when he died, I had it dyed blue. That's where my things go to. Here, Sarah! Sarah Jane! Sarah Jane Field! Thieves! Norah, Norah! Thieves!

Norah. (*Outside*, R.) Coomin', coomin', mam!

[*Enter* NORAH, *dressed in short red petticoat, which discloses a pair of men's heavy cowhide boots; an overskirt of calico, made to "stick out" by a half-concealed work-basket of good size; a green shawl on her shoulders; a wide-awake hat on her head, adorned with a peacock's feather; white cotton gloves and an umbrella. The whole should be made very ridiculous.*]

Susy. (*Starting from sofa.*) Gracious! What have we here!

Aunt Debby. Land of liberty sakes! What a looking critter!

Norah. If you plase, it's "the Gracian Bind," which Miss Bessie gave me.

All. "The Grecian Bend!"

Enter MRS. FIELD, R.

Mrs. Field. Aunt Debby, what on earth are you yelling so for? Gracious! I didn't know you had company. Why, Norah, what are you doing here? I've been looking for you for the last half hour. Here's my washing not out yet.

Norah. If you plase, mam, I couldn't help it. Miss Bessie said I must have "the Gracian Bind," or I'd lose my situation.

Mrs. Field. But who are these ladies?

Aunt Debby. Ladies? They're thieves! They've been at my things. That's my bunnet, and that's my shawl and petticoat.

Mrs. Field. But they're friends of Miss Susy.

Susy. Indeed they're not. I never saw them before, and I never want to see them again.

Mrs. Field. Pray, what is your business here then?

Jenny. I came to help you wash.

Kitty. And so did I.

Mrs. Field. To help me wash? But who are you?

Jenny. (*Takes off her bonnet.*) Miss Short.

Kitty. (*Takes off her bonnet.*) Miss Long.

Mrs. Field. Jenny! Kitty!

Aunt Debby. That's the Long and the Short of it.

Susy. What! you girls rigged up in that fashion?

Jenny. It's the last new sensation, Susy.

Kitty. A little secret. You understand, Susy.

Mrs. Field. Well, I'd like to know what this is all about.

Aunt Debby. It's a regular mystification.

Kitty. Susy understands it — don't you, Susy?

Susy. I understand you have been laughing at me, and I'm not surprised at it; for, of all the contemptible fashions that ever were invented, I think "the Grecian Bend" exceeds any thing I ever heard of. At any rate, you shall never see or hear any more of it during my stay here.

Jenny. I'm glad you are not offended, Susy; for it was only a little bit of fun.

Kitty. With a bit of a moral.

Susy. Ah! there's a moral — is there?

Kitty. Yes: that there's but one step from the sublime to the ridiculous.

Susy. I'll accept the moral; but what's to be done with Norah?

Norah. If you plase, I'd like to be undone: the thing on my back is killing me intirely.

Enter BESSIE, R.

Bessie. Please, mother, may I have "a Grecian Bend?" All the girls are going to have them.

Mrs. Field. I'll give you a "bend" that you'll remember, for taking Norah away from her washing. Mercy sakes! I shall never get my washing out. Was there ever such a plague as a house full of girls!

Aunt Debby Never! My sixth husband —

Mrs. Field. Oh! never mind him. Who's going to help me with the wash? I shall never get the wash out. Who will help me?

Kitty. I will, mother.

Jenny. And I, aunt.

Susy. And I; for I think it would be very useful to me.

All. Useful!

Susy. Yes: for, in the first place, I shall learn to wash; and, in the second place, I'm conviuced it is just the exercise necessary to prepare me to bear with resignation, when I reach home, the latest iufliction of fashion, — "A Grecian Bend."

SITUATIONS.

R. BESSIE, NORAH, MRS. F., KITTY, JENNY, SUSY. L.

SNOW-BOUND.

AN ENTERTAINMENT FOR FOUR PERSONS.

CHARACTERS.

Brown, Jones, Smith, Miss Robinson, — Travellers.

COSTUMES.

Brown, Jones, Smith, — Overcoats, slouched hats, comforters, and thick gloves.
Miss Robinson, old-fashioned brown cloak, "pumpkin-hood."

Scene. — *Parlor of an Inn. Grate, with fire burning,* c. *Chairs,* r. *and* l. *of Grate. Piano,* l. *Chair and small Table,* r.

Brown. (*Outside,* r.) Here! Landlord, chambermaid, boots.

Jones. (*Outside,* r.) Boots, chambermaid, landlord! Here!

Brown. Humbug! I tell you this is my room, first to the right.

Jones. No, sir! Mine: positively and unequivocally mine! If a man hasn't got any rights —

Brown. (*Enters* R., *followed by* JONES.) Oh, bother your rights! Humbug! Do you suppose I'm going to stand shivering in that entry, when there's a good rousing fire and comfortable quarters here? No, sir.

Jones. Now, look here! Business is business, and fun is fun. Here we are, after a hard day's ride in a blustering storm, stuck fast — positively snow-bound, at a wayside inn, with a strong probability of being so for the next three days.

Brown. Well, what do I care about that? Blast the storm, confound the inn, and bother you!

Jones. But I don't choose to be bothered. I got out of the coach first. I engaged the best room: I am directed to this —

Brown. And here you are. But I tell you what, sir: there's but one decent room in the house; and if you are the man to selfishly secure the most comfortable quarters, to the exclusion of your fellow-travellers, to leave your companions out in the cold, I am not the man to selfishly see you do it. So here I stay. (*Sits* R. *of fire.*) I've had a pretty good blowing from the storm outside: if you can beat that, why, blow away.

Jones. Now, isn't this pleasant? This comes of attempting a journey in that played-out vehicle of locomotion, the stage-coach, mixing one's-self with nobody knows who. Look here, sir, this is my room: you'll oblige me by leaving it quietly.

Brown. No, sir: "My foot is on my native *hearth*, my name's Micaber."

Jones. Oh, murder! Your foot's on my corns. Look here, Mic-what's-your-name: there's quite enough of that. (*Sits* L. *of fire.*) Now, come, do go, that's a good fellow. The landlord's got a nice room on the next floor.

Brown. Has he? Then you take it: you've higher ideas than I have.

Jones. Now, this is too bad. Is it not enough that I've been jostled all day in a stage-coach? —

Brown. I should say it was quite enough. Confound all stage-coaches! say I.

Jones. And confound all bothering travellers, who get into other people's room!

Brown. Confound them, with all my heart.

Jones. Oh, dear! Can't I get rid of him? Must I endure your delightful society for the next three days?

Brown. Three days! If you get out of this in a week you'll be lucky.

Jones. A week! I can never stand that.

Brown. You don't look as though you could stand much of any thing.

Jones. Now, what do you mean by that? Isn't it enough that I've been jostled all day —

Brown. Oh, pooh, pooh! don't ride over that road again.

Miss Robinson. (*Outside*, R.) Well, I do declare, I'm so thankful to get near a fire again.

Jones. Heavens! there's that old woman coming here.

Brown. Confound her! Haven't we got rid of her yet?

Enter Miss Robinson, r.

Miss R. Oh, lud! Oh, dear! I'm eenamost gone. Do somebody ketch me, quick. I'm going to faint, sartin sure.

Brown. Here, you, why don't you catch her?

Jones. Catch me, that's all.

Miss R. Do run and git me some camphire.

Brown. Come, come, old chap, run for the camphire.

Jones. No, I thank you: I prefer this fire.

Miss R. Ain't anybody going to catch me? Well, if this ain't human nater, right eout and eout. Let a poor lone woman, eenamost tired to death, stand here, and not even offer her a cheer.

Jones. But, I tell you, you don't belong here: this room's engaged.

Miss R. Engaged! Well, p'r'aps I am, and p'r'aps I amn't. I'd like to know what business that is of yours?

Brown. The old lady is a little hard of hearing. Come, come, be civil, and give her your chair.

Jones. Your corner is the warmest: give her yours.

Miss R. Ain't you going to let me sit down by the fire, neither? Here I've travelled all day, and I'm eenamost froze.

Jones. Oh, come, come! go to the landlord: he'll put you somewhere on the next floor, or give you a room in the attic.

Miss R. Rheumatic! Yes, well, I should say so. I've got 'em dreffful bad. You don't know what a poor sufferin' creeter I am.

Brown. You don't suffer any more than I do at present.

Jones. Now, my good woman, do make yourself comfortable somewhere else.

Miss R. Make myself comfortable? Well, that's kind of you, anyhow, and I'll jest take a cheer, and toast my feet right here. (*Wheels a chair to fire, and sits with back to audience.*) It seems to me you are taking a leetle too much of the fire.

Jones. It seems to me this is a remarkably cool way to take possession of my room.

Brown. Your room! I like that. Mine, you mean.

Jones. No, sir: mine (*seizes poker*); and I am prepared to defend it against all intruders.

Brown. Oh, you are! (*Seizes brush.*) Well, two can play at that game.

Miss R. Massy sakes! I do believe there's going to be a massacree here.

Smith. (*Outside*, R.) That's right, landlord. Fish, flesh, and fowl. Cook them all. "I am as hungry as the sea, and could digest as much." We're good for a week here; so set your ovens roaring, your spits turning, and your tea-kettle singing. Ha, ha! this is fun.

Jones. Now, there's our noisy fellow-traveller!

Brown. Yes, and coming this way, sure.

Enter SMITH, R.

Smith. Hallo! here you are. I've been looking for you. Why, what's the matter?

Brown. Matter! I should think you'd ask that.

Jones. Shipwrecked in a snow-storm, — that's what's the matter.

Smith (taking off his hat, coat, and gloves). Well, here we are, a coach-load of distressed travellers, snow-bound, dumped at the door of a nice little inn.

Brown. Yes: we're nicely taken in.

Smith. Come, ain't you going to throw off your over-coats and wrappers? We're good for a week here.

Jones. Good for a week? Thunder!

Brown. A week! Just my luck!

Smith. Yes, a week. There hasn't been such a storm in the memory of the oldest inhabitant; and it's coming faster and faster. Isn't it fun?

Jones. Fun! I don't see much fun about it.

Brown. I confess I am unable to see the precise spot where the laugh comes in.

Jones. It's outrageous!

Brown. It's diabolical!

Smith. Oh, come! this won't do, now. Don't get in a passion. It can't be helped, you know: the snow would come down, the coach couldn't come on, and so here we are.

Brown. Well, you do take it cool.

Smith. Of course I do. If the ride we've taken to-day wouldn't make a man cool, then I've little faith in the cooling properties of snow and ice.

Jones. But, I tell you, I shall be ruined. I must be ten miles from here this very night.

Brown. And so must I. A very particular engagement. There must be some way to get out of this.

Smith. Yes, there is one. Shovel yourself out. It's no use, fellow-travellers: here we are, and here we must stay; so throw care to the winds. We'll bid farewell to the hollow, heartless world, and, in our comfortable quarters, eat, drink, and be merry.

Jones. Oh, yes! this may be all very well for you. You evidently like being "out in the cold."

Smith. "Out in the cold!" Where's that? A man can never be "out in the cold" when he carries a warm heart, a cheerful temper, and an earnest purpose.

Brown. Humbug!

Jones. Bosh!

Smith. Oh! come, come, fellow-travellers, don't give up so. Why, when we started this morning, you were as gay and as jolly as schoolboys on a frolic. You remember it, don't you?

When the sky was blue above, and the snow was white below,
The clear, cool breezes blowing, and our hearts were all aglow, —

we were all on top, — sent the driver inside to talk to the old lady. I took the reins, and off we started.

Brown. Nearly upsetting us the first thing.

Jones. We did spin along tolerably fast, though.

Smith. Spin? We flew. Up the hill and down again, across the bridge, and along the road, a clear stretch of three miles, with our horses on the keen jump. We passed every thing on the road.

Brown. Yes, frightened all the old women.

Jones. Upset three farmers and a milkman, and scattered a crowd of boys in all directions.

Smith. Then the driver stuck his head out of the window, and shouted —

Brown. The rival coach is coming up. That's where I took the whip. (*Jumps up.*)

Jones. And I commenced to yell. (*Jumps up.*) Didn't I yell?

Smith. Didn't you, though? But we let the rival coach come up.

Brown. 'Till the leaders were almost on the rack.

Smith. And then I gave them the reins.

Brown. And I the whip.

Jones. And I the yell.

Smith. (*Imitates driving.*) Now, my beauties, go along there; show your training.

Brown. Hy, hy!

Jones. Hy, hy!

Smith. Lively, now, Dobbin. Show yourself, old Jack. Step out, Dexter. Lively, now, lively!

Brown. Hy, hy!

Jones. Hy, hy!

Smith. And then they went to work. Away, mile after mile, and the rival coach —

Brown. The rival coach was far behind.

Jones. Yes, on her beam-ends, in a gully. Wa'n't it jolly?

Smith. And then the storm came on, and here we are, snow-bound.

Brown. Yes, confound it, snow-bound. (*Goes back to chair.*)

Jones. Dead stuck. It's too bad. (*Goes back to chair.*)

Smith. Now, don't say that. It's the same snow we sped over so merrily this morning. There's a little more of it, to be sure; but then, you know, you can't have too much of a good thing. So what's the use of fretting?

We've nice, comfortable quarters here; the landlord is a whole-souled fellow, who will let us do just as we please. So let's be jolly, laugh at the storm, and, like true philosophers, make the best of it. We've all lost something by the delay, and I'll just tell you what I've lost. I had a letter, three days ago, from a friend of mine who is stopping some ten miles from here, making sketches of snow-scenes, I believe. He's got a little lonesome, and wanted me to come and see him. He had invited a nice little party: we were to have a masquerade, private theatricals, bring out a new piece, and have a good time generally. I started off this morning, got too late for the train, as usual, and took the stage-coach to go to my friend Robinson's —

Brown. Robinson! Not Tom?

Smith. Exactly.

Brown (*coming down front*). Well, this is queer. I was bound for the same place. I've all the costumes for the masquerade. I was to assist in getting up the theatricals —

Jones (*coming down front*). And I was to lead the orchestra, — one piano and a bass drum.

Brown. You!

Jones. Yes: I was bound for the same place.

Smith. Well, this is capital: all bound for the same place, and all snow-bound here. We can't go, you know, so let's make ourselves comfortable. We should have become sociable at Tom's: let's be so here. We can entertain each other.

Brown. So we can; that's capital.

Jones. An idea worth entertaining.

Smith. In spite of the storm, we'll be gay and — what is the song?

Brown. (*Sings.*) "Gay and happy, gay and happy, we'll be gay and happy still."

Smith. That's it. Off with your wrappers.

Brown. Here goes. (*Throws off coat and hat.*) I'll do my best for the entertainment of the party.

Jones. And so will I. (*Throws off coat and hat.*)

Smith. And I. And who knows but what, in endeavoring to entertain ourselves, we may entertain angels unawares? By-the-by, speaking of angels, there's only one thing necessary to make us perfectly happy.

Jones and Brown. What's that?

Smith. A presiding genius, one of those fairy mortals whose presence beautifies a desert, and whose smiles can make any spot on earth the dearest; for, where she is, 'tis always home.

Miss Robinson. (*Sings.*)

> "'Mid pleasures and palaces, though we may roam,
> Be it ever so humble, there's no place like home."

(*Then rises, throws off cloak and hood, and appears in evening dress.*)

Smith. Well, well: here's a masquerade!

Brown. My dear madam, do let me offer you a chair.

Jones. Let me take your cloak.

Miss R. Your pardon, gentlemen: I fear I intrude. The landlord will, no doubt, be happy to show me a room in the attic.

Brown. Ah, madam, if we had suspected!

Jones. Which we didn't, I assure you.

Miss R. Ah, gentlemen, I fear your politeness is governed by age. But I'll forgive you. Perhaps I should explain the meaning of this masquerade. My brother, the gentleman to whom you have just alluded, wrote me while I was visiting a relative, that he should expect me home to-night, to assist him in entertaining company which he had invited. I was to have had a protector in travelling; but at the last moment he found it impossible to leave. Knowing my brother would need my services, I determined to start without him, and, that I might be unmolested, adopted the disguise which I have just thrown off. Gentlemen, like you, I am snow-bound. It would have been a great pleasure to me to have entertained you at my brother's: will you allow me to hope that I shall be no intruder here, but may be allowed to assist you in your endeavors to amuse and entertain each other?

Smith. Madam, Miss Robinson, allow me, in behalf of the proprietors of this establishment and my fellow-travellers, to bid you a hearty welcome, and to assure you that during your stay you will be a guest whom we shall be proud and happy to entertain and protect.

Brown. All of which is heartily seconded by yours, truly.

Smith. Allow me to present my friends, here. Miss Robinson, Mr. ——, Mr. ——

Brown. Brown.

Smith. Mr. Brown; and this is Mr. —— Mr. ——

Jones. Jones.

Smith. Mr. Jones; and myself, Mr. Smith.

Miss R. Gentlemen, delighted to make your acquaintance.

Jones. But ain't we going to have some supper?

Smith. In just half an hour. The landlord has assured me that we shall have the best in the house, as soon as it can be prepared. While you are waiting supper, suppose you try that piano. It looks well, and, I have no doubt, can sound its own praises. Mr. Jones, a song will be very acceptable.

Miss R. Oh, do sing, Mr. Jones!

Jones. I'll do my best; but, remember, I've left my notes at home.

Song, MR. JONES.

Brown. That's good. Give us another.

Jones. Suppose, by way of variety, you try your musical voice.

Brown. Oh, certainly! if there's any thing here I can sing. Ah! here's my old friend, "The Bashful Young Gentleman." How will that do?

Jones. Capitally. Let's hear from "The Bashful Young Gentleman."

Song, MR. BROWN.

Smith. Good. Give us another?

Brown. Suppose you try your voice?

Smith. I don't sing.

All. You don't sing!

Smith. I don't sing.

Brown. What can you do?

Smith. Not much of any thing. Yes, I'll tell you a story.

Recitation, MR. SMITH.*

* Of course it is optional with the *characters* to sing or recite.

And now, Miss Robinson, as we of the masculine gender have tried our best to entertain you, we trust that you will favor us —

Miss R. With all my heart.

Song, MISS ROBINSON.

Brown. Now, let's go over it again.

Smith. Hold on. Variety's the spice of life. It has just occurred to me that I have in my right-hand pocket the manuscript of the new play, which was to have been performed at our friend Robinson's.

Brown. Good! read it.

Jones. Yes, let's have it.

Miss R. "The play, the play's the thing." Do read it!

Smith. Read it! we'll do better than that: we'll act it.

Brown. A good idea: let's form ourselves into a dramatic company. I'll be the scenic artist.

Smith. So you shall. Mr. Jones and Miss Robinson shall look after the music (*sits the table*, C.), and I'll copy the parts. So let's to work (*takes paper from pocket*). Here's the manuscript: "Alonzo the Brave and the Fair Imogene."

Brown. Ah! We shall want a castle for that.

Smith. Yes: and a trap.

Brown. I'm not up to trap. Hallo, here's one right under our feet!

Smith. Then go to work. I'll copy the parts.

Brown. Now, what shall I do for a castle? I'll make a voyage of discovery. (*Exit*, R.)

Smith. Now to work. (*Sits at table and takes pencil.*) Alonzo, Imogene, Baron Brumagem, Baron Boz,

Miss R. Oh! this will do capitally: try that.

(MISS R. *sings*, MR. J. *plays very loud. If the piano is not on the stage, let both sing.*)

Smith. Oh, come, my dear friends! I can never write if you make such a noise as that.

Enter BROWN, R., *with a clothes-horse.*

Brown. That's the best I can do for a castle.

Smith. That will do capitally. "Act 1, Scene 1: Castle Klaushaus, with a view of Mt. Washington in the distance."

Brown. Mount Washington! Where will you get that?

Smith. (*Pointing to picture at back.*) Well, there's Washington, about to mount. We shall have to make that do.

Brown. What an *a-mount* of imagination you have!

Smith. Castle, L., Imogene discovered at window of Castle. (MISS R. *sings*, JONES *plays*, BROWN *hammers.*) My dear friends, don't make such a noise: "Ye cruel fates, that unrelenting play." (MISS R. *sings*, JONES *plays*, BROWN *hammers, till curtain falls.* SMITH, *jumping up.*) Oh, confound it! I can't write with such a noise as that. Ladies, Miss Robinson; gentlemen, Mr. Jones, Mr. Brown, will you oblige me —

(*Curtain falls, with music in full blast.*)

ALONZO THE BRAVE AND THE FAIR IMOGENE.

CHARACTERS.

BARON BRUMAGEM, manager of the "Fair" (Mr. Jones).

ALONZO, sometimes called "the brave," sometimes "the green" (Mr. Brown).

IMOGENE, sweet sixteen, as may be seen (Miss Robinson).

BARON BOZ, the baron all covered with jewels and gold (Mr. Smith).

COSTUMES FOR THE PLAY.

BARON. Long brown shirt, white tights, brown shoes, white wig and beard, cap and cane.

ALONZO. Act 1, White shape dress (doublet and trunks), white tights, white shoes, cap and feathers, moustache. Act 2, armor-suit.

BARON BOZ. Blue shape dress, white tights, blue shoes, wig and beard to imitate Charles Dickens.

IMOGENE. Rich dress.

The costumes and wigs for this piece can be procured in Boston, of Mrs. M. A. Wilson, Costumer, No. 52 Chambers Street. The "Castle," and other pieces of scenery, of D. A. Story, No 72 Sudbury Street.

ACT I.

Exterior of Castle Klaushaus.

SCENE, *same as first, with stage all clear, and a castle,* L., *made by covering a large clothes-horse, painting it on one side to represent a castle, on the other a door and window, with painted sign,* "ORIENTAL TEA COMPANY:" *a practical window to open.*

(IMOGENE *at the window in castle.*)

Im. Ye cruel fates, that unrelenting play
On earth's fair lawn your frolicsome croquet,
Pity the sorrows of a forlorn maid,
Locked up all day, because her pa's afraid
She'll make a *faux-pas*, her fond sire will euchre,
And wed for love, and not for filthy lucre.
Ah, me! was ever maid in such distress?
I can't get out to purchase a new dress;
And silks and satins are so very low,
It is a shame I can't a-shopping go.
A stern old Roman, if he is my pa,
Why does he seek my pleasures thus to mar?
To be like him I'm sure I ne'er intend:
I'm more inclined to have a Grecian Bend.
These gilded bars and bonds I can't abear:
I'd rather have a gilt band for my hair.
Oh, for some gallant knight! — handsome, of course,
With lance and shield, upon a noble horse,
To free this luckless maid from her vile prison:
How gladly would I say my life was his'n.

Song, IMOGENE. *Air*, "*Kissing at the Gate.*"

Oh, dear! I once did have a beau:
A gallant knight was he,
Who with the army marched away,
And crossed the stormy sea.
He left me sadly here alone,
And went in search of fame:
A tall and handsome cavalier,
Alonzo was his name.
Alonzo was his name, Alonzo was his name;
A tall and handsome cavalier, Alonzo was his name.

Ah, me! I often sigh for him,
  And wish him at my side:
It is so grand to have a beau
  To with you walk or ride;
To bid him come or go at will,
  His whole attention claim.
Ah! such a beau I once did have:
  Alonzo was his name.
Alonzo was his name, Alonzo was his name;
A tall and handsome cavalier, Alonzo was his name.

Now I feel better. Dear me! here comes pa:
I'm quite resolved to have a family jar;
Proclaim for woman's rights, preserve my station,
If necessary, make a grand oration. (*Exit.*)

Enter BARON BRUMAGEM, R.

Baron. Now, by my castle-walls, this news, if true,
Is morter*f*ying, and makes me feel blue.
Down at the "public," with mine host I sat,
To quaff my ale, and have my usual chat,
When, with a grin most horrible to see,
A lad slipped in this telegram to me:
"To Baron Brumagem, rich, hale, and balmy,—
The king has drafted you into his army."
The king be ——. There's nobody about.
If walls have ears, just let 'em 'ear it out.
The king be blowed. I'm driven to a corner:
Let him protest, this draft I will not honor.
He hales me hale. There'll be a hail-storm here,
When from my h'ale he drags me to my bier.
And must I leave you, my ancestral halls,
To pine and moulder when my country calls?

Not as I knows on. Young ideas may shoot,
But not I, dears, while there's a substitute.

Song, Baron. *Air*, "*Walking down Broadway.*"

The toughest thing in war, —
And no one dare say nay, —
In column or platoon,
Is marching all the day.
My substitute shall go,
And fight or run away;
But I prefer my ease
To marching all the day.

(*Speaking.*) Oh, no! I couldn't think of it. The idea of Baron Brumagem, with knapsack on shoulder and musket on his back, —

Marching all the day, the hot and dusty day:
The O. K. thing, I think, is not marching all the day.

Let young blades fight and run,
And all the glory win:
I am too old a chick
To be so taken in.
Where cannon-balls fly fast,
The glory does not pay
For all the pains you get
In marching all the day.

(*Speaking.*) No, 'twould never do for me. If I must be a soldier, I'll join the Home Guard; for, in that Ancient and Honorable company, there's no —

Marching all the day, the hot and dusty day:
The O. K. thing, I think, is not marching all the day.

Im. (*At window.*) Why, pa, so soon returned? What has gone wrong?

Bar. Why ask you that? I told you in my song.

Im. The import of your song I scarce could hear:
You sing so badly out of tune, my dear.

Bar. And so you importune me. Bah! I say.

Im. I fear you've seen too many bars to-day.
Do let me out, that is a parent dear.

Bar. To keep you in I pay a dear rent here.

Im. To feel the fresh, sweet airs upon my brow.

Bar. My sweet, I think you've airs too many now.
Young woman, no! To guard you well I'm bound:
In me a fond and loving sire you've found.
Kind and indulgent, I'm your legal keeper:
Gals should be kept at home, it's so much cheaper.

Im. Now, dear papa.

Bar. Shut up.

Im. Do let me out, I pray.

Bar. If I let out, there'll be the deuce to pay.
(*Drops cane.*)
I'm coming in, so stop your horrid clatter, —
Lay out that cold fowl on the pewter platter.

(*Unlocks door of castle.*)

Im. O pa, your cane! You've left your cane!

Bar. Dear me,
What canes are good for, I'm not able to see:

(IMOGENE *slips out of door, and slips behind it.*)

I'm coming in, just mind what you're about.

(*Exit into castle*, IMOGENE *claps to door and locks it.*)

Im. If there are callers, pray say I've stepped out.

Bar. (*Inside.*) Come, come, young woman, have no joking, dear.

Im. Jo King! there's no young man of that name here.

Bar. O Immy! immolate your father thus?

Im. I have no farther use for you: don't make a fuss.

Bar. Open that door.

Im. It's locked.

Bar. You've got the key.

Im. I mean to keep it too.

Bar. We'll see, we'll see.
This is rebellion.

Im. This is woman's right,
When teasing fails, to take up arms and fight.

Bar. Oh, dear! you've listened to Geo. Francis Train.

Im. I have, and mean to go and list again.
You'll find your cold fowl on the pewter laid:
I won't go far, so don't you be afraid.

Bar. Cold-hearted chicken, thus your sire to fret:
Where's that cold fowl? I will be happy yet.

(*Duet*, BARON *and* IMOGENE. *Air*, "*The Last Rose of Summer.*")

'Tis the last chick of Christmas,
Left sadly alone;
All its plump little fellows
Devoured and gone:
No vestige of turkey,
No wild-goose is nigh;
But this sad little chicken
Forsaken doth lie.

Im. So fair and foul a day I have not seen:
Oh! if I could but meet Alonzo Green,

We'd hie together to the Skating Rink,
Of pleasure's fount to take an ice-cold drink.
Now isn't that pretty? that's a metaphor:
If I don't meet him soon, there'll be a thaw.
Off to the wars so long, I'm very sure
There never was so long a time before.
Good gracious! who's that coming down this way?
'Tis a poor minstrel, wandering all the day,
One of a Band, that's organized to slay
Music (not Gilmore's) in a cruel way.
Though of return they have a ready knack,
And should be popular, tho' so Of-fen-bach,
His notes won't pass, so aside I'll slip,
Or he'll post here, and I must then post scrip.

Enter ALONZO, R., *disguised in a domino, turning the spit of an old-fashioned tin-kitchen hanging from his neck.*

(*Song*, ALONZO. *Air*, "*Gaily the Troubadour.*")

Daily the organ-man
  Roams through the streets,
Begging a nickel
  Of all that he meets:
Singing "From Hoveltine,
  Hither I flees,
Lady dear, lady dear,
  One nickel, please."

Daily the organ-man
  Sad turns away,
With the rude throng,
  That never will pay:
Singing, "Your airs are bad,
  You're out of tune,
Organ-man, organ-man,
  Go away soon."

The wheel of fortune is a gay machine,
No greater novelty was ever seen:
Like Paddy's pig, it has a curious knack
Of getting forward oft by turning back.
It's back on me; for, turn it as I will,
It leaves me where I started, standing still.
Back from the wars, as poor as when I went,
To turn an honest penny, I invent
This wondrous apparatus, so bewitchin',
Which is a very musical tin-kitchen;
But all in vain, no tin it brings to me,
Though I do tinkle it where'er I be.
A knight of chivalry, I once was bold
At shivering lances, now am shivering cold.
I can't get on; and so, my friends, you see
The wheel of fortune's wheel and woe to me.

Im. What wheedling voice is that?

Alon. A lady gay!
Madam, will it please you hear my humble lay?
A curious instrument you see —

Im. Cureious, I'm sure:
It seems to me more like to kill than cure.
No airs for me. Your voice, it strikes a chord —

Alon. I have a striking voice, upon my word.

Im. A chord of memories —

Alon. Lady, you make me smile.
A cord! why don't you measure by the mile?

Im. Gentle musician, let me see your card.

Alon. No cards.

Im. Your pardon, it is hard
To mock your poverty. I forgot you're poor.

Alon. I'm in the fashion, any way, I'm sure.

Im. That voice again, — that form, — Oh go, go, go!

Alon. I am disguised.

Im. In liquor?

Alon. No, no, no!

Im. That voice again — you are —

Alon. I am.

Im. 'Tis he!

Alon. Alonzo Green, from o'er the dark-green sea.

Im. Oh, oh, oh! (*Rushes towards* ALONZO.)

Alon. Stop one moment, just for fun:
We'll have this melo-dramatically done.

(ALONZO *goes extreme* R., IMOGENE, L.)

Alon. That face, those form, —

Im. That eyes, those nose, —

Alon. 'Tis she!
Immy —

Im. Lonny —

Alon. Now: one, two, three. (*Embrace.*)

Im. But, dear Alonzo, why this coarse disguise?

Alon. Coarse! Of course it looks so in your eyes.
Listen, dear Immy. Now I've older grown,
I would be lov*ed* for myself alone,
So laid aside my gilded traps of war, —
My shining armor.

Im. To be, — ah, more sure.
I see it all. And could'st thou doubt thy Immy?

Alon. Nay,
Dearest one, I never could, by Gemini!

(*Looks at her tenderly, places her up stage, and indulges in a soliloquy.*)

To pop, or not to pop: that's what's the matter.
Whether 'tis better now to cut it fatter,
By marrying her, or pop off out the way.
Her pop is rich; has coupons, so they say:
He coops her up, he keeps her very quiet, —
She's like to die, she's kept on such low diet.
I'm poor and proud, called brave, and have a name, —
'Tis all I have, yet 'tis well known to fame.
She's in distress, — may die, — 'tis good to give:
I'll give my all, — my name, — and she shall live.
My heart, fair Immy, at your feet I fling,
And while it beats 'twill be good time to sing.

(*Duet*, ALONZO *and* IMOGENE. *Air*, "*Guaracha.*")

Alon. Just listen to me now, my fair Imogene,
And nestle up close to my side.
You're the sweetest young lady I ever have seen:
O dearest! O dearest! wilt thou be my bride?

(*Air*, "*Sonnambula.*")

Im. Sounds so joyful, bliss revealing,
Chloroform-like o'er my senses stealing,
Like wilting I'm very sure I'm feeling:
Dearest Alonzo, you must ask my respectable papa.

Alon. Ask him? What, face old Baron Brumagem? I couldn't do it.

Im. Yes you can, dear: come.

Alon. 'Tis worse than medicine.

Im. Which you must take.

Alon. I'd rather take you.

Im. Then you would mistake.
Good boys first take the medicine; so don't frown, —
A lump of sugar then —

Alon. To keep it down.
I see the point: obedient I'll be found,
And take this ugly medicine by the pound.

(*Pounds on castle.*)

(*Song*, ALONZO. *Air*, "*Who's dat knocking.*")

Alon. Old man, I love the little girl
You've christened Imogene:
Of all the lasses in this town,
She's the fairest I have seen.
Her eyes so bright, they shine to-night,
To steal my heart away.
I'd like to wed this little maid, —
Old man, what do you say?

Enter BARON, *from castle.*

Bar. Who knocks so loud? My friend, you'd better steer
For Leonard's auction, with such knocks shun here.
Alon. Behold in me a knight.
Bar. Well, knight, good-day.
Alon. My name's Alonzo; on the Gramp — ah —
Bar. Shut up, I say.
I'm not your grampa, nor your uncle, — so look out!
Just go to Brattle Square, if you would spout.
If you've a story, prythee cut it shorter.
Alon. I will. I want to cut off with your daughter.
Bar. Ha, ha! And darest thou, then,
To beard old Brumagem within his den?
Alon. Oh, cut your beard! I'd whisk 'er off, old man
To Hymen's altar.
Bar. I forbid the banns.

Cut off yourself, and in a jiffy too.
My daughter's not for any knave like you.

Alon. The deuce she's not.

Im. Whist, dear Alonzo, whist.

Bar. You cur.

Alon. I can't, my queen.

Bar. From your pursuit desist, —
A suitor for my girl in such a dress!

Alon. Hardly a winning suit, I must confess;
Yet I've her love. My heart, with trumpet-shout,
Cries —

Bar. Hearts are not trumps here, so your hand's played out.
My daughter's not for you: your game is blocked.
The girl shall straight be in a dungeon locked.
I'll stop her squalling, and her saucy raillery.

Alon. He's going to put his daughter on low cellery.

Im. Stay, jailor, stay and hear my woe.

Bar. Shut up your bawling!
Into the house, — a heavy dew is falling.

(*Exit* BARON, *dragging* IMOGENE.)

Alon. O Baron, Baron! when I settle with you,
You'll find, my friend, there is a heavy due.
What's to be done? I cannot lose her thus,
And yet I hardly like to make a fuss.
This Baron puts on airs within his castle stout:
To spite him, then, I'll try an air without.

(*Song*, ALONZO. *Air*, "*Up in a Balloon.*")

Old Brumagem frowns upon my love,
And hurries her off from my loving sight;

But I'll batter the walls of his castle stout,
And carry her off this very night.
He'll find that a lover danger can face,
And humbug papas with a very good grace;
And, should he pursue, he'll find very soon,
His daughter is off for a trip to the moon.

(*Spoken.*) By the latest style of locomotion.

Up in a balloon, up in a balloon,
With the Baron's little star, sailing round the moon.
Up in a balloon, up in a balloon,
A splendid place, with Imogene, to spend the honey-moon.

O cruel Baron, pause a while,
Ere you the brave Alonzo snub:
Should I your daughter bear away,
'Twill cause a hub-bub in the "Hub."
The papers will tell of our sudden flight,
After we're fairly out of sight:
Detectives will scour the country around,
But this truant young couple ne'er will be found.

(*Spoken.*) Only Prof. Allen can tell that they're —

Up in a balloon, up in a balloon,
All among the little stars, sailing round the moon.
Up in a balloon, up in a balloon,
Won't it be a pleasant place to spend the honey-moon?

Enter IMOGENE, *with bundle.*

Im. Dearest Alonzo, partner of my heart,
I could not bear to see you thus depart,
And so have bundled up my little store,
To follow you, my love, the wide world o'er:
Your Imogene will go where'er you ask her.

Alon. My love, we'll start at once for cool Alaska.

Enter BARON, *with club.*

Bar. Will you? Not if I know it. I've a word to say,

The knight is long that never finds the day
Of reckoning; so, my gallant knight, I reckon
This gal ain't going off at your mere beckon.
When clubbed together you are strong, I'll own:
I'm strong on clubs myself, so'll play it alone.

(*Combat,*—BARON *thrown down.*)

Alon. You're euchred, Brumagem, and gone to grass:
Next time you hold that suit you'd better pass.
Im. Pa's on the ground. Oh, dear! what shall we do?
Alon. Into the castle I will pass with you.
Spoils to the victor always do belong,
I've knocked that castle down for a mere song. (*Exeunt.*)
Bar. (*sitting up*). Astronomy is a grand study: 'tis, I'm sure.
I never saw so many stars before.
Where have they gone? I'll take myself to bed:
I feel quite shaky, specially my head.
(*Goes to castle-door — locked.*)
Hallo! I do believe I'm really fastened out.
What's this? Hallo! within.
Alon. Hallo! without.
Bar. What means this outrage?
Alon. Don't inrage yourself,
I've put your chicken on the upper shelf.
Bar. Mutiny, rebellion! Give me back my child,
My castle, and my chicken.
Alon. Draw it mild:
Your child is well content to stay with me;
Your castle's stayed already, as you see.
Here goes your chicken.

Bar. What are you about?
This fowl proceeding —

Alon. (*Throwing chicken out of window*). This fowl's proceeding out.

Bar. Confound your nonsense: let me in, I say!
O Imogene! you well shall rue this day.

Im, Me, pa! why, what's the matter? Now, I'm sure
We're doing our best to guard your little store.
Don't blame me, pa: you know I try to please you.
Don't mind Alonzo, — he's but trying to tease you.

Bar. Tease, store! this may be fun, I'll own,
But I prefer a tea-store of my own.
Young man, forbear: you're really acting queer.

Alon. I'm doing my best to act "*ad interim*" here.

Bar. Are you? We see you're keen as any razor.
Remember Samson, and the gates of Gaza.
Remember Dio Lewis has a place in town;
And, mind your head, this castle's coming down.
Remember Dr. Windship, and beware,
For, young "Ad Interim," you can't stay there.
If you can find that tease is made to pay,
I'll just set up a tea-store o'er the way.

(*Folds up castle, takes it to* R. *of stage and sets up* "ORIENTAL TEA STORE.")

Im. Oh, dear! Oh, say! where are we now?
Alon. Don't know.

Im. If that's a sign, at Copeland's, Tremont Row.

Alon. This sire of yours is really getting bold.

Bar. Hallo, "Ad Interim," left out in the cold.

Alon. I say, old man, why do you take up there?

Bar. Consult The Tea-cup.

Im. Well, I do declare,
Did ever any body see the like of such?

Alon. 'Tis evident he's taken a drop too much.
I'll blow him up with Nitro-Glycerine.

Im. He's filled with Gunpowder: you had best resign.

Alon. I'll parley. Old Shouchong, parley if you please.

Bar. Parley, Young Hyson? Parly-vous Chinese?

Alon. I can't do that. I'll give you French or Danish.

Bar. You can't talk Chinese? Then you just walk Spanish.

Alon. No: I'll give in. 'Tis useless to hold out,
With such a store of gunpowder about.
You'll blow me up —

Bar. Well, then, I'm content,
And, like the Arab, I will fold my tent.

(*Folds up castle, and sets it up as before,* L.)

Imogene, my daughter, as I'm your pappy,
I'm very much inclined to make you happy.
Just watch the house. Now, do go in, my dear:
There's something of a draft now going on here.

(*Exit* IMOGENE.)

And now, Alonzo, sometimes called the brave,
About my daughter you're inclined to rave.
You want to marry?

Alon. By my —

Bar. Don't palaver.
I wouldn't buy you. I will let you have her
On one condition.

Alon. Name it.

Bar. No: it shall be sung;
So open your ears, my friend, and hold your tongue.

(*Duet*, ALONZO *and* BARON. *Air*, "*Sprig of Shillalah.*")

Bar. Now hearken, Alonzo, as well as you can;
For, to gain my consent, I have hit on a plan
By which you may marry my child, Imogene.
The wars, they are on: I'm drafted, I'm told.
I once was a soldier, but now I am old;
So I tell you, Alonzo, if you will go there,
As my sub in the army, I do not much care
If I give you permission to wed Imogene.

Alon. Now, Baron, I think it is hardly the thing,
On such a young blade such an old trap to spring,
Because he's in love with the fair Imogene.
To the wars I will go, as your sub I will serve;
But, regarding your daughter, I beg you'll observe
Her hand must be mine, with a thousand or two,
Which you will plank down when I come back to you,
So impatient to marry the fair Imogene.

Bar. 'Tis well. My daughter, then, is yours — by and by;
So, in the coming battle, mind your eye.
Immy, come here. (*Enter* IMOGENE.) Look at this young man well:
Light beats his heart, though he's a heavy swell.
He'll be your husband —

Im. Oh, my!

Bar. When the war is over.
So say good-by to your devoted lover.
Go in, my lad, and win: don't be afraid;
Send me the news by mail, with postage paid.

(*Exit into castle.*)

Alon. And now, farewell: to glorious feats of arms
I turn my feet. Thrice welcome war's alarms, —
The rolling volley, and the piercing fife,
All pomp and circumstance of martial life.
Farewell, sweet Immy, —

Im. Alonzo, part we so?
Leave me your photograph before you go.

Alon. Here 'tis, sweet angel, wear it next your heart.
I'll take my horse, and leave with you my carte.
Should I be slain when I the foe attack,
You'll find the negative with Mr. Black.

(*Duet*, ALONZO *and* IMOGENE. *Air*, "*Lucy Long.*")

Alon. O Imogene! you're handsome, and, Imogene, you're young;
And you have heard what your pa just said, or rather what he sung.
I know my lot is cruel; but believe, my dearest life,
I'll be your father's substitute, and claim you as my wife.

Both. Then good by, dearest Immy, / dear Alonzo, I know your love is / brave and strong,
I'll / So go and be a soldier, and will / do not stay too long.

(*Air*, "*Believe me, if all these endearing young charms.*")

Alon. But, ah, dearest Immy, if to-morrow I go
To fight in a far distant land,
Some other may claim you, and you will bestow
On some wealthier suitor your hand.

Im. Oh, cease these suspicions! am not I your bride?
If e'er for another my heart should decide,
Forgetting Alonzo the Brave,
I hope that, to punish my falsehood and pride,
Your ghost at my wedding may sit at my side, —
May tax me with perjury, claim me as bride,
And bear me away to the grave.

(*Repeat chorus to first stanza.*)

Then good-by, dear Alonzo, &c.

Alon. And now farewell: my steed impatient waits,
And, while I pause here, paws without the gate.

Im. Good-by, Alonzo.

Alon. Good-by, love. (*Exit*, R.)

Im. He's gone,
Leaving his Imogene to weep forlorn;
But, as he rides, I'll have a parting word,
And give, as an excuse, my father's sword.

(*Exit into castle.*)

Enter ALONZO, R., *dragging a rocking-horse, on which he mounts. Enter* IMOGENE, *from castle, with a tin sword.*

(*Song*, IMOGENE. *Air*, "*Sabre de mon père.*")

Behold this small-sword of my pa's,
Bind it, Alonzo, to your side:
Worthy to guard a son of Mar's.
Cherish it, O Lonny dear with pride!
Amid the din and smoke of battle,
Flourish it with right good will:
My father oft did make it rattle,
For 'tis the sword, the sword of Bunker Hill.

Chorus. Take, then, the small sword, the small sword, the small sword,
Take, then, the small sword, the small sword of my pa.

(*Quick curtain.*)

ACT II.

Room in the BARON'S *castle.* BARON *discovered at the piano*, L., *playing.* IMOGENE *at table*, C.

Im. Now, pa, do stop, you're making such a clatter:
Pray, are you practising an operatta?

You rattle so. It really is too bad:
I do believe you have gone music-mad.

Bar. Madam, I've not: so don't get in a passion.
To take to music now is all the fashion.
All that amuses must the muses court;
And so do I, though music's not my forte.

Im. Nor is piano, now you have passed forty.

Bar. Immy, my dear, you're really talking naughty.

Im. Round that piano you are ever lingering.
Such an attachment —

Bar. Surely needs some fingering.
Music's my idol.

Im. 'Tis a shame, I say,
To pass your time in such an idle way.
Your hair's become as gray as it can be.

Bar. My locks being turned, the more I want a key.

Im. For such an old man, you act basely here.

Bar. As you're a minor, you are trebly dear.

Im. O pa!

Bar. Well, child.

Im. Do you know 'tis o'er a year
Since my beloved Alonzo went from here?
And not one line, by telegraph or post.
He's given me up.

Bar. He's given up the ghost.

Im. No, no! It cannot be: he won't come back.
Must I wear sackcloth?

Bar. If he's given you the sack,
Of course you must. So, Immy, drop a tear
To his fond memory, while I practise here.

Im. Oh, don't, don't, father! If you must rehearse,
Play an accompaniment, while I sing a verse.

(*Song*, "*This kiss I offer*," IMOGENE.)

Bar. Humbug! My daughter, you are very wrong:
This brave Alonzo isn't worth a song.
Not worth a rap. (*Knock*, R.) Hallo! What noise is that?

Im. A rat! A rat!

Bar. A postman's rat-tat-tat.

Im. Who knocks so loud?

Bar. Why don't you go and see?
And bid him welcome, whosoe'er he be. (*Exit* IM., R.)
A year and more Alonzo's been away:
No longer will I in my plans delay.
This girl must wed — I'll find a way to make her —
The first rich man that offers, he shall take her,
From this wild love-match I the girl will wean;
We'll have no more of this Alonzo Green.

Enter IMOGENE, R.

Im. O pa! such an arrival! Dear, dear me!

Bar. Such an arrival! Who, dear, can it be?

Im. The greatest man, I'm sure, that ever was.
He wears such jewels: 'tis the Baron Boz.
Two B's upon his trunks.

Bar. Well, this is queer.
Two B's, or not two B's: what does he here?
The Baron Boz, — who is he?

Im. With great stir
He comes. I think he is a Roman, sir.

Bar. A Roman? Goodness gracious! what an answer.

Im. Excuse the emphasis, I meant romancer.

Bar. Well, let him come: we'll give him welcome, dear;
But what the dickens is he doing here?
No matter what, his coming will delight.
Just look, my dear, and see the lights all right.

Enter Baron Boz, *with book, who goes to table, and reads in imitation of Dickens.*

Boz. Alonzo is dead, to begin with —

Im. Oh!

Boz. Very much dead.

Im. Oh!

Boz. Run through the body, and shot through the head.
There cannot be the least doubt about that.
Not a trace of him left, not even his 'at:
Very much dead, my doggrel to curtail,
Alonzo the Brave's as dead's a door-nail.
Or, to make my allusion a little more 'andy,
A very dead duck is Alonzo the dandy.

Im. Hung be the heavens in black: this blow is cruel.

Bar. Heavens! Don't hang your head, my precious jewel.

Im. My Alonzo dead! My, I — I — I — I —

Bar. Now save your eyes, my love, and do not cry.

Im, My Louny's dead, and I must put on black,
Just when my new moire-antique's come back.

This news will drive me mad, 'tis very plain:
Take off this net, I'm very much insane.

Bar. Why, so you are! Dear me, do see her stare!
What do you want, love?

Im. Why, I want the air.

(*Song*, IMOGENE. *Ophelia, in Hamlet.* "*He's dead and gone, lady.*" *Sits*, R.)

Boz. Baron, a word. If I have rightly read,
Your daughter has a singing in her head.
Some remedy you must very quickly find
To ease her ravings, and restore her mind.
This brave Alonzo's dead, and gone to boot:
As he was yours, I'll be his substitute.
Console your daughter with my hand and heart.

Bar. Will you? Dear me, consols have taken a start.
You have my blessing: there, go in and win.
Stay. How's your income really coming in?

Boz. Come in and see, when you come o'er the water.
Excuse me, I would speak with your fair daughter.
Fair maid, a fairer image ne'er was seen
Than by the light I view fair Imogene.
I am the Baron Boz.

Im. Now, go away:
Barren of sense you see I am to-day.

Boz. "I'd offer thee" —

Bar. Now, please, hold on a minute:
Just let me strike the chord ere you begin it.

Boz. Why, what's the matter?

Bar. Ain't you going to sing?

Boz. I'd offer thee, fair maid, a wedding-ring.

Bar. Oh!

Im. To be my Alonzo's widow, I would rather.
Besides, you're old enough to be my father.

(*Crosses to* BAR., L.)

Bar. Girl, you have lost your senses; listen to his pleading.
He's made two hundred thousand by his reading.

Im. And wouldst thou, father, sell thy child for gold?
Why, pa, he doesn't look so very old.

Boz. Fair Imogene, "An Uncommercial Traveller" you see.
I've "Great Expectations" that you will take me,
A "Haunted Man," away from my "Bleak House,"
And, with your smiles, will bid "Hard Times" vamouse.
My heart is called an "Old Curiosity Shop;"
But all its treasures at your feet I drop.
I am the owner of "Two Cities," where,
Without you, through them there's "No Thoroughfare."
My "Copperfield's" to me a golden one:
My bankers are the well-known "Dombey & Son."
Of friends I've plenty, "Nickleby's" a score,
Who to my coffers many "nickles" pour.
To name them all would be the merest folly, —
"Mark Tapley's" one: you know him, always jolly.
With old "Micawber," and good "Little Dorrit."
I love them all, you do not blame me for it.
Their efforts always aid and comfort lend:
They'll come for to go for to be "Our Mutual Friend."
But time is pressing, and I must desist;
For you, fair maid, my heart is "Oliver Twist." *

* All of a twist.

From all these friends of mine, pray take your pick;
But pick me first, and do, dear maid, "Pickwick."

Im. Baron, such volumes of rich love you pour,
I never shall read you through, I'm very sure.
He's rich as Crœsus, and he keeps a carriage.
What do you publish next?

Boz. I hope, our marriage.
And now, fair maid, quickly your answer speak,
That we together may my fair land seek.
For my boat is by the shore, and my bark is on the sea:
"Barkis is willin';" so, pray thee, come with me.

Im. Oh! isn't that splendid? So original.

Bar. Quite.
Before you take your bark, we'll take a bite.

Im. If you would marry me, just ask papa:
A barrier he may find.

Bar. A barrier? Bah!
Take her in welcome. Soon as you are able,
Send me some cake by the Atlantic cable.

Boz. What say you, then, fair Immy, — shall we wed?

Im. Well, baron, if I must.

Alonzo. (*Outside.*) Your oath.

Im. Oh, my!

Bar. What's that you said?

Boz. I said nothing. 'Twas the wind, I'm sure.

Im. Well, then, —

Alon. Your oath.

Im. Oh, dear!

Bar. Baron, you swore.

Im. What shall I do? my spirits are quite low,
Those spirits underneath annoy me so.

Baron, my hand is yours. This very day
Let's to the parson go, without delay.

Bar. Do it at once, and then come back and sup,
For fear Alonzo may be turning up.

Boz. Come, then, my love, we'll straight our footsteps turn
To Hymen's altar, where the festals burn, —
Where love awaits the fond and loving pair.

Bar. Baron, baron, what are you doing there?
Stopping to make a book, I do declare.

Boz. What am I waiting for? Why, don't you know?
We want the wedding march before we go.

(*Wedding march.* BARON BOZ *and* IMOGENE *march to* R. ALONZO *appears.* IMOGENE *faints, and falls into* BOZ'S *arms.*)

Im. Oh, my! what horrid spectre have we here?
Alon. Spectre! Ha, ha! You didn't 'spect me, dear?
Boz. I know him: 'tis Marley's ghost.
Im. Pa, lay him, do.
Bar. I can't. I think he comes to parley you.
Im. It is Alonzo!
Alon. Yes, 'tis Alonzo. Maiden, you are fickle.
Bar. Alonzo here! This is a precious pickle.
Alon. You recognize me, do you? Once the brave,
The gay, and jocund; but I've grown more grave.
Old man, you sent me off to have me killed:
The grave has given me up, your gravy's spilled.
I am the spirit.
Boz. My friend, now do be candid:
If you're a spirit, you should be well branded.

All spirits here are subject to a fine:
We ma-dear-a hold you, if you do not whine.
If you're a spirit, make your title true:
'Tis clear we cannot even see through you.
Alon. I am a spirit —
Boz. That you said before.
Alon. Yes; and, my friend, I'll say it one time more.
At raising spirits you've a wondrous knack,
And all you raise do richly pay you back.
Don't trouble yourself, I beg, romantic Charley,
I didn't come up here with you to parley.
This fair maid I'll take, for better or for wus:
Baron, I think you had better accompany us.
I claim the promise by you freely spoken:
Was it, like pie-crust, made but to be broken?
I'm in a hurry.
Im. Now, Lonny, don't say so:
I really am not in a state to go.
The new berage I ordered hasn't come.
Alon. If you don't start, I shall be raging some.
Im. I really have not got a thing to wear:
My trunks all want fresh locks.
Alon. They'll have a change of *h*-air.
You should have thought of this; 'tis too late now:
I come to claim fulfilment of your vow.
Don't try to escape, no more for mercy crave:
Don't jest; this matter's getting very grave.
My carriage waits below; so come, my love.
Im. There let it wait: I'll stay, myself, above.
Alon. But you must come.
Im. Your hand release.

Alon. Quick!

Bar. Baron, be kind enough to call the police.

Im. Police, police!

Boz. Dolby, Dolby, here!

Alon. In vain you call this Doll: be mine, my dear.
Baron, farewell: your daughter may be found
"At Home" on April first. Down, down, I'm bound.

(*Song*, ALONZO. *See* "*Alonzo the Brave and the Fair Imogene.*" — COWELL.)

Recitative. Behold me! You told me
You'd be true, and you've sold me.
List to your own broken vow.

(*Air*, "*Down among the dead men.*")

You hoped that, to punish your falsehood and pride,
My ghost at your wedding might sit at your side,
Might tax you with perjury, claim you as bride,
And bear you away to the grave beside.
So, since your oath you did forego,
Down among the dead men, down among the dead men,
Down, down, down, down,
Down among the dead men you must go.

Brown. Down, down, I'm bound. Confound it! What's the matter with the trap?

Smith. Sh, sh! Kick it. (*Brown kicks.*)

Jones. Jump on it. (*Brown jumps.*)

Voice. (*Outside.*) Look here, up there! Do you suppose I'm going to have my house pulled to pieces in this manner? Guess not! (*Nails.*)

Brown. Whoa, there!

Smith. Stay, nailer, stay, and hear his woe. (*Exit,* R.)

Brown. Well!

Miss Robinson. Well!

Jones. Well! your bound is no bound. We're stuck again.

Brown. What's to be done?

Jones. Give it up, of course.

Miss R. What, ain't I going down to see the curiosities?

Jones. This is a pretty way to end a play.

Enter SMITH, R.

Smith. Hurrah! we're all right again. The road's open once more; the coach has come up; and in half an hour we shall be on our way rejoicing.

Jones. Pooh, pooh! But the play?

Miss R. Yes: what's to become of Imogene?

Smith. I can't imagine. I forgot all about the play. We'll leave it in the same condition in which we found it, "snow-bound," until some mightier plougher — I mean power — can break his way through to the end.

Brown. But I don't like ending a play that way.

Miss R. Nor I.

Jones. Nor I.

Smith. Then let's end it in the usual way, by thanking our kind friends for their sympathy while snow-bound here, — thanks which know no bounds; take our positions, and let the curtain fall.

Miss R. After the chorus.

Smith. Certainly, after the chorus.

(*Finale. Air, " Beautiful Bells."*)

Miss R. Merry sleigh-bells, O merry sleigh-bells!
Ringing so sweetly to greet us again:
A welcome of joy your merry sound tells,
Chiming a musical strain.
Soon, soon, we go o'er the crispy snow:
Oh! happy and light all our hearts are to-night,
As over the road we so swiftly go,
While the moon on our path beams bright.

Chorus. Merry sleigh-bells, O merry sleigh-bells!
Jingling so sweetly to greet us again:
Merry sleigh-bells, O merry sleigh-bells!
Musical, musical, musical bells.

Air, " The Bells they go ringing for Sarah."

The bells go a-ringing for sleighing, sleighing, sleighing:
The bells go a-ringing for sleighing, we'll bid you all good-night.

Alon. 'Tis time that to-night we should leave you,
For midnight doth slowly draw near:
To entertain you we have all done our best,
And we trust our endeavors please here.
As Alonzo, with the fair Imogene,
Together now bid you adieu,
We trust you will cheer them at parting,
Baron Boz and old Brumagem too.

Full Chorus. The bells go a-ringing for sleighing, &c.

(*Curtain falls.*)

NOTE.

This entertainment was originally performed by the author and his friends, the parties using their real names. If "Jones" and "Miss Robinson" are competent to play accompaniments, no other person is required; otherwise, a pianist is necessary; and, in that case, the piano should not be upon the stage. Most of the music is taken from Cowell's medley song, "Alonzo the Brave and the Fair Imogene," to be obtained at the music stores.

SPECIMEN PROGRAMME.

MUSICAL AND DRAMATIC.

SNOW-BOUND.

DRIFT FIRST.

Introduces a party of travellers at a wayside Inn, shows how they got in, why they got in, and their doings therein, with the following incidents thrown in.

1. **BALLAD..MR. JONES.**
2. **SONG..... ....MR. BROWN.**
3. **RECITATION ....MR. SMITH.**
4. **SONG.. MISS ROBINSON.**

DRIFT SECOND.

A new edition of the wonderful and tragical history of

ALONZO THE BRAVE

AND THE

FAIR IMOGENE.

Adapted from the well-known song, dramatized without permission of the author, and now first presented, with Musical, Comical, Whimsical, Punical, Scenic, and Equestrian effects. In two parts.

BARON BRUMMAGEM, Manager of the "Fair,"..................MR. JONES.
ALONZO, sometimes called the "Brave," oftener the "Green,"..MR. BROWN.
BARON BOZ, known in history as the "Baron all covered with jewels and gold."..MR. SMITH.
FAIR IMOGENE, sweet sixteen, as may be seen ....MISS ROBINSON.

PART FIRST.—*CASTLE KLAUSHAUS, with a distant view of Mt. Washington.* A captive maiden. SONG.—*Imogene*, "Alonzo was his name." A drafted Baron. SONG.—*Baron*. "Marching all the day." A Rebellious daughter. In doors and out. Woman's rights. A wandering minstrel. SONG.—*Alonzo*, "Dally the organ-man." The recognition. "Ask my pa." TRIO.—"Who's dat knocking at de door?" Rejected addresses. SONG.—*Alonzo*, "Up in a balloon." A devoted damsel, an enraged parent, and a winning youth. Capture of the castle, and the Baron's store. Rally of the enemy, and

GRAND TRANSFORMATION.

"Out in the cold." A parting. DUET.—*Baron and Alonzo*, "Now, listen, Alonzo." A treaty. DUET.—*Alonzo and Imogene*, "O Imogene! you're handsome." Off to the wars. FINALE—*Imogene and Alonzo*, "Take now this small sword."

A period of "a year and a day" is supposed to elapse.

PART SECOND.—*INTERIOR OF THE CASTLE.* A pupil of the conservatory. Imogene out of tune Puns and pianos. SONG.—*Imogene*, "This kiss I offer" "A knocking at the outer gate." The mysterious visitor. Who the Dickens is he? A new way to tell bad news. Incipient insanity and its cure. The Baron Boz "pops." An accepted suitor. Hush! that voice. Matters getting grave. Off to the parson's. Wedding March. THE UNWELCOME GUEST. Alonzo back again. SONG.—*Alonzo*, "Behold me!" A terrified maiden. "Police! Police!" The suitor that didn't suit her. Down among the dead men—almost! SNOW-BOUND AGAIN. "Merry Sleigh Bells."

BONBONS.

A MUSICAL AND DRAMATIC ENTERTAINMENT.

CHARACTERS.

CHROME, }
EASEL, } Amateur Painters.
PALLETTE, }
MARIE, a French bonbon seller.

COSTUMES.

CHROME. Dark pants; white shirt, with rolling collar; black velvet coat.

EASEL. White pants; neat breakfast-jacket, white, trimmed with blue; white smoking-cap, trimmed with blue, blue tassel.

PALLETTE. Blue sailor trousers; drab breakfast-jacket, trimmed with red; drab smoking-cap.

MARIE. Short dress, white hose, slippers, hat.

The stage should be hung with curtains, with openings at back and side, and no other scenery used throughout the piece, except such pieces as are designated.

The original apparatus used in the piece can be obtained of D. O. Story, 71 Sudbury Street, Boston, with all the properties required for its performance; the original costumes, of Mrs. M. A. Wilson, No. 52 Chambers Street, Boston.

SCENE.—*A Studio.* R., *an easel, at which sits* EASEL, *painting; beside him a vase of flowers.* L., *an easel, at which sits* PALLETTE, *painting; beside him a basket of fruit. Sofa,* C., *back.*

Easel. Beautiful! Superb! Magnificent! That rose comes out so perfect, I can almost smell it. (*Sings.*) "I had a rosebud in my garden growing."

Pallette. Oh, bother! Can't you paint a rose, without cackling like a hen over a new-laid egg? Your confounded noise distracts me. Look at that peach! You've made me paint it blue!

Easel. Fit type of your unhappy disposition, Pallette. You'll never be a painter: you're too irritable. Art delights in all that is serene, beautiful, calm—

Pallette. Precious little delight it takes in you, then,—a noisy, squalling—

Easel. Pallette, you've no ear for music.

Pallette. Easel, you've no voice. I'd as soon listen to the bark of a dog.

Easel. (*Sings.*) "My bark is on the sea"—

Pallette. Keep it off the high C's, or 'twill surely crack. I tell you, it's impossible for me to paint, with that unearthly squall forever ringing in my ears. Will you oblige me by being silent?

Easel. Certainly. If the *noise annoys* you, I'll be silent as the grave. Any thing to oblige.

Pallette. Now, that's spoken like a good fellow. Quiet is as necessary to a painter's existence— Hallo! Where's my ochre? Who's been at my paints? I say, Easel! Easel! Easel! Confound it, are you deaf?

Easel. Hallo! Who's making a noise now?

Pallette. Have you seen my ochre?

Easel. (*Sings.*) "Tapioca, tapioca."

Pallette. There you go again! I tell you, I've lost my ochre!

Easel. Oh, you're always losing something! Here, take mine. (*Throws cake across.*)

Pallette, Murder! Right on my canvas! You've ruined that peach, — totally ruined that peach!

Easel. I do confess the soft impeachment. No matter, try again. (*Sings.*)

> "If success you would achieve,
> Try, try, try again."

Pallette. Easel, you try my patience to an alarming extent. You're a noisy, turbulent fellow.

Easel. "Call me pet names, dearest; call me a bird."

Pallette. Humbug! I've done with you. I'll pack up my goods and chattels, and leave for some retired spot, some desolate island.

Easel. —

> "Like poor old Robinson Crusoe;
> O Pallette! how could you do so?"

Now, don't. I'll put myself on my good behavior, and we'll smoke the pipe of peace together.

Pallette. Smoke, will you? A fine mixture, truly! Flowers and tobacco!

Easel. Fine-cut: fine cut flowers, and fine-cut tobacco.

Pallette. How can you so debase yourself?

Easel. My boy, 'tis the economy of art; for while I color my flowers, at the same time I color my meerschaum.

Pallette. You'll not color your meerschaum here. Either that pipe goes out, or I do.

Easel. The pipe is already out. Come, Pallette, smooth that wrinkled brow, and I'll be as quiet as — as — our friend Chrome.

Pallette. Chrome! He's a pretty specimen of a quiet man, *he* is. Always in an uproar, always some new idea — and I do detest ideas — agitating his cranium. He quiet! He's as uneasy as a weathercock, and as noisy as old Boreas himself.

Easel. (*Sings.*) "Cease, rude Boreas, blustering railer."

Pallette. There you go again! Between you with your squalling, and Chrome with his infernal ideas, this place is more like Pandemonium than an artist's studio. I tell you, I've done with you! I'll go to some lone spot, where no voice can break the stillness —

Chrome. (*Outside.*)

> "Now, I swear, by the light of the comet-king's tail,
> If again with these magical colors I fail,
> The crater of Etna shall hence be my jail,
> And my food shall be sulphur and fire."

Enter CHROME, R.

Pallette. Speak of, — you know whom, — and here he is.

Chrome. Such an idea! Throw aside your brushes, cast loose your canvas, and listen to the words of wisdom from the lips of the sage and reverend Chrome.

Easel. Ye that have ears to hear, prepare to stretch them now.

Pallette. Easel, don't make a donkey of yourself! What's the matter? Whose house is on fire?

Chrome. The house I live in. The slumbering embers of genius in my bosom have burst into flame, — a flame that can never be quenched.

Easel. Get an annihilator.

Pallette. Call out the fire-department.

Chrome. Our fortunes are made. Already around my brow I feel the laurel twine. Fame's trumpets ring in my ears —

Pallette. Put up your trumpet, and talk sense.

Chrome. 'Tis useless to throw pearls before swine. Listen. 'Tis now some three weeks since we three ambitious individuals, filled with the desire to immortalize ourselves, and feeling within our bosoms the glow of that seraphic fire, which, leaping to the brain of Raphael Titian —

Easel. Oh, come, Chrome! I petition for something a little more cooling.

Pallette. Don't attempt to fire up the ashes of the great.

Chrome. 'Tis three weeks since we three, fired by ambition, determined to astonish the world as painters. We had had little experience in the art; but that was nothing.

Easel. No, indeed.

Pallette. Anybody can become a painter.

Chrome. You, Easel, had used the brush a little.

Easel. Yes: I was always great on blinds.

Chrome. And blind ambition will yet make you great. While you, Pallette —

Pallette. Well, I did a little glazing.

Chrome. Your painful tasks shall lead to greater lights. I knew nothing of the art; but you kindly consented to take me by the hand, and share with me your knowledge. We formed a coalition, swore eternal friendship, fitted up this studio, spread our canvas, and sailed in. You, Easel, being of a verdant disposition, took to grasses and flowers, and have spoiled many yards of canvas in vain attempts to imitate nature.

Easel. Well, I like that!

Chrome. Do you? Well, I'm glad of it. While you, Pallette, being a man of an unbounded stomach, took to fruit, and have not only destroyed much canvas, but devoured your pomological subjects with the greatest gusto.

Pallette. Well, that's cool!

Chrome. Ah! you like it? While I, being naturally of a roving disposition, took to the water. My first ambitious scheme was to paint a sunrise on the water, — the mighty orb of day majestically rising from his morning bath. How glorious! But then, not being an early riser, I had never seen this moving spectacle. Of course, this fault must be remedied. Filled with this sublime marine and sub-marine idea, I embarked one dark night with a jolly tar, who was perfectly familiar with the water; but, having become a little too familiar with whiskey on this occasion, his whiskey and the water got rather mixed. 'Twas dark as pitch. A gale came on. The jolly tar called it a stiff breeze. I believed him, for it made me very stiff. Nature, whom I went to visit, did not receive me kindly. She made me very sick. She upset our boat, and for six mortal hours I clung to the keel, wet, cold, and hungry. Nature gave me the cold shoulder; in fact, she gave me two, and I turned my back on her forever. I saw the sun rise, but came home cured of any desire to put it upon canvas. Nature's a humbug!

Easel. Come, Chrome, don't abuse Nature.

Pallette. The artist's storehouse, whence he draws — he draws —

Chrome. Well, draw it mild. Don't be sentimental, Pallette: it doesn't become you. Nature's a humbug!

Pallette. Let Nature rest in peace.

Chrome. She rests too much: that's what's the matter. Occasionally she gets up an earthquake or tornado, fires off a volcano, or swallows an island; but, as a general thing, she's too old, too sluggish, to match the ruling spirit of the age, — Sensation.

Pallette. Oh, stuff! Nonsense!

Easel. Bah! Humbug!

Chrome. How perfectly we agree. If we would be painters, we must leave Nature in her solitude, and study the wants of the age we live in. Sensation rules it. Art has plodded along in the old ruts, filling canvas with mountains, cataracts, ruins, and saw-mills, that nobody cares to see. It wants stirring up. Who cares for a sunrise? It's not lively enough. Let some shrewd Yankee rig an apparatus to bring it up with a jerk. That will draw.

Easel. Chrome, you're a fraud. You a painter!

Pallette. You a worshipper of the Muses!

Chrome. Not much. The nine old maids of Mount

Olympus can be matched by modern belles, any day. No tame Nature for me. I'm going to endow Art with a new era. I've got a magnificent idea for a sensational picture that will astonish the world: a great idea. 'Twill take forty yards of canvas. What do you think of Washington Allston's "Paint King?"

Easel. What, the story of fair Ellen and that Vampire?

Chrome. Yes. I'll read it to you. "Fair Ellen was long" —

Pallette. The little coquette, who hailed a painter passing by?

Chrome. Exactly. "Fair Ellen was long" —

Easel. Yes. He gave her a picture of himself.

Chrome. Precisely. "Fair Ellen was long" —

Pallette. Oh, I remember it! She fell in love with the picture, and swore if it would only step out of the frame —

Chrome. She'd step out with him. "Fair Ellen was long" —

Easel. He did step out, seized her in his arms, and carried her off to his studio.

Chrome. Yes, yes. "Fair Ellen was long" —

Pallette. Pulverized her, made paint of her, and painted the picture of somebody else.

Chrome. I'll tell you all about it. "Fair Ellen was long" —

Pallette. Don't trouble yourself. I know it all by heart. You can never make a picture of that.

Chrome. Oh, but I can! The Paint King's studio, dark, sombre, mysterious, — splendid background. Two figures, "The Paint King and Fair Ellen." He in towering majesty, as, —

> "Seizing the maid by her dark auburn hair,
> An oil-jug he plunged her within."

(*Seizes Pallette's hair.*)

Pallette. Confound you! That's my hair! I'm not fair Ellen, and I'm not going into oil.

Chrome. Ah, Easel, Pallette! sensation is our forte. There glory waits us.

Pallette. Glory will wait a long time before I meet her there.

Easel. (*Sings.*) "Meet me at the gate when the clock strikes nine."

Chrome. I tell you, there's fame in "The Paint King." I've got the idea, if I can only work it out. I must have living models and costumes to work from.

Easel. Models! Living models! You don't mean to say you'll have them here!

Chrome. Certainly I do.

Easel. 'Tis profanation! This temple of art is sacred to the study of Nature.

Pallette. And costumes! Theatrical costumes! Oh, horror! We can't have it! We won't have it!

Chrome. You don't like my sensational scheme?

Pallette. No: I do not. He who would be a painter must draw inspiration from Nature alone.

Easel. Sensation! Humbug! There's nothing to be compared to quiet, peaceful Nature, and, in Nature, nothing so beautiful as flowers.

Pallette. Yes, there is. Fruit is quite as attractive, and far more profitable, for that can be eaten.

Easel. That's why you take to it, — hey, Pallette?

Pallette. Now, what do you mean by that? Why will you make yourself disagreeable?

Chrome. That's a conundrum. You'd better give it up. Come, leave those daubs, and help me with the "Paint King."

Easel. Not I. Nature alone has charms for me.

Pallette. Nature's my mistress. Chrome, you can't get up a sensation here.

Chrome. Can't I? He'll see. Why, Easel, you've got into the vegetable world. What a monstrous cabbage!

Easel. Cabbage? Don't you know a rose by its color?

Chrome. I thought it was a red cabbage.

Easel. No, sir. That's a perfect copy of that rose, — that beautiful rose.

Chrome. 'Tis a beautiful rose, I declare. Well, you may keep the copy, and I'll take the original to deck my buttonhole. (*Takes rose from bouquet.*)

Easel. Confound you! You've ruined my bouquet, — totally ruined my bouquet.

Chrome. What's that on your canvas, Pallette? I declare! A turnip! I never saw such a turnip.

Pallette. Turnip! Turnip! Why it's a peach, — a perfect peach! A copy of that in the dish.

Chrome. You don't say so! That is a fine peach. I'm very fond of peaches; and, as you've so fine a copy, I'll take this. (*Takes peach from dish.*)

Pallette. My peach! My matchless peach! Chrome, you've ruined me! You're a swindler!

Easel. A confounded nuisance!

Pallette. A double-dyed villain!

Chrome. Who says we can't get up a sensation here?

Easel. Pallette, let's put him out.

Pallette. Agreed.

Easel. We'll give you a sensation.

Pallette. Yes: sensation No. 2.

Easel. Out you go.

Pallette. Instanter.

Chrome. Indeed! Then two against two is fair play. Sensation No. 3. (*Raises stool. Knock.*) Hallo! Hallo! Whom have we here?

Marie. (*Outside.*)

(*Air, "Prima Donna Waltz."*)

Come buy, come buy bonbons!
Come buy, come buy bonbons!
From La Belle France I bring you now,
Ze charming, sweet bonbons.

Enter, L., *with a tray hung about her neck, on which are a variety of "Costume bonbons."* *

In colors bright and gay arrayed,
So sweet and fresh, to you I bring,
Wizin my basket, neatly laid,
To tempt your taste, bonbons I sing.
Come buy, come buy bonbons!
Come buy, come buy bonbons!
From La Belle France I bring you now,
Ze charming, sweet bonbons.

* Sold by Russell, Tremont Street, Boston.

Pallette. Bombs! Bombs! Why this must be a vivandière.

Easel. She's a nice little dear. That's my idea.

Marie. Pardon me, Messieurs, if I am *de trop*,—vat you call ver mooch in de way. I am ver miserable, ver poor. No l'argent, no monie, no vat you call de greenbacks. I have leave now our countree in France, to come wiz mon père across ze water to zis great countree, zis grand republique. Mon père, he be ver mooch indisposée, vat you call seek. He lose in de flesh; he has ze choak in his troat, and de coff, and de wheeze, and all ze l'argent dat he bring to zis grand coutree vanish in ze air. Ah, Messieurs, but ze poor must live; and I tink, vat vill I do to help mon père? Zen, Messieurs, I tink of ze pretty bonbons, ze charming bonbons, zat mon père have bring from France to please his Marie; and I say, I vill be brave, I vill go to ze great American peoples, and I vill tell zem of mon père, and I vill show to zem mes bonbons, and I vill sing zem ze little song, "Come buy, come buy bonbons," &c.

Easel. Capital!

Pallette. Splendid!

Chrome. Welcome, little France, to great America. The great American people hold forth their arms to embrace the unfortunate of every land.

Pallette. Yes: here's a pair of 'em.

Chrome. Now, don't you be troubled about mon père. He shall be taken care of. Your bonbons — by the by, what are bonbons?

Pallette. Something good to eat?

Easel. Pooh! They're nothing but sugar-plums!

Pallette. Oh, pshaw!

Marie. Sugar-plums? Vat you call sugar-plums? I no comprend sugar-plums! Zay are nice leetle confections.

Pallette. I wonder if they're Southmayd's.

Easel. No. They are the French maid's.

Pallette. Well, I want none of them. They don't agree with me.

Easel. Nor I. They keep me awake nights.

Marie. You no buy mon bonbons? Zat is too bad, — ver mooch too bad!

Chrome. I'll buy them, Marie. I've no doubt they are very nice. Go with a snap too! But what are these?

Marie. Ah! zay are ze latest sensation, — Costume Bonbons.

Chrome. Sensation! Hallo! That interests me.

Marie. In my own contree, at ze fêtes, ze costume bonbons be ver mooch ze rage. Ze bonbon-seller sings ze little song, and all ze company takes ze bonbons, ze harlequins, ze masks, ze dominoes, and zey dress zemselves in ze characters, and ven zey fail to make zem fine, zey pay ze forfeets.

Pallette. Well, I like that. I'd like to have a character myself. I'll take a bonbon.

Easel. And I. There's fun in the idea.

Chrome. Gentlemen, gentlemen, remember your vocation! In Nature, the great storehouse of the artist, there are no such things as bonbons.

Pallette. I tell you, there's inspiration in the idea!

Chrome. "He who would be a painter must draw inspiration from Nature alone."

Easel. Oh, bother Nature! I'm going to have a costume.

Chrome. Costumes! Theatrical costumes? In this place? 'Tis profanation!

Pallette. But this is a case of real distress.

Easel. Yes, genuine charity.

Chrome. Which covers a multitude of sins. Gentlemen, your sentiments honor your hearts. Marie, we'll take all your bonbons, at your own price, on condition that you help us to dispose of them.

Marie. Ah, thanks, Messieurs! But I no comprend deespose. Vat you mean by deespose?

Chrome. I'll tell you. You hold the tray. These two gentlemen and myself will each take a bonbon, retire, and appear in the costume enclosed. He who fails to personate, to your satisfaction, the character which falls to his lot, shall pay for the contents of your tray.

Pallette. Suppose we all fail?

Chrome. Fail! "In the Lexicon of youth" — we'll patch up.

Easel. That's fair. Pallette will have to pay the bill.

Pallette. Will he? I want you to understand there's a great deal of character in me.

Easel. No one would ever dream it.

Pallette. Now, what do you mean by that?

Marie. And zat is what you call deespose? I like deespose.

Chrome. Then dispose yourself on that stool, and, while we are preparing, give us one of your sweetest songs. Now, then, all ready? One, two, three. Go!

(*They take bonbons and exit*, CHROME, PALLETTE, L. EASEL, R.)

Marie. Zay have deespose zemselves ver mooch.

(*Song*, MARIE. *Introduce any thing that will please.*)

Enter PALLETTE, L., *as a sailor; blue trousers, sailor shirt, blue jacket, and tarpaulin hat.*

Marie (*clapping her hands*). Ha! ze jolly tar! Zat is ver nice.

Pallette. Shiver my timbers, blast my hies, and keel-haul me, if this here land-lubbery terryfirmy ain't as unsteady as a seventy-four in a nor-nor-easter, her jib-booms under main-hatches, and her caboose lashed to the top royals amidship!

Marie. Ah! jolly tar, how you vas all ze vile? Vhere you come from, hey?

Pallette. From a four years' cruise.

(*Song*, PALLETTE. "*A wet sheet and a flowing sea.*")

Marie (*clapping her hands*). Bravo! Bravo! Zat be ver nice. You be von fine, jolly Jack-tar.

Enter EASEL, *as an old woman; calico dress, black shawl, front, and cap.*

Pallette. Hallo! Here's old Mother Hubbard! (*Exit*, L.)

(*Song*, EASEL. "*Blessed Rheumatics.*")

(*At the end of song, exit*, R., *and return immediately in first costume. Enter* PALLETTE, L., *in first costume.*)

Pallette. So far, so good. But where's Chrome?

Chrome. (*Outside*, L.) Play away, forty-four! Hold on, nine! (*Rushes across stage.*)

Easel. Here, here! There's too much noise altogether.

Pallette. Yes. We don't want any roughs here.

Chrome. Roughs! Ay, you're right. Rough hands, rough frames, rough faces; but beneath the red jackets beat hearts that move all these to do such deeds as make us honor and applaud their claims to true nobility. (*Exit* MARIE, R.)

(*Recitation*, CHROME. "*The Red Jacket.*")

Exit CHROME, L., *changes to first costume, and returns before the end of* MARIE'S *song.*

Easel. So far, so good. But where's Marie?

Music. *Enter* MARIE, R., *in French national costume.*

(*Song*, MARIE.)

All. Bravo! Bravo! Bravo!

Pallette. I like this. Let's try another bonbon.

Easel. What an appetite! Are there any more left?

Marie. Ah! you like my bonbons? You be very hungry.

Chrome. They're capital, Marie, and must be wholesome: they lead one into such good habits. Shall we try again!

Pallette. Certainly.

Easel. There's nothing like them.

Chrome. Ready, all! One, two, three. Go! (*Each takes a bonbon.* CHROME'S *very small. Exit*, PALLETTE, L., EASEL, R.) Hallo! What's this? The last, and certainly the least! What do you call that?

Marie. Zat leetle bonbon?

Chrome. Yes: "zat leetle bonbon."

Marie. Ah! Zat is ze most wonderful of all ze bonbons. Zat is "La Triumph."

Chrome. I want to know! And pray what is "La Triumph," and what is it for?

Marie. I sall tell you. It is ze charming leetle bonbon, ze inspiring leetle bonbon! If you cannot eat your dinner or your breakfast, it will give you ze appetite.

Chrome. Thank you. I don't need it. I can eat my breakfast and my dinner. I'll take it to Pallette. He needs it.

Marie. No, no! Keep it yourself; keep it yourself! If you have ze sweetheart, it will inspire your heart wiz ze greatest love.

Chrome. Well, I'm not in the sweetheart business. I'll give it to Easel. He's got lots of them.

Marie. No, no! Keep it yourself; keep it yourself! If you have something in your head —

Chrome. Something in my head! Is it an exterminator?

Marie. Ze zensation in your head —

Chrome. Neuralgia?

Marie. No, no! Ze imaginazion, — ze idea, — zat you cannot express. You are a painter! You vish to paint ze picture: you have ze idea, but you vant ze power.

Chrome. Oh, I see! It's a patent stimulating brain-scrubber. It's just what I want, for I've a splendid idea, "The Paint King"!

Marie. Capital! Capital! "La Triumph" vill fill your soul vith spirits.

Chrome. Spirits? Ah, Marie, be careful! Dealing in spirits without a license is strictly prohibited.

Marie. You vill paint ze most beautiful picture. Ze earth vill be filled viz beauty, and ze heavens glow viz light.

Chrome. And I shall see stars! Come, then, "La Triumph," show your power; inspire my brush, and you will triumph indeed. (*Snaps bonbon, and takes from it a small vial. Drinks.*) Bah! "Sedlitz powders." Booh! it makes me shiver! (*Yawn.*) How my head spins! (*Yawn.*) I see a yawning gulf. (*Yawn.*) Who cares? You can't beat mine. (*Yawn.*) "Fair Ellen was long"— (*Yawn.*) I wonder if she was as long as that! "The delight of the fair." (*Yawn.*) "No damsel could with her compare." (*Yawn.*) Marie, your bonbons overpower me. (*Yawn.*) Sailor bonbons. (*Yawn.*) Rheumatic bonbons. (*Yawn.*) Fiery bonbons. (*Yawn.*) What next?

Enter PALLETTE,* L., EASEL,† R. (CHROME *falls upon sofa.*)

Pallette. Charles hof the Hoxfords, you know.

Easel. Hedwin hof the Hoxfords, my boys.

(*Curtain.*)

* As Charles of the Hoxfords. See costumes in cut.

† As Hedwin of the Hoxfords. See costumes in cut.

Bonbons.

THE PAINT KING.

A MUSICAL EXTRAVAGANZA.

PART FIRST.

FAIR ELLEN, romantically inclined to be loved for herself alone.

PRINCE WEAZEL, affected by her possessions, and anxious to possess her affections.

COUNT PALATINE, the lady's big brother, fond of the national game.

The PAINT KING, a medium controlled by evil spirits.

COSTUMES.

FAIR ELLEN, white satin dress, pearl necklace, flowing tresses.

PRINCE WEASEL, white shape dress, trimmed with green velvet; white tights, green shoes, white cap and green feather.

COUNT PALATINE, blue shape dress, trimmed with silver; blue shoes, white tights, blue cap and feather.

PAINT KING, chocolate-colored shape dress, with tights to match; black shoes, cap.

SCENE. — *Exterior of* COUNT PALATINE'S *residence, with a view of the bay-window*, R. ELLEN *seated in the window, sewing.*

Ellen. Heigho! The weary sun has gone to rest
Behind the cloudy curtains of the west;
Nature's grand orchestra, melodious frogs,
Are buckling on their armor in the bogs,

To assail the coming of the silver moon
With silver notes from cornet and bassoon.
Ah, happy frogs! Music hath power to warm
Your miry homes with an admired charm;
But I, poor hapless maid, must sit and sew,
Watching the fleeting shadows come and go;
Or climb the winding stairs the livelong day;
Pore o'er the "Atlantic" in this little "bay,"
Skim from the dailies all their choicest cream,
Or scribble for the weeklies by the ream.
'Tis all in vain! Nothing will give me rest.
Skullcap, valerian, Mrs. Winslow's best,—
All have I tried; and yet full well I know
My *h*arrowed heart requires a guiding beau.
Of fulsome flattery I have tired grown,
I would be loved for myself alone.

(*Song*, ELLEN. *Air*, "*Coming thro' the rye.*")

If a body would be happy,
Sitting in the bay,
Place a lover close beside her,
Sitting in the bay.
There's a charm about these fellows,
No one can say nay.
Oh for a swain to smile on me,
While sitting in the bay!

If a body would be happy,
Sitting in the bay,
Place a loving arm about her,
In a manly way;
Whisper in her ear sweet praises;
Bid her name the day.
Oh! such a beau I'd ne'er refuse
While sitting in the bay.

O Fortune! if you love me, send along
Some sir or answer to my loving song.

Enter PAINT KING, R., *with a covered picture on his arm.*

P. K. Good old Dame Nature, like all country-bred,
Has early sent her bouncing son to bed.
In seas of gold he sinks beneath the sky,
Which proves that he has speculation in his eye.
For one so steady, this is very queer:
So many've sunk in gold this fiscal year.
Of all you raise, we'll very freely borrow,
Good night, old Sol, turn up again to-morrow:

Ellen. Heigho! Thou glorious sun, still tarry near:
Don't leave me solitary sitting here.

P. K. One touch of Nature kinship doth inspire
Between the setting sun and sitting sigher.
What sweet enchantress do I now espy,
Chanting her "high-hows" with such dignity?
'Tis the fair Ellen! comely and divine,
The airy heiress of the Palatine.
At humble people she doth jeer and scoff:
I'll straightway leave, ere she doth take me off.

Ellen. Ahem! Ahem!

P. K. With other hems her needle's found:
That needless hem was meant to turn me round.

Ellen. Stay, gentle stranger! Whither would you flee to?

P. K. I am pursued!

Ellen. By what?

P. K. A huge mosquito!

Ellen. Nay, stay, and list to Nature's matin song:

Her feathered songsters' sweetest notes prolong;
The insect hums, the dripping water sings —
P. K. What are their hums to their confounded stings?
Ellen. I dote on Nature.
P. K. Do you? So don't I.
Ellen. Pure are the charms that in sweet Nature lie —
P. K. Pure! I fear 'twould Southmayd shock,
There's so much *terra alba* in her stock.
Ellen. She's ever busy: like the spider, weaves —
P. K. I've spied her often when her work she leaves.
Ellen. So orderly and neat each flowery mead!
P. K. Neat? You forget she's partial to the weed.
She has such force to back her when she shoots,
Cigarcity should tell you that she roots.
Ellen. So graceful in her motions!
P. K. Not at all:
She can't get through the year without a fall!
Ellen. You rail at Nature. Your revilings quit.
P. K. Madam, I've finished. My last rail is split.
Ellen. Who are you? With a proud, offensive gait,
You rove unbidden o'er my wide estate.
P. K. My name is Norval.
Ellen. Of the Grampian?
P. K. No:
For he, alas! was murdered long ago.
Ellen. A distant relative?
P. K. I thank you, nay.
Too many relations put him out the way.
My name is Norval. In an attic small,
My father fed his flock, — sixteen in all.
It was his constant care, in this retreat,

With awl and waxed-ends to make all ends meet;
To make the last loaf ever last the more,
And keep me trotting to the grocery store.
For I had heard of painters; and I longed to rush,
And at the canvas have a passing brush.
Blind Fate soon granted what my pa denied,
And with impartial interest took my side.
This moon, this silver moon, which rose last night,
Showing a quarter to our wondering sight,
Had scarcely filled his horn across the bar, —
The horizontal bar which stretches far
'Twixt earth and stars, — when, by its glare,
A band of fierce whitewashers climbed the stair!
Into our attic rushed! the walls assailed!
Till they, beset by pails and brushes, paled.
My parents fled for safety; but defiant, I,
Seizing their implements, my hand did try.
Watching their movements while I held position,
I whitewashed like a first-class politician.
With triumph filled, 'twas then I did disdain
My father's sole employ, which brought no gain;
And, having heard that Childs paid heavy salary
To artful men who furnish his Art Gallery,
I packed my carpet-bag, and off did hurry,
For an Adirondac tour with Mr. Murray.
There did I sketch, and scratch my humble name,
And do the deed which gilds this little frame.

Ellen. Oh! hum —

P. K. Ma'am?

Ellen. Humbly do I pray
To see your picture.

P. K. Nay, nay, nay!

Ellen. Is it a horse piece?

P. K. No, upon my honor:
The best horses are taken by Rosa and Robert Bonner.
Mine is a modest subject.

Ellen. Then, 'tis plain,
It must be a portrait of Geo. Francis Train.

P. K. You mock me, lady; but we'll let it pass.
I am no sculptor, and can't work on brass.

Ellen. Do let me see it, Mr. Norval dear!

P. K. I can't. It has no worth nor value here.
Good Mr. Childs would fly to arms should I display
His purchased treasures in this open way.

Ellen. That is all nonsense! Nothing need you fear.
Children in arms are not admitted here.
That picture I must see!

P. K. I must away.

Ellen. You do refuse me?

P. K. Still I must say nay.

Ellen. I shall get angry!

P. K. Passion won't avail.

Ellen. I'll buy it.

P. K. This canvas' not for sale.
I have another I will bring to-night, —
A subject far more pleasing to your sight.

Ellen. Then I'm content. If you will bring it here
I'll purchase it.

P. K. You'll find it very dear.

Ellen. You're very poor, I see.

P. K. In flesh, you mean?

Ellen. Nay, in your purse.

P. K. My purse is rather lean:
Yet I am proud. I scorn the filthy trash
That men call greenbacks —

Ellen. Then you sell for cash.
(Aside.) This youth is poor: he knows that I am rich.
Wouldst wed for money?

P. K. Gold or greenbacks, — which?

Ellen. Either.

P. K. Well, — neither. I'm very poor, I own;
But when I wed, I'll wed for love alone.

Ellen. Your scorn of wealth is noble.

P. K. Fare you well.

Ellen. You'll bring the picture that you have to sell?

P. K. It shall be here in half an hour, sure.

Ellen. You'll bring —

P. K. Or send it by the Messenger Corps.

Ellen. Be sure you bring it.

P. K. It is so heavy, and so far away —

Ellen. Then bring yourself, and let the picture stay.

(*Exit*, R.)

P. K. Ha, ha! I smell some mice. 'Tis very clear
The painter, not the picture, 's wanted here.
She little dreams, that, 'neath these humble clothes,
A wily schemer doth a while repose,
Who one "lost art" again has brought to light,
And paints his pictures by a patent right.
Farewell, fair sewer, you shall soon behold
Whether my picture or yourself is sold. (*Exit*, L.)

(PALATINE *and* WEAZEL, *outside*, L.)

"See the conquering heroes come,
Sound the timbrels, beat the drum."

Enter at L., WEAZEL *with a large ball*, PALATINE *a bat.*

Wea. Behold the champion ball! We've won the day.
Our score was forty —

Pal. Hip, hip, hip, hooray!

Wea. Don't bawl so loud! The muffins we subdued.
Two was their score —

Pal. A case of forty-tude.
I muffed four balls, and caught one on the fly.

Wea. You caught it well.

Pal. It lodgéd in my eye.

Wea. It was a hot one.

Pal. Ay, it was a stinger,
That made me basely bawl, though no base singer.

Wea. Of all the glories manly sports can yield,
Give me the glories of a base-ball field.
Laud, if you will, the Muses as divine:
They're not so striking as our modern Nine.

Pal. O Weazel, Weazel! I am sore afraid
These bruiséd limbs their last home-run have made.
This buoyant game, of which we've been partakers,
Though on a little field, has many acres.
O glorious game! How can I pass thee by?

Wea. You look upon it with a swelling eye.
You know the pitcher that too often goes
Into this field is sure to break his nose.
Don't be put out when accidents befall —

Pal. I ne'er was put out by so foul a ball.

Wea. You're getting chicken-hearted.

Pal. You are wrong:
I'm going to run my base —

Wea. How?

Pal. With a song.

(*Song*, PALATINE. *Air*, "*Old Oaken Bucket.*")

How dear to my heart is the green-covered ball-field,
  When good rival captains their men rightly place!
The pitcher, the catcher, the right field and left field,
  The good men and true men we place on each base.
The short-stop so lively! The centre-field ready!
  The bat, and the striker who aims to send high!
But dearer than all, to the hearts of true fielders,
  Is the leathern-clad base-ball we catch on the fly.
The well-covered base-ball, the jolly old base-ball,
  The leathern-clad base-ball, we catch on the fly.

Enter ELLEN, L.

Ellen. Who dares disturb our rest? Base bawlers, cease!
Your roars uproarious break our quiet peace.
Why, 'tis my brother! with triumphant tread
And conquering arms —

Pal. Ay, and a swelling head.

Ellen. He comes!

Pal. Now, cease your clamor, sister.

Ellen. But this is bliss.

Pal. My eye calls for a blister.
Bring me a cracker moistened.

Wea. Hold! Be steady!
That eye of yours has crack ernough already.

Ellen. A stranger!

Wea. Introduce me, Palatine.

Pal. Prince Weazel, sister; captain of our nine.

Ellen. Delighted, captain.

Wea. Happy to meet fair Ellen.

Pal. Bring me that cracker. How my eye is swelling!

Wea. Bewitching maid, those eyes of heavenly blue,

My youthful heart have piercéd through and through.
They put me out.

Pal. Now, this is too severe!
If you're put out, she'd make a short stop here.

Ellen. If, Captain Prince, they have a piercing glance,
Don't let them put you out of countenance:
With air so noble, and moustache so curled,
I wouldn't cut you, really, for the world!

Wea. O charming maid! I'd gladly call you mine.

Ellen. A prince, I think you are?

Wea. I am.

Ellen. Pray, of what line?

Pal. Prince of Good Fellows.

Ellen. That line's very long.

Wea. To cut it short, I'll spin out with a song.

(*Song*, Weazel. *Air*, "*Five o'clock bus.*")

They call me Prince Weazel: the fortunes I bear
Are lands (under water), and castles (in air).
My coffers with precious (few) jewels are filled:
In modern accomplishments I am well skilled.
I drive my fast horses, I sing, and I dance,
Promenade every day, and devour romance.
But dearer to me is this title of mine;
For I'm captain, you know, of the Silk-Stocking Nine.

Chorus. — For the Silk-Stocking Nine
Upon every field shine;
And I'm captain, you know,
Of the Silk-Stocking Nine.

What is life but a game, with its pitch and its toss,
Here scoring a run, and there making a loss!
Full of muffins and byes, that daily rally,
Mocking our efforts to make a good tally.

Yet they serve best in the field to-day,
Who, joining their forces, make double play:
Then do, Fair Ellen, be partner of mine,
And you captain shall be of the Silk-Stocking Nine.

For the Silk-Stocking Nine, &c.

Ellen. Your very flattering offer me delights:
'Tis an acknowledgment of Woman's Rights.
She aims to lead. I really feel elated,
As a base-ball captain to be nominated.
The good time's coming fast when men can yield
The foremost place to her on any field.
Wea. You do accept me?
Ellen. Well, I'll think it over.
I'd quite resolved never to have a lover
Who kept fast horses, dealt in fancy stocks,
Deposited in banks which have no locks.
Checks on such banks the longest purses harrow.
Wea. O Moses!
Pal. Hush! That was a hit on Faro.
Ellen. The greatest happiness that can be known
Is to be lovéd for one's self alone.
So, hark you! When I do my hand bestow,
My money to the Consumptive's Home must go.
Wea. "Love in a cottage."
Pal. Bah! That's gone by.
You'll never find the man.
Ellen. I've one in my eye.

(*Song*, Ellen. *Air*, "*Eupidee.*")

The shades of night were falling fast,
As by my window just now passed

A youth, who bore a picture-frame,
And answered, when I asked his name,
Chorus. — Eupidee, &c.

His dress was poor, his purse was low,
Yet proudly walked he to and fro:
He kept his picture very nice,
And answered, when I asked the price,
Eupidee, &c.

Oh! should I meet that youth again,
This swelling heart could ne'er refrain.
I'd cast all prudish arts away,
And unto him would boldly say,
Eupidee, &c.

Pal. Nonsense! Here's a pretty how-d'ye-do!
Wea. I wish that Longfellow had been cut in two!
Pal. Hark you, Miss Ellen, I am master here.
Ellen. I want to know!
Wea. Now, Pal., don't be severe.
Pal. My will is law.
Ellen. Law, now, do tell!
Pal. This is Prince Weazel. Look upon him well.
He's the best catcher of our famous Nine.
Ellen. He can't catch me, though.
Wea. Nay, now, do be mine!
Pal. Silence! Now, by our royal name,
I will be umpire in this little game.
Miss Ellen Palatine, do you behave:
This youthful prince is noble, rich, and brave, —
Very accomplished, — ay, and more than that,
He has a striking air.
Ellen. Then send him to the bat.

Pal. He's learned, highly skilled in foreign lingo.

Ellen. Send him to France.

Pal. You marry him, by jingo!
So get your silks and muslins into trim:
Thursday, at 2, P.M., you marry him!

Ellen. But —

Pal. Silence, I say!

Ellen. Oh, fiddle-de-dee!
With my own muslins you can't muzzle me.
I'm a free-born woman, and I pay my taxes:
Do you think I'll marry the first man who axes?
Oh for some champion, these brutes to smother!
Some Anna Dickinson, or any other.
I'll marry whom I please! now, mark you that.
If you are sharp, you'll find I can be flat.
So get your parson: when the bargain's closed,
Just mention that the bride is indisposed. (*Exit*, R.)

Wea. And then the band struck up —

Pal. The hussy's made a stir.
Band or no band —

Wea. I ne'er can husband her.

Pal. She will come round. I think this is a feint.
Hard fare and locking up will cure —

Wea. It ain't.
She reads "The Revolution;" and you bet
"*Hard fare* ne'er won *faint* lady yet."
An offer of my hand I did parade:
How can I win her?

Pal. Try a serenade.

Enter PAINT KING, L., *dragging on a trick picture, which should be a frame seven feet high, five wide; at the back a black cloth, on which is painted the statue of a woman on right side. In front is a green curtain, which conceals it when brought on. Space should be left between the frame and the back for the* PAINT KING *to take his place. It should be placed at the back of the stage, in front of the opening in the curtain, and so arranged that the* PAINT KING *can get into it without being discovered.*

Wea. Confusion!

Pal. Oh, my eye again!
Murder!

Wea. His painting's struck my brain!

Pal. Fellow, are you insane? or are you blind?

P. K. No: only in an uneasy frame of mined.

Pal. A slim excuse, although your frame is stout.

Wea. That's the Longfellow she does rave about.

Pal. Ha! Say you so? We'll take his highness down.
You're poaching on my manor, you base clown.

P. K. If that's your manner, it requires polish:
So mean a base as that you'd best abolish.

Pal. He mocks me, Weazel. Oh, with rage I choke!
My blood is boiling!

Wea. Don't a broil provoke.
You're very *stew*pid: coolly treat the joker;
Don't let your choler be to you a choaker.

Pal. I will be cool. Hark you, young painter swell!
What want you here?

P. K. Your blooming sister, Nell.

Pal. She's not at home.

Wea. She's gone out for the day.

P. K. I'll tarry, then.

Wea. You'd better turn away.

Pal. She sees no strangers, so no longer tarry:
When she gets home I will your message carry.
I am her guardian, for she has no other —

P. K. Ah! what is home without a homely brother?
Your fond affection, count, doth touch my heart:
It moves me strangely!

Wea. Then, why don't you start?

P. K. Well, really, prince, I am not good at guessing.

Pal. The naked truth is, that you want a dressing.
Oh, how my fingers itch his face to spoil!

P. K. I'm not a salad, though I mix with oil.

Pal. Will you be gone?

P. K. Your tongue is very glib,
But from it just now there rolled off a fib.
Your sister is at home; so here I stay:
As Count Unreliable you count any way.

Pal. An insult to my face!

Wea. 'Tis very plain
This painter chap we've "interviewed" in vain.

Pal. You've laid upon my patience heavy tax.
Your fate is sealed.

Wea. Ay, sealed with heavy wax.

P. K. Come on! Come on! Your strongest man shall fly
From his first base almost as soon as I.
Here am I fixed, and here I mean to stay;
So, fiery youths, go in, and blaze away.

Wea. Well, here's my compliments! (*Raising ball.*)

Pal. And here are mine! (*Raising bat.*)

Enter, ELLEN, R. *Takes* C.

Ellen. Hold! villains, hold! enough! this quarrel's mine.
"Who touches a hair of his *black* head,
Dies like a dog. March off!"

P. K. She's read!
A Whittier maid ne'er came in hour of need.

Ellen. Why, it is Norval!

P. K. Yes, it is indeed!
Behold my picture: 'tis of goodly size;
May it be precious in thy precious eyes!
Bestow it in your album, guard it well,
Think often of the giver, and — farewell!

Ellen. Why, you're not going!

P. K. Ay, I must away.

Ellen. But you're not paid —

P. K. I'll call another day.
Good-night, my roaring blades, you have my blessing.
Some other time I'll take that promised dressing.

(*Exit*, L.)

Pal. Miss Ell —

Ellen. Hold, brother, stay!
Don't speak in that Miss Ellaneous way.

Pal. But I will speak, in spite your bold defiance.
Miss Ellen, you shall make no mésalliance.
The bones of our great ancestors indignant rattle,
To hear you with a base plebeian prattle.

Ellen. Pooh! Who cares for all their sighs and groans!
You just walk round here while they play the bones.

Pal. With indignation I am almost choking.

Wea. This little Nell is really quite provoking.
A simple painter! Shouldn't you look higher?

Ellen. He's full six feet. What more could I desire?
But where's my picture?

Wea. Here, against the wall.

Ellen. A gem of high art!

Wea. It is rather tall.

Ellen. Will you be courteous, and the curtain raise?

Wea. Pleased to obey you: I remove the baize.

(*Raises curtain. The* PAINT KING *discovered, looking intently upon the statue as a part of the picture.*)

Pal. Horror!

Wea. 'Tis he, himself!

Ellen. Isn't it splendid?
How nicely in it light and shade are blended!

Pal. The color in the face is rather weak.

Wea. The painter's failing is too much of cheek.

Ellen. Now, isn't it a duck?

Wea. It skill doth lack.
This duck of yours is but a canvas-back.

Pal. Quick, close the curtain, Weasel.

Ellen. What for, pray?

Pal. That I may drag this filthy daub away,—
Bestow it in some corner out of sight.

Ellen. Nay, it has found a corner in my heart to-night.

Pal. Now, quit your ravings, and obey my will:
No more your little head with nonsense fill;
But make one of the party I have planned,
And take Prince Weazel for your husband.

Wea. Oh, do, dear Ellen, with me share my lot!
This heart is blasted if I have you not.

Pal. With such a blasted lot of blarney, sure
You can't refuse to share his little store.

Ellen. Ay, but I do. Your prince doth make me faint,
He's so much troubled with the heart complaint.
Hark you, my brother: if from out that frame
Could step the youth who bears an humble name,
I'd go with him, your guardian will to spite.

Pal. You wouldn't.

Ellen. Yes, I would, this very night.

Wea. Why, this is nonsense!

Pal. Foolish girl, forbear!

Ellen. Ay, and I'd marry him. I would, I swear!

(*Gong.* P. K. *steps from frame.*)

P. K. Fair Ellen, thank you. What you freely proffer
I'll freely take, and here embrace the offer.

Pal. Hallo! Here's witchcraft!

Ellen. Do my eyes deceive?
I quake with fear!

Wea. My friend, you'd better leave.

Ellen. Can this be Norval? I am much afraid
I've been deceived.

P. K. You have, mistaken maid,
By an old character I oft assume.
I am the Paint King. (*Gong.*) Norval's my *nom de plume.*

Wea. It is no feather in your cap, I'll swear.

Ellen. Mercy! Mercy! O Mr. Paint King, spare!

P. K. By your own swearing you are mine, fair Nell;
So to your loving brother say farewell.
Nothing can save you from my magic art:
She is the Paint King's prize, who gives her heart.

Ellen. Oh, this is horrible! What shall I do?

Wea. Get up a faint, and that may bring him to.

P. K. The dew is falling.

Wea. Do fall in a swoon.

Pal. Yes, give him fits: 'twill spoil his honeymoon.

(*Song and Chorus. Air,* "*Shoo Fly.*")

O dear, O dear, my head does ring,
O dear, O dear, my head does ring,
O dear, O dear, my head does ring,
My senses now are on the wing.
I feel, I feel, I feel a swimming in my head.
My senses now go spinning round,
I'm going out of my head.
Paint King, don't bother me; Paint King, don't bother me;
Paint King, don't bother me, for I'm going to faint away.
I feel, I feel, I feel, I feel I'm going to faint;
I feel, I feel, I feel, I feel I'm going to faint.

(*Falls into* PAINT KING'S *arms. Quick curtain.*)

ACT SECOND.

COSTUMES.

FAIR ELLEN. Same as before.

WEAZEL and PALATINE. Long Shaker coats and broad-brimmed hats, umbrellas, concealing their "studio" dresses.

PAINT KING. Long purple robe, purple smoking-cap, concealing his "studio" dress.

Dummy figures of Fair Ellen and the Paint King are required for this scene, made to look as much like them as possible.

SCENE. — PAINT KING'S *studio. At back representation of a caldron, marked* "OIL," *which conceals sofa used in the studio scene;* R., *a large canvas frame, on which are painted nine cat's heads, labeled* "THE NINE MEWSES;" L., *another frame, covered, representing a canvas prepared for painting, — the upper half should be arranged to let down.* ELLEN, *seated* C.

Ellen. O champions of my sex! do drop a tear,
As that drop rising shows me sitting here.
This dark and gloomy cavern, that you see,
Of Woman's Rights is all that's left to me.
I've nobly struggled, but defeat befell,
And of my air-built castles made this cell.
Imprisoned here, I mourn my hapless fate,
And, almost dying, on my woes dilate.
This lonesome place of joy is void and null, —
What ho! Without! That "ho" is very dull.
My voice is weak; and yet I will be brave,
And stave my fears off with a joyous stave.

(*Song*, ELLEN. *Selected.*)

From my misfortune, now, dear misses, take
This warning: Don't acquaintance make
With picturesque young men when passing by;
But look upon their wares with wary eye.
Though poor their garb, when they've addresses paid,
Their suits are poorer yet, though custom-made.

(*Duet*, PAL. *and* WEA., R., *and enter.*)

To the rescue now we go,
  Hunki-dorum, doodle dum day!
The base Paint King to overthrow,
  Hunki dorum, doodle dum day!
Peaceful garbs about us flow,
  Hunki dorum, doodle dum day!
Yet we're prepared for war below,
  Hunki dorum, doodle dum day!

We come to set Fair Ellen free,
The Paint King's power to break, you see;
And, for the wrongs endured by her,
A swift revenge to take, be sure.
To the rescue, then, we go,
  Hunki dorum doodle dum day, &c.

Ellen. Methinks I've heard those foreign airs before:
"Hunki dorum,"—that's Italian, sure.
They must be Strakosch's singers, often round
With opera, operating where stray cash is found.
Gentle musicians, pass on.

Wea. Bless my eyes!
Her long-lost brother she don't recognize.
Behold your brother, Pal.

Pal. 'Tis palpable, my sister,
I am your loving brother.

Ellen. Don't palaver, mister,
My brother doesn't look a bit like you.
He is a blonde.

Wea. This blonder makes him blue.
Nay, nay, fair maid, 'tis Palatine.

Pal. Ne'er doubt it.
I'll prove my claim.

Ellen. Then quickly set about it.

Pal. Who took you from your cradle bed,
And gently by the hand you led, —
Then let you fall and break your head?

Ellen. My brother!

Pal. Who always filled your little cup,
When at the table you did sup,
Then — boldly took, and drank it up?

Ellen. My brother!
Enough! One touch of Nature sets me right.
Brother!

Pal. Sister!

Wea. This is a touching sight.

Pal. Now, sister, that our joyful meeting's over,
Allow me to present your gallant lover.

Wea. Still your devoted.

Ellen. Are you, really!
Then your devotion I shall test severely:
For I've had wrongs —

Wea. Confess your sorrows, sweet.

Ellen. He doesn't give me half enough to eat;
Keeps me on mouldy bread —

Wea. That staff's unsteady
To one so finely moulded and well-bred already.

Ellen. Water's the only liquor that I swallow
To liquidate my thirst!

Wea. Why, what a fellow!
I'll tear him limb from limb.

Pal. That's Bowery, you see.

Ellen. Oh, do, dear prince! and send his trunk to me.
This hand is yours when his quietus' made.

Wea. My soul's in arms, and eager for the trade.
Where is the villain?

P. K. (*Outside.*) Now, my hearty,
Fire up the engine.

Ellen. Hush! Here comes the party

Pal. Oh, mercy!

Wea. Dod-rot it, if this is he,
Then too much steam he's getting up for me.

Ellen. Ingenuous youth, the Paint King comes this way.
Now, tear him, prince!

Pal. We'd better tear away!

Wea. That's my opinion, seasoned with a moral,
That men of peace should never seek a quarrel.

Ellen. What, cowards! would you fly and leave me thus?
Where is your boasted valor?

Pal. Don't you make a fuss:
'Tis always wise to choose the better part.

Wea. And that's — discretion.

Ellen. Then you'd better start.
You'll meet the Paint King as you pass the door,
Who two whole men of peace will cut in four.

Pal. Your words are sharp.

Wea. So cutting, it is clear
We'd better stop and face the music here.

(*Chorus*, "*Masaniello.*")

Behold the Paint King swiftly coming!
Though hard our lot, we'll face the foe.
To spoil his game, and send him humming,
We'll save the maid, and lay him low.
He comes! He comes! Now courage show!
Take heed, and whisper low!
Look out and trap him unaware:
Take heed, and whisper low!
The foe we seek we'll soon, we'll soon ensnare,
The foe we seek, &c.

(PAL. *and* WEA. *conceal themselves* R. *and* L.)

Enter PAINT KING, R.

P. K. Fame's a good thing, either in rhyme or reason;
A cure for many ills when taken in season.
'Twas often lauded by that famous "poic"
Whom Mrs. Stowe has tried to prove no stoic, —
A bold endeavor, savoring of the frantic,
For Byron can't be drowned by the "Atlantic."
Vain the attempt so strong a "Childe" to smother,
And fame's not made *Byron*ning down another.
Yet fame is sought for, and so I, to-night,
Would fain secure it with a patent right.
With this philosophy: In Modern Art,
Our foremost painters win the public heart
By mixing colors from all sorts of earth,
And from these meaner clays give fancy birth.
Bedeck our studios with Nature's graces,
And charm our senses with bewitching faces.
If such results from poor old earth are gained,
What grander triumphs yet may be attained
By pounding up our models, which combine,
Of course, all colors which we think so fine?
That's new philosophy!

Ellen. It's old and loose.
To get the golden eggs, you'd kill the goose.

P. K. Aha! Fair Ellen, meet we once again?
Your pretty face shall make this matter plain.

Ellen. You are a villain!

P. K. Prithee, say no more.

Ellen. You vowed you loved me.

P. K. Nay, 'twas you who swore.
The course of true love ne'er runs true, I grant.

Ellen. Then, if you love me, take me to my aunt.

P. K. She's not at home.

Ellen. My uncle's!

P. K. He's quite sick.

Ellen. Then take me somewhere, and do take me quick.
I shall go mad!

P. K. Then you'll go somewhere, surely.
Nay, nay, Fair Ellen, here you stay securely.
There is no other course.
'Tis quite well known
You would be loved for yourself alone.

Ellen. I would, I would! It is my fond desire.

P. K. Your wood is very green: it should be dryer.
Well, I will take you for yourself.

Ellen. You will?

P. K. As an expounder of my artist skill.
Behold you brazen dish! 'Tis filled with oil.

Ellen. This is some wicked snare.

P. K. Nay, don't recoil.
Beneath are mighty wheels.

Ellen. There's mischief here:
Something's revolving 'neath that wicked sneer.

P. K. Quick tripping hammers there unceasing pound.

Ellen. It is no wedding trip on which they're bound!

P. K. If thou wouldst have me paint the home
To which I'd bear thee, this way come.

(*Points to caldron.*)

Ellen. Nay, base dissembler, your wild jestings cease!
No Yankee girl could find a home in Greece.

P. K. Unbending maiden, you must straightway go
To explore the mysteries which lie below.
My canvas waits for colors.

Ellen. What care I?

P. K. Your charms and graces must my wants supply.
I have an order for a fancy sketch,
And want your picture.

Ellen. You can't have it, wretch.

P. K. Ay, but I must. (*Seizes her hands.*)

Ellen. Unhand me, villain!

P. K. Don't complain.
Nothing is gained by this unhandsome strain.

Ellen. Oh, spare me! Spare me! I am weak and faint.
Life is so short!

P. K. And I am short of paint:
So you must go where welcome waits for you
Within that oil-well we are coming to.
'Tis sweet for art to die, my artless maid:
Plunge boldly in, and do not be afraid.
Time swiftly flies!

Ellen. Then I will try a race
'Gainst time, and swiftly fly this place. (*Runs off*, R.)

P. K. Nay, not so fast, for you awake my wrath:
Naught's so refreshing as a cooling bath.

(*Follows her off, and quickly returns with a "dummy," which he flings into the oil-caldron.*)

She sinks! She's gone! and, free from toil,
A martyred heroine plunges into oil.

Farewell, sweet maid: when next your face I view,
'Twill give much color to the deed I do. (*Exit*, R.)

(PALATINE *and* WEAZEL *approach from* R. *and* L., *and look into the* "OIL" *caldron.*)

Pal. Weazel!
Wea. Palatine!
Pal. The axe has dropped!
Wea. Methinks, my friend, it's time this thing was stopped.
Pal. Oh, what a fall was there!
Wea. It was severe.
Pal. He's made a sardine of my sister dear.
Wea. The knell of all my hopes he's badly sounded.
Pal. My little sister Nell he's gone and drownded.
Wea. To be so foully wronged! It's quite distressing.
Pal. She wasn't a salad, though so fond of dressing.
I shall go wild with grief!
Wea. You do look bad.
Pal. Pray, are there no detectives to be had?
Wea. I scarce detect your meaning. What for, pray?
You'll want the coroner without delay.
Pal. Oh, I did love her so!
Wea. That I don't doubt.
Pal. Get some official, quick, and fish her out!
Wea. A brother's love so pure, now who would mock it?
Pal. I want her, for she's got her bank-book in her pocket.
I cannot live without her; so, dear fellar,
Just end my troubles with this umberella!

Wea. I do not see the point; so, Pal, delay,
And keep that refuge for a rainy day.
Dry up that tear, it is a watery waste:
Reflect at leisure, ere you die in haste.
This saucy Paint King by our hands must die,
And with his life we'll end his sorceri.

Pal. But I can't see it. Oh, this bitter cup!

Wea. Then go it blind. Revenge shall drink it up!
He comes again!

Pal. O Christopher! Let's travel.

Wea. Nay, here I stick, this mystery to unravel.
This Paint King hankers for the trump of Fame:
We'll find a trump to block his little game.

(*Conceal themselves as before.*)

Enter PAINT KING, R., *with pallette, on which are daubs of paint, and brushes.*

P. K. White for the brow as alabaster pure,
Yellow for golden ringlets sweeping o'er,
Vermilion for the lips, blue for the eyes,
All hues and colors that true artists prize
So quickly gained! Now, by great Julius Cæsar,
This rivals Masser's famous Ice-Cream Freezer!
Now to the test. If wisdom guides me right,
Great Mumler's photographs are out of sight.

(*Goes to canvas,* L., *and paints. As he paints, the canvas opens, disclosing* FAIR ELLEN.)

(*Song,* WEA. "*Still so gently.*")

Still so gently o'er him stealing,
What his pallette is revealing;
Spite of peril I've a feeling
That I'll block him, quickly block his little game.

P. K. Fly fast, good brush: my colors show
Beneath your touch a very bristling row.

(*Song*, WEA. *Repeat as before, and add* —)

There's another brush to warm thee,
O Paint King, I'd inform thee!

"*Ten Little Injuns.*"

Four little paint cakes lying there I see,
Steal away one, and then there are three:
Four little paint cakes, one a cake of blue,
Steal away that, and no eyes for you.
One little paint cake, two little paint cakes,
Three little paint cakes stay.
Fourth little paint cake, blue little paint cake,
Pretty little paint cake, I take you.

(*Removes paint from pallette.*)

P. K. Now triumph's certain! One touch, and behold,
In liquid blue Fair Ellen's eyes unfold.
Confusion! Where's my blue?

Pal. Mark how he's shook:
He seems quite ill.

Wea. He has a bilious look.
It was a bitter pill for him to face.

P. K. I'm lost! lost! lost!

Pal. It struck a hollow place.

Wea. Nay, you are not lost, for we have found you out. (*Draws cutlass from his umbrella.*)

Pal. With all the wickedness you've been about.

(*Draws cutlass from his umbrella.*) (*Canvas shuts.*)

P. K. And who are you, that, with defiant air,
Unbidden seek the Paint King in his lair?

Your garbs are peaceful, but your manners rough.

Wea. Humbug!

Pal. Silence! We have heard enough.
I am Count Palatine, that lady's brother,
The little goose whom you did lately smother.

Wea. What's sauce for goose is sauce for gander too:
You martyred her; we come to martyr you.
With these good swords we will your picture spoil.

Pal. Nay, hadn't we better finish it in oil?

P. K. Whose funeral is this? Hadn't you better wait?
For I would have a voice in this debate.
As I'm the villain of this tragic play,
Poetic justice, could it have its way,
Would lay me low; or speaking by the card,
Foil vice, and give to virtue its reward.
But Boucicault gives vice a foremost place,
And bids it triumph in Formosa's case.
Fate shows that strength, not justice, 's sure to win;
So, while I have the strength, I'll just pitch in.
With flats and sharps defiantly before us,

(*To leader of orchestra or pianist.*)

You sound the pitch, and we will pound the chorus.

(*Combat, to the tune of "The Anvil Chorus."* PAINT KING *disarmed. They seize him and struggle off,* L.; *immediately return with the dummy of the* PAINT KING, *which they throw into oil-caldron; then exit,* R. *and* L. *Side scene-pieces and caldron disappear, and discover* CHROME *upon sofa, just awakening.*

Chrome. Give me another sword! Quick! I smother! I die! (*Wakes.*) Hallo! What's this? The studio, Easel's pallette, and Pallette's easel, — but where's the oil? Where's —

Enter PALLETTE, L., EASEL, R., *in costume of first part.*

Pallette. Confound you, Chrome, you've wakened the whole neighborhood.

Easel. The police are here in full force. What's the matter with you?

Chrome. But where's the picture? Where's the patent machine? Where's the oil?

Pallette. Why, the man's crazy!

Easel. Come, come! Wake up, Chrome! You've been dreaming.

Chrome. Well, I believe I have, prince.

Pallette. Hallo! Easel, you've got a title.

Chrome. But look here. How long have I been asleep?

Pallette. About an hour. What have you been dreaming?

Easel. Of your famous Paint King — hey?

Chrome. Paint King! Have I been dreaming? Ain't you the captain of the Silk-Stocking Nine? Didn't you get stung in the eye?

Pallette. Oh, nonsense! Wake up! It's time you were about your painting, — your great sensational painting.

Chrome. Nonsense! I've had enough sensation to last me for the rest of my natural existence. But where's Fair Ellen?

Easel. And who's Fair Ellen, pray?

Marie. (*Outside*, L.)

"Come buy, come buy bonbons," &c.

Enter, L.

Chrome. Ah! here she is. No: it's the French girl.

Marie. Ah, Messieurs, you have made mon père's heart jump wiz ze joy it feel when I bring him ze greenbacks zat you pay me for my bonbons. Ah! I sall nevar forget ze kindness of ze great American people. Nevar! Nevar! You have poured ze oil upon ze troubled vaters of his soul.

Chrome. Oil! Ah, she little knows how deeply she's been into it. Marie, that last bonbon of yours has completely cured me of any desire to speculate in sensation.

Easel. But your great picture?

Chrome. Is finished. As Byron says, "I had a dream which was not all a dream." Easel, Pallette, you're right. Nature's the true guide to lead the artist on to grand achievements; for the scenes she spreads to his enraptured gaze have sense and substance, while sensation's but a maddening dream, whose shifting colors fade before the artist's brush can fasten them upon the canvas.

Easel. Well, Chrome, I do believe you've been dreaming.

Pallette. He's had the nightmare. That's what's the matter.

Chrome. Let's stick to nature; for sensation's sure to lead us into oil — I mean hot water.

Easel. But sensation's a good thing in its place.

Chrome. But a little of it goes a great way.

Pallette. So you intend to give it up altogether?

Chrome. No; for it has served to while away an hour with me. And, when we are tired of work, we'll send for Marie, here, to amuse us.

Easel. With her Costume Bonbons. That's good.

Marie. Oui, oui! I sall come avec plaisir; and I vill bring my bonbons; and, when you are tired of work, I vill sing, —

"Come buy, come buy bonbons," &c.

EASEL, R. CHROME AND MARIE. PALLETTE, L.

(*Curtain falls.*)

SPECIMEN PROGRAMME.

MUSICAL AND DRAMATIC.

BONBONS.

PART FIRST.

AMONG THE ARTISTS.

CHROME .... } ....
EASEL.................... } Amateur Painters. } ....
PALLETTE................. } ....
MARIE. — A French "Bonbon" Seller..

With the following incidentals: —

SONG. — "A wet sheet and a flowing sea"......................PALLETTE.
SONG. — "Those blessed Rheumatics"..............................EASEL.
RECITATION. — The Red Jacket....................................CHROME.
BALLAD...MARIE.

PART SECOND.

CHROME'S DREAM.

THE PAINT KING.

A very free dramatization of Washington Allston's poem, in two acts, full of moving accidents and incidents, produced with all the splendor of machinery and scenery that a limited income would admit of.

FAIR ELLEN, anxious to be loved for herself alone.................MARIE.
PRINCE WEAZEL, affected by her possessions, and anxious to possess her affections.......................................EASEL.
COUNT PALATINE, the lady's brother, with an eye for the national game...PALLETTE.
PAINT KING, disturber of the Piece..................................CHROME.

ACT 1. EXTERIOR OF COUNT PALATINE'S RESIDENCE, WITH A VIEW OF THE OPEN BAY. — A fair soul, solus. SONG. — *Ellen*, "Sitting in the Bay." The Paint King on his travels. Nature and art. A gentle hint. The silk-stocking nine. See the conquering heroes come. A bat in time saves nine. A blind bat. SONG. — *Palatine*, "The leathern-clad base-ball we catch on the fly." An interruption. SONG. — *Weazel*, "I'm captain you know of the silk-stocking nine." The coming man. SONG. — *Ellen*, "The shades of night." Woman's rights. A moving picture Readings from the poets. A woman's oath, and what came of it. Tragic denouement. CHORUS. — "Paint King, don't bother me," to a new tune.

ACT 2. THE PAINT KING'S STUDIO. — The deceived Ellen. DUET. — *Weazel and Palatine*, "To the rescue now we fly." The recognition. A touching picture. Valor and discretion. CHORUS. — *Ellen, Weazel, and Palatine*, "Behold the Paint King quickly coming." The plot unfolds itself. The patent machine. The plot thickens in oil. The struggle, and the dreadful doom of the deceived damsel. The picture. The Paint King at work. SONG. — *Palatine and Weazel*, 'Still so gently from him stealing.' Now all looks blue, and now it don't. Foiled. The struggle, and the Paint King's painful predicament.

TRANSFORMATION SCENE,

(of course), and Home Again.

LIGHTHEART'S PILGRIMAGE.

AN ALLEGORY.

FOR FEMALE CHARACTERS ONLY.

CHARACTERS.

LIGHTHEART, the pilgrim.
CONSCIENCE, the guide.
FRIVOLITA, queen of the Valley of Pleasure.
MIRTH, SPORT, FOLLY, FALSEHOOD, SHAME, and other dwellers in the valley.
CELESTA, guardian of the Heights of Wisdom.
REASON, RELIGION, and other dwellers on the heights.

This allegory is particularly designed for school exhibitions. A chorus of "dwellers on the heights" should be seated on the platform, R. *Chorus of "dwellers in the valley,"* L. *An open stage should be left between, for the speakers.*

SCENE. — *A place where two roads meet.*

(*Solo and chorus. Air, "Come forward with pleasure."*)

(*During which, enter,* L., FRIVOLITA, MIRTH, SPORT, *and other dwellers in the valley.*)

Friv.
Bright spirits of pleasure,
With light hearts advance,
And join in the measure
Of song and of dance.

Chorus. — Bright spirits, &c.

Friv. With roses upspringing your footsteps to greet,
While sweet woodland songsters their welcomes repeat,
Bright spirits of pleasure with gay hearts advance,
And join with full heart in the song and the dance.

Chorus. — Bright spirits, &c.

Frivolita. Thanks, joyous spirits: you our bidding greet
With rare obedience. Our most fair retreat,
Pleasure's bright valley, wakens to new life,
Warmed by your hearts, with glee and gladness rife.
All's bright and happy in our fairy home,
And joy attends our feet where'er we roam,
Save on this spot, where heartless, cruel fate
Marks daily conflicts to annoy my state.
Pilgrims of life, who, crowding thickly, press
In search of havens of true happiness,
With bounding footsteps hurrying o'er a road,
Which, till it reaches here, is smooth and broad,
Now pause, perplexed to find the way divide
To two strange paths, that stretch on either side.
One leads o'er rocky, dark, and dismal steeps:
There false Celesta watchful vigil keeps.
The other, winding down, 'mid groves and flowers,
Conducts the pilgrim to our blissful bowers.
Quick choice were made, where glowing beauties sweep
In happy contrast to a toilsome steep,
But that Celesta, with her polished art,
Weaves a mysterious influence o'er the heart,
Robbing my sceptre of its power to bless
The longing pilgrim with true happiness.

(*Music, piano.*)

But hark! she comes: that mournful, solemn strain
Proclaims Celesta, with her sober train.

(*Chorus. During which enter*, R., CELESTA, REASON, RELIGION, *and other dwellers on the heights.*)

(*Air*, "*The quiet night.*")

Adown the heights advancing,
  In marshalled ranks we come,
To guide the toiling pilgrim
  To Wisdom's peaceful home.
In Duty's footsteps treading,
Nor care nor danger dreading,
  To battle for her rights,
  To battle for her rights,
For Wisdom's rights, for Wisdom's rights.

Celesta. Frivolita, once more we meet in strife
In this marked spot, upon the path of life.
Upon the road of youth I just espied
An eager pilgrim, full of faith and pride.
Soon must she reach this spot: here choice must make,
Which of two roads, the right or left, to take.
I marked her face: 'twas earnest, thoughtful, bright.
Left to herself, she'll surely choose the right.
Upon her path set not your glittering snares
Of senseless joys to trap her unawares,
But let her freely pass up Wisdom's road,
To rest securely in her grand abode.

Frivolita. Nay, false Celesta, thine's a foolish tale:
True happiness is found within our vale,
Where mirth and laughter, revel, dance, and song,
On lightsome pinions move the groves among;
And not in Wisdom's staid and sober hall,
Where irksome duties joyous hearts appall.
They who would drink at Happiness' pure fount,
Adown the vale must glide, not climb the mount.

Gay, smiling Pleasure I pronounce the queen
Of joys unnumbered, happiness supreme.
In her just cause I throw the gauntlet down,
Prepared to win this pilgrim for her crown.

Celesta. Firm in the faith that Wisdom's ways are true,
Fearless I arm, your temptings to subdue.
Throw round the pilgrim all your flowery spells;
Bring Mirth and Laughter from their echoing cells:
I'll meet you with the pure, unsullied joys
That sober Wisdom quietly employs.
Calm, clear-eyed Reason, with her watchful care;
Spotless Religion, with her earnest prayer, —
These be my champions in the coming fight:
Marshal your force; let Justice guard the right.

(*Chorus. During which all march off,* — FRIVOLITA *and attendants,* L., CELESTA *and attendants,* R.)

(*Air, "Soldiers' Chorus."* — FAUST.)

Arm you to fight for the queen you prize,
In whose kingdom true happiness lies.
Just is our cause, and steadfast we stand:
Yes, ready to fight, or ready to die, at her command.

(*Semi-chorus,* CELESTA *and attendants.*)

Who lacks courage to dare at Wisdom's call?
Who would falter or quail till her foes shall fall?

(*Semi-chorus,* FRIVOLITA *and attendants.*)

Who would turn from a queen so loving and true,
When foes would assail the fair fame of the vale
So fondly we view?

Chorus. — Arm you, &c.

Enter — C., *if possible; if not*, R. — LIGHTFOOT, *followed by* CONSCIENCE.

Lightfoot. How sweet it is, life's pleasant path to tread:
Earth, with its gayest covering thickly spread;
Heaven bending o'er me in its cloudless blue;
Flowers springing forth in ever-changing hue;
The song of birds, the fragrant scented air, —
Gladness and beauty stretching everywhere!
O happy pilgrim! that such joy can feel,
Press on thy journey with redoubled zeal.
But here I pause in doubt; for, stretching wide,
The smooth, straight road behind doth here divide:
This to the right in tortuous windings creeps,
O'er rugged paths, up high and rocky steeps;
While to the left a grassy path doth wend
Through groves of trees that intertwining blend.
The left I'll take: its light, attractive air.
Foretells the passage to a land more fair.

Conscience. (*Stepping before* LIGHTHEART.)
Lightheart, forbear! ere you a step advance,
Consult your guide, trust no unlucky chance.

Lightheart. Who dares to check my purpose? Who are you,
That start up in the path I would pursue?

Conscience. A true and trusty friend, — Conscience, thy guide,
Whom that old sage, Good Counsel, at thy side
Fastened for life: thy "better part," indeed,
To warn, to aid, to succor thee in need.
In search of happiness, O pilgrim! you
These wise instructions ever keep in view:

All outward splendor is an empty show,
A glittering crust, that hides the void below.
The dullest earth, by labor dug away,
Brings richest jewels to the light of day.
Choose wisely, pilgrim. Duty's path is plain:
By toilsome steps the lofty height we gain.

Lightheart. Thy words are wise, grave Conscience, and anon
The stern and rocky path I'll journey on:
Here let me pause a while, and blissful stand
Upon the precincts of this fairy land.

(*Chorus*, L. *Air*, "*Come again to father-land.*")

Come, pilgrim, join our happy throng;
Pilgrim, come, pilgrim, come,
Where merry dance and joyous song
Fill our fairy home.
No dull cares our hearts assail:
Pleasure's spell guards us well.
Beautiful our festive vale,
More than tongue can tell.
Come, pilgrim, &c.

Lightheart. What joyful sounds! Sure, Happiness dwells there,
Where such bewitching notes float in the air.

Conscience. Trifler, forbear! 'Tis Pleasure's siren call:
Turn, ere its mystic power your heart inthrall.

(*Chorus*, R. *Air*, "*The Rose.*")

Sweet the power of Wisdom's spell,
Lovingly caressing,
Shed, with free and lavish hand,
Peace and joy within our land,
Ever richly blessing.
Peace and joy within our land,
Ever richly blessing.

Conscience. List to the welcome of the good and pure.
Shun false allurements; Wisdom's ways secure.

Lightheart. 'Tis but a sober strain: no joy it brings,
Such as from Pleasure's merrier measure springs.
And see! from out the grove, with dancing feet,
Three smiling strangers come this way to greet.

Enter, L., FRIVOLITA, SPORT, *and* MIRTH.

Frivolita. Welcome, young pilgrim, to our happy grove,
Where joyous spirits all unfettered rove:
Pleasure's fair land, in all attraction bright,
Shall ope to thee a realm of sweet delight.
Enter thou in. No task or toil severe,
No base, depressing cares, annoy thee here;
But never-ending joys from sun to sun.
Pilgrim, thy search is o'er, thy journey done.

Sport. No land so fair, no realm so bright and free,
As this, that stretches welcomes warm to thee.
With bounding sports we quicken sluggish hours,
Frolic in woodlands, dance amid the flowers,
With feasts and revelry new charms array,
And at the founts of song our thirst allay.

Mirth. Thrice welcome, pilgrim, to the fairy dells
Where Mirth's resounding laughter joyous swells.
Grim old Sobriety here hides his face,
And shuns the spot where jovial spirits race
In madcap glee. Pilgrim, life's brightest dress
Is gayety, the garb of happiness.

Lightheart. Thanks for your welcome: surely peace and rest
Await me in a land so richly blest.

Conscience. Lightheart, beware of Pleasure's smiling face:
Pitfalls lie hidden 'neath this seeming grace.

Enter, R., CELESTA, REASON, *and* RELIGION.

Celesta. Young stranger, by this rude and rocky road
All zealous pilgrims reach the grand abode
Where Wisdom dwells. Her pure and loving arts
Attract her subjects and subdue their hearts.
The way is stony, rough, and hard to keep;
But sturdy Duty aids them up the steep,
While streams of knowledge, with refreshing play,
Their rugged pathways smooth, their thirsts allay.
Her palace gained, the pilgrimage is o'er:
The precious treasures of her bounteous store
For them are poured, and, in refreshing rest,
Their search for happiness supremely blest.
If thou hast strength to climb the mountain side,
Reason will counsel, and Religion guide.

Reason. Lightheart, she speaketh well; her words are true:
Straight up the rugged way thy search pursue.
I, Reason, counsel; for no joys are pure
But those which strong Endeavor can secure.
Pleasure's smiles fade before the test of trial:
Life's first great victory's gained by self-denial.

Religion. Take me, O pilgrim! for thy trusty guide
In thy rough journey up the mountain side:
I'll fill thy soul with calm and holy zeal,
Sweet ways of pleasantness and peace reveal,
With holy prayer thy weariness dispel,
With Hope uphold, with Faith will guide thee well.

Conscience. Be wise, O Lightheart! their instructions heed:
They'll serve thee well in darkest hour of need.

Frivolita. Behold how bright the valley spreads below!

TABLEAU. — FRIVOLITA *takes* LIGHTHEART'S *left hand with her right, turns her to* L., *and points off with her left hand.* SPORT *puts her left arm around* LIGHTHEART'S *waist, and points* L. *with her right.* MIRTH *stands behind, with her right hand on* LIGHTHEART'S *shoulder, pointing with her left. All stand motionless, while the music of "Come forward with pleasure" is played very softly.*

Conscience. 'Tis but a mockery, and a senseless show.

Celesta. Above the clouds the domes of Wisdom tower.

TABLEAU. — CELESTA *places her left hand on* LIGHTHEART'S *right shoulder, turning her to* R.; *with her right hand she points off* R. LIGHTHEART'S *right arm around* CELESTA'S *waist.* RELIGION *falls on one knee beside* LIGHTHEART, *pointing* R. REASON *stands just behind* CELESTA, *pointing* R. *All motionless, while the music of "The Rose" is played very softly.*

Conscience. Emblems of solid and unfailing power.

Frivolita. Pleasure's bright spirits at her bidding come
To welcome thee to her alluring home.

Chorus. — "Bright spirits of pleasure," &c.

Enter, L., *dwellers in the valley.*

Celesta. Wisdom's choice spirits at her bidding meet,
To guard and guide thee to her grand retreat.

Chorus. — "Adown the heights advancing," &c.

Enter, R., *dwellers on the heights.*

Lightheart. Kind friends, fair promises of peace and joy
To lure my steps you eagerly employ.
How shall I choose? Each claims the better part;
Each with attractions rare enchains my heart.
Wisdom's grand temple dim and distant lies,
To longing souls a rich, alluring prize;
But from the road before, so rough and drear,
My trembling spirit shrinks with doubt and fear.
Here Pleasure's valley, beautiful and sweet,
Spreads flowery pathways for my tender feet.
To reach *her* realms is no unwelcome task:
Freely her joys are given all that ask.
Two paths to happiness you thus disclose:
One steep and rough, the other smoothly flows.
I am but mortal: where sweet pleasures rise
I'll take the gift, to others leave the prize.
Thou, fair Frivolita, shall be my guide
To all the joys that in your home reside.

Frivolita. Pilgrim, your hand: a happy choice you make;
At Pleasure's feast come freely and partake.

Conscience. Stay, Lightheart, stay! list to my warning voice:
There's sin and danger in your foolish choice.

Lightheart. Conscience, away; your voice is harsh and cold:
Break not the charm that doth my heart enfold.

Conscience. There's danger in the path thy feet would tread, —
Pitfalls beneath, and darkness overhead,
If thou wilt go, I'll with thee to the vale,
With shame will goad thee, with remorse assail,
Till back thou turn to Wisdom's better way.

Lightheart. Conscience, I heed thee not: away, away!

Enter, L., FOLLY, FALSEHOOD, *and* SHAME, *who crowd and jostle the dwellers of the valley, and force themselves to the front.*

Lightheart. But who are these who recklessly appear,
To make confusion 'mid the dwellers here?

Folly. I'm Folly, daring spirit of the dell:
Within the vale you'll learn to know me well.
They seek to keep me from their sports away:
I'm always there, the noisiest in the play.
I lead them by my arts where pitfalls lie,
And laugh and shout to see them sink and die.

Falsehood. Falsehood's my name. I'm Folly's trusty friend:
Together ever we in mischief blend.
O'er all unsightly things a veil I throw,
Flimsy and weak, but gorgeous in its show.
I robe the valley in a gay disguise
That hides the rottenness which in it lies.

Shame. In a dark dell the cave of Shame is found,
By weeping willows thick enclustered round,

Near to the lake o'er which, with wild despair,
Grim Fates, relentless, wearied spirits bear.
When Pleasure's smiles lose their delusive spell,
Come, hide your sorrows in Shame's gloomy cell.

Conscience. Lightheart, this heavy burden must you bear;
With Folly, Falsehood, Shame, your pleasures share.

Lightheart. (*To* FRIVOLITA.) Are these the joys to which you would invite?
Vanish, false Pleasure, from my aching sight.
Your smile's a mockery, and your joy's a snare
To lead my soul to darkness and despair.
Back to your groves! Lightheart the welcome spurns
That points the way where sin unholy burns.

(*Exeunt* FRIVOLITA *and attendants*, L.)

O fair Celesta! with repentance meet (*kneels*),
I lowly bend me at your steadfast feet.
Lead me in Wisdom's path: if rough or fair,
I'll toil with energy, with patience bear.

Celesta. (*Raising* LIGHTHEART.) Thou hast but looked on Pleasure's mocking face:
On thy fair fame she leaves no blasting trace.
Temptation overcome doth fit thy soul
To battle bravely for the promised goal.

Conscience. Thou hast done well: henceforth the path is sure
For thy young soul to happiness secure.
Where Reason and Religion point the way,
Step forth with courage, and with joy obey.
Upward and onward be thy watchwords ever:
Pure pleasures spring alone from wise endeavor.

Celesta. Forward, brave pilgrim! to the pure and true,
Wisdom gives power to conquer and subdue.

(*Chorus. Air,* "*Chorus of Pilgrims.*")

(*During which characters march off;* R., *in the following manner: First,* REASON *and* RELIGION, *hand in hand; then* LIGHTHEART, *with* CELESTA *on her right,* CONSCIENCE *on her left. Dwellers in the heights follow.*)

To our home, pilgrim brave, we will guide thee,
With its power of joy thee alluring:
Let no duty or danger appall thee
A haven of rest from securing.

Semi-chorus.

To the pilgrim, who, bold and enduring,
Bravely treads in the pathway of duty,
Her mansions of wondrous beauty,
Attractive and beautiful gleam.

Semi-chorus.

Fairest home, where purified pleasures
Sweetly gladden the heart that secureth,
Ever pouring its bountiful treasures
In blessings of peace and of joy.

Semi-chorus.

Then press onward, bold pilgrim, onward:
To the joys that our loved home bestoweth,
The rough pathway of duty secureth;
For the toils of the pilgrim sweet rest,
For the toils of the pilgrim sweet rest,
Yes, sweet rest, pilgrim, sweet rest.

(*Curtain falls.*)

NOTE.—The tunes used in this allegory may all be found in "The Grammar School Chorus," published in Boston, and sent by mail, post-paid, by Oliver Ditson & Co., on receipt of one dollar.

THE WAR OF THE ROSES.

AN ALLEGORY.

FOR FEMALE CHARACTERS ONLY.

CHARACTERS.

GENTILLA, the wanderer.
CAMELLIA, queen of the flowers.
RUBA (the red rose), emblem of love.
EGLANTERIA (the yellow rose), emblem of jealousy.
VIOLA (the violet), emblem of modesty.
LILIA (the lily), emblem of purity.
COLUMBINE, emblem of folly.
AMARYLLIS, emblem of pride.
POPIVA (the poppy), emblem of sleep.

(*This allegory is particularly designed for school exhibitions. Choruses should be seated on the platform,* R. *and* L. *An open stage should be left between, for the speaking.*

SCENE. — *The Garden of Youth. Decorate the platform with plants in pots, hanging baskets, small trees, &c., with a green bank at back. The characters should be adorned with emblematic flowers.*

Chorus.

(*During which, enter* Ruba, Viola, Lilia, R.; Eglanteria, Columbine, *and* Amaryllis, L.)

(*Air, "The herd-bells.*")

From mossy beds upspringing,
Fair queen, we gather now,
Our flowery tributes bringing
To grace thy regal brow,
With crystal dew-drops gleaming,
With fragrance rich and sweet,
Pure as the love we bear thee:
We lay them at thy feet.

Enter Camellia, C. *Repeat chorus.*

Camellia. Beloved subjects, to our willing ear
Your loyal greetings come in tones sincere.
In love we welcome all the love you sing,
And for that love the tributes that you bring.
Your blooming faces, ever bright and fair,
Adorn the earth with beauty rich and rare.
Your graceful forms attractive ever prove;
Your virtues waft their fragrance as you move.
When love and loyalty go hand in hand,
What realm can equal our bright, flowery land?

Ruba. With joy, fair queen, *your* orders we obey:
Fondly we own your gentle, loving sway.
Your smiles, refreshing as the summer showers,
Reward the tasks you set our humble powers.

Eglanteria. Proudly, fair queen, thy sovereign will we own,
And bend submissively around thy throne:
The chosen ruler of our tender race,
Thou rul'st supreme with dignity and grace.

Camellia. Since Nature gave to us the charm to grace
And deck with varied hues the earth's broad face,
Youth's first attraction was the realm of flowers,
The fairy garden of life's sunny hours.
With gratitude should we accept its love,
With bounteous hands our grateful feelings prove.
Just stepping into Life's bewildering hours,
An earthly maiden strays among the flowers,
Gazing enraptured where our treasures lie,
Fearing to pluck, yet loath to pass them by.
This maid to welcome 'tis our high decree,
Ruba, that you our messenger shall be.
Choose from our royal court companions fair
To aid you in the task: then quick repair,
With our dear love the happy maiden greet,
And lay your floral tributes at her feet.
Remember, not alone to charm the sense
Do we our regal offerings dispense:
That which is lovely do we wisely prize
For some fair virtue that within it lies.
Forget not, that, within our beauteous land,
Poisonous flowers all unblushing stand.
For her adornment use your highest art;
With sweetest fragrance bless her youthful heart.

Ruba. Eager I haste, sweet queen, the maid to greet:
Your royal welcome shall my lips repeat.
Viola and Lilia, my companions fair,
With your approval shall my mission share.

Camellia. Ruba, thy happy choice we well approve:
Over the garden on your mission move.

(*Chorus. Air, "Over the billow.*")

Over the garden merrily dancing,
Seek the bright maiden hither advancing;
Over the garden joyfully moving,
Meet her with greeting, peaceful and loving:
Flowers bright blooming, sweetly perfuming,
Welcoming her coming, greet her with love.

Repeat.

(*Exeunt* RUBA, VIOLA, LILIA, R. QUEEN, C.)

Eglanteria. Again preferred! Ruba, the simplest rose,
The plainest flower, that in our garden grows!
Methinks our gracious queen is lacking taste,
Her favors on this senseless thing to waste.

Amaryllis. Ay, Eglanteria, 'tis a cruel shame,
This insult to your proud ancestral name.
You, of the roses the most bright and fair,
Our sovereign's favors have a *right* to share.

Columbine. Sweet Amaryllis, doth not *your* proud heart
Rebel to be so coolly set apart,
While Viola and Lilia, tame and meek,
Usurp the places our high names bespeak?

Amaryllis. Ay, sister Columbine, with bitter pain
My heart is moved; yet why should we complain?
Our sovereign's will is law, there's no denial:
What comfort can we seek in this sore trial?

Columbine. When monarchs recklessly the sceptre wield,
Justice, the higher law, should be our shield:
Fair Eglanteria's wrongs give ample cause
To seek rebellion 'gainst unholy laws.
Some solace for our woes we yet may gain
By open war 'gainst Ruba and her train.

Eglanteria. Thanks for your sympathy in my sore need.
Ay, Columbine, a bitter war indeed
Henceforth 'twixt Ruba and myself shall wage,
Not e'en Camellia's power can assuage.
While Ruba seeks the maid, with ready art,
To plant the germs of virtue in her heart,
Devouring passions I will mingle there,
To check their growth, their tendrils to insnare.
Grant me your aid, my true and loving friends,
And for your wrongs I'll quickly make amends.

Amaryllis. Ay, Eglanteria, with a willing heart,
Proud in your triumph thus to have a part.

Columbine. Thy wrongs are mine: show me the way to serve;
Thy trust and counsel I will well deserve.

Eglanteria. Again my thanks. Ruba the maid will charm
With loving blandishment and virtues warm;
Teach her the secret powers which dwell within
The heart of youth to guard from guile and sin.
This be *our* task: sleepy Popiva's aid
Shall fast in Slumber's arms enfold the maid;
Then to her bosom shall our gifts be pressed,—
Pride, Jealousy, and Folly there find rest.
Come, then, my sisters, we'll the maiden greet:
For cruel wrong revenge is fair and sweet.

Trio. Air, "Love of country."

Come, sisters, with united hearts,
Against the foe before us
Boldly advance: our wily arts
To peace shall quick restore us.

For cruel wrongs revenge is sweet,
Oppression's power defying:
Fearless we go the foe to meet,
Quick victory descrying.
Chorus. Come, sisters, &c.

(*Exeunt* EGLANTERIA, LILIA, *and* VIOLA, L.)

Enter GENTILLA, R.

Gentilla. A paradise of flowers! How sweet to rove
O'er sunlit meadow, through the rustling grove,
By murmuring fountain, drinking with full heart
The joyous beauty each and all impart!
The leaves' soft rustle in the summer breeze,
The song of birds among the bending trees,
The bee's swift hum, the cricket's chirping voice,
In Nature's language bid the heart rejoice.
The flowers alone in silent beauty stand,
The fairest treasures of this bounteous land;
Yet legends tell us they've the magic skill
Youth's opening life with richest truths to fill.
If this be true, O pretty flowers! impart
The purest teachings of your mystic art:
Plant in my tender heart the germs of truth,
To guard and guide aright the steps of youth.

Song. Air, "Ye merry birds."

Gentilla. In gardens, where soft breezes blow,
Are pretty flowers which sweetly grow.
Within each soft and tiny shell
Is hidden a rare and curious spell
To guard and guide the steps of youth,
And fill the heart with germs of truth.
Come, pretty flowers, so bright and free,
Whisper your secrets unto me,
Your highest arts employ
To fill my soul with peace and joy.

(RUBA, LILIA, *and* VIOLA, *outside*, R.)

Yes, gladly will we to thy heart
The secrets of our race impart:
If thou wilt guard what we bestow,
Around thee shall life's blessings flow,
Sweet peace and joy thy soul shall know.
Along life's path our flowery spell,
If thou but guard, shall guide thee well.
Yes, happy maid, so bright and free,
Our secrets we'll disclose to thee,
Our highest arts employ
To fill thy soul with peace and joy.

Full chorus.

Repeat. — "Yes, happy maid," &c.

Enter RUBA, LILIA, *and* VIOLA, R.

Ruba. Our royal queen, Camellia, bids me greet
The youthful wanderer in her fair retreat:
Her bounteous realm, in all attractions bright,
Welcomes thee, maiden, with a fond delight;
Here mayst thou rove, where all is pure and fair,
Gather our treasures, and our pleasures share.

Gentilla. Thanks for your welcome; yet I fain would know
Where in your realm the mystic flowers grow
That warm the breast of youth with pure desire,
And Virtue's holiest attributes inspire.

Ruba. (*Presents rose.*) Thy wish is wise, fair stranger: here behold
A gem far richer than a mine of gold, —
A simple rose, emblem of purest love,
The holy power that rules in heaven above.
With this true happiness is freely bought;
Without it all the world is less than nought:

Keep it unsullied in thy youthful breast;
'Twill guide thee to the mansions of the blest.

Gentilla. Thy blooming gift, fair messenger, shall be
A precious talisman of power to me,
All base and selfish passions to subdue,
To gain the good, the beautiful, and true.

Viola. (*Presents violet.*) This violet, a simple shrinking flower,
Within its petals holds a mighty power.
In beds obscure it hides a blushing face,
Yet wafts the richest perfumes of our race:
Fit type of Modesty, a gem of worth,
No more unselfish spirit e'er had birth.
Take it, fair maid: whatever life secure,
This simple flower shall make more rich and pure.

Gentilla. Beside the rose, fair stranger, it shall bloom,
Freshening Endeavor with its sweet perfume;
So fair without, so rich and pure within,
A guide to virtue, and a guard from sin.

Lilia. (*Presents lily.*) This lily that I bring contains a spell,
Within thy youthful heart to guard thee well, —
Emblem of purity, the pearl of price,
A weapon strong 'gainst Folly's gay device.
All heaven-born virtues own its gentle sway,
All vices from its presence shrink away.
Cherish it, maiden: on life's battle-field
'Gainst all invaders 'tis a spotless shield.

Gentilla. Your precious gifts, sweet friends, I hold most dear:
To your fair queen pray bear my thanks sincere.

Tell her Gentilla breathes this heartfelt prayer:
Long may she live to rule a realm so fair!

TABLEAU. — GENTILLA *stands in front of bank, looking at the flowers in her hands.* RUBA *steps upon the bank, places roses in her hair, and looks into her face.* VIOLET *kneels at* R. *of* GENTILLA, *and fastens a bunch of violets on the skirt of her dress, looking up into her face.* LILIA *passes behind* GENTILLA *to the* L., *and places a girdle of leaves and flowers around her waist, looking up into her face. Bright, smiling, happy expressions on all faces. Take positions quickly, and stand immovable, while the pianist plays softly,* "THE ROSE."

Ruba. Gentilla, all the graces we bestow
Only by careful nurture fruitful grow.
The germs of worth, if thou unceasing guard,
Protect, and cherish, bring a rich reward.
Neglected, their fair tints will fade away,
Their fragrance vanish, and their powers decay.
Farewell! the richest blessings life can give,
If thou be faithful, shall thy trust receive.

(*Exeunt* RUBA, VIOLA, *and* LILIA, R.)

Gentilla. (*Sits on bank.*) Neglect thee! tender flowers, believe it not:
Henceforth for thee and me a common lot.
Now that I know the language of thy race,
Each whispered word of counsel I'll embrace.
Thou, rose of love, with all thy sweetness warm;
Thou, modest violet, with thy fragrance charm;
Thou, pure, sweet lily, with thy virtue glow;
And round life's path shall countless blessings flow.

Enter POPIVA, C.

Popiva. To serve the crafty Eglanteria's will,
A magic potion must my art distil,
In drowsy chains this maiden fast to keep,
And waft her gently to the arms of Sleep.

(POPIVA *waves a poppy around the head of* GENTILLA, *who falls asleep.*)

Song, POPIVA. *Air*, "*The image of the rose.*"

Come, Sleep, on drowsy pinions flying,
This maiden lull to sweet repose:
The land of dreams around thee lying,
To charm her senses, brightly glows.
There fairy visions, soft entrancing,
In changeful measures sport and play:
Sleep, by thy magic power advancing,
Within thy arms bear her away.
Magical sleep, bear her, bear her, oh, bear her away!

Enter EGLANTERIA, AMARYLLIS, *and* COLUMBINE, L.

Popiva. My task's accomplished: in a sleep profound
The tender victim of your wiles lies bound.
Popiva's power no mortal can withstand:
Softly approach and deal with gentle hand.

Eglanteria. (*Places yellow rose in* GENTILLA'S *breast.*)
Now, by your leave, my sweet and gentle maid,
By Ruba's fancy modestly arrayed,
I'll place within your breast this yellow rose:
Emblem of Jealousy, it hotly glows.
When love shall coldly turn with frown and sneer,
Thou'lt find in Jealousy a friend sincere:
Love gave it birth, 'gainst love it fiercely wars,
And by Suspicion's aid all joy it mars.

To swift revenge 'gainst all insulting foes,
With fiery passion, recklessly it goes.

Amaryllis. This flower of regal birth, emblem of Pride,
Viola's modesty I'll place beside.
Type of nobility, it stately stands,
Bends to no will, but royally commands.
Wear it: 'twill teach thee all thyself to know,
And, knowing all thy worth, thy worth to show.
In no obscurity it hides its face,
But boldly blossoms with a conscious grace.

Columbine. (*Places flower in her hand.*)
Folly's gay flower, the fickle Columbine,
With Pride and Jealousy let me entwine.
Unlike its sisters, ever bright and gay,
'Twill teach thy steps in Pleasure's paths to stray.
Nothing so fair but it will freely face;
Nothing so foul but it will quick embrace.
Reckless of peril, 'tis a sportive sprite,
That dares the lowest depth, the loftiest height.

TABLEAU. — GENTILLA *moves.* POPIVA, *behind bank, leans forward, with her finger on her lips.* EGLANTERIA, *at head of bank, kneeling, looks to the left.* AMARYLLIS, *at foot of bank, front, kneeling, looks to the right.* COLUMBINE, *kneeling behind bank, watches* GENTILLA. *All but* POPIVA *should take these positions when they place flowers in* GENTILLA'S *bosom. When* GENTILLA *moves, all take attitudes as described, with frightened, anxious, guilty expressions of faces. Music as before. When* RUBA *speaks, all start up.*

Ruba. (*Outside*, R.) Sisters, awake! there's treason in our realm!
Advance, Rebellion's power to overwhelm.

(*Exit* POPIVA, L.)

GENTILLA *awakes.* *Enter* RUBA, VIOLA, *and* LILIA, R.

Ruba. Vile Eglanteria, with unblushing shame,
Thou dost disgraceful mar our mystic fame:
Within this maiden's breast our sovereign's will
Gave me the power all virtues to instil.
With crafty art and traitorous intent,
A mad and wicked plot thou didst invent,
With my pure flowers to mingle base alloys,
And rob sweet promise of its richest joys.
Speak, traitress! can thy wicked spirit plead
Aught to extenuate so base a deed?

Eglanteria. Insulting Ruba, dost thou basely dare
To flaunt and clamor with so proud an air?
Dost think to school me with thy pettish ways?
Me, over whom the royal colors blaze?
The same almighty power has given us all
The right vain hearts of mortals to inthrall.
The favorite of a queen, thou canst bestow
Only such gifts as her commands allow.
While freely I endow, with quickening fire
The slumbering passions actively inspire.

Ruba. Vile are your gifts, base Eglanteria; cease:
Unworthy art thou of this realm of peace.
No right have we to give but what is pure,
To sweet and lasting happiness secure.
I do pronounce thee traitorous to our cause:
Thy acts unholy mock our righteous laws.

Quick, make amends: in Queen Camellia's name
Thy poisonous gifts I bid thee now reclaim.

Eglanteria. I own no queen: defiantly I stand
The peer of any power in Flower-land.
My gifts shall bloom, base Ruba: thou shouldst know
None can reclaim what once we free bestow.

Ruba. Then will I pluck them with this loyal hand.
Guardians of virtue, firm around me stand.

Eglanteria. Come, sister spirits, to the rescue fly:
Our gifts bestowed, securely they must lie.
Of Eglanteria's power, base slaves, beware.

Ruba. My strength 'gainst thine to match I boldly dare.

(RUBY *and* EGLANTERIA *approach* GENTILLA.)

Gentilla. Hold! brilliant flowers, a moment cease your strife.
You both claim mystic power o'er my young life.
Thou, gentle Ruba, and thy sisters twain,
Taught me with blooming gifts sweet peace to gain.
Thou, Eglanteria, on my slumbers pressed
Passions which ever war within the breast.
While 'tis your power to give, 'tis mine to take:
Of all your bounties this free choice I make.
On Jealousy I look with fear and dread;
Cold-hearted Pride too lofty holds her head;
Folly's a flower of ever-changing hues:
These, crafty Eglanteria, I refuse.
Deceitful gifts, I cast ye off with scorn:

(*Throws away flowers given her by* EGLANTERIA, AMARYLLIS, *and* COLUMBINE.)

Ye gain no homage, yet the true heart warn.
The power of Love already o'er me steals;

The power of Modesty its charms reveals;
The power of Purity my choice controls, —
Three guardian virtues for all longing souls.
These will I wear within my youthful heart,
Richly to flourish, never to depart.

Enter QUEEN, C.

Queen. Well said, Gentilla: thine's a happy choice;
May all its blessings make thy heart rejoice!
As thou hast found within these realms of joy
Unholy passions mingle base alloy,
So wilt thou find along the path of life
Upspringing foes of virtue, armed for strife.
Guard well thy treasures with a tender care:
Of Slumber's toils be watchful and beware.
(*Gives japonica.*) Accept our royal token: let it be
"Type of perfected loveliness" to thee, —
The highest honor mortal can attain;
Then onward press with Hope and Faith to gain.
Then shall our flowery virtues never cease
To fill thy youthful soul with joy and peace.

Chorus. Air, "Boatman's return."

Joy, joy, ever be near,
Sweetly fall o'er thee;
Peace, Peace, guarding from fear,
Warmly infold thee.
Love, warm and endearing, with sweet modesty glow,
With Purity cheering Life as you go.
Joy, joy, &c.

(*Form, and march off* R., *led by* QUEEN.)

NOTE. — The tunes used in this allegory may all be found in "The Grammar School Chorus," published in Boston, and sent by mail, post-paid, by Oliver Ditson & Co., on receipt of one dollar.

THIRTY MINUTES FOR REFRESHMENTS.

CHARACTERS.

JOHN DOWNLEY, a bachelor.
CLARENCE FITTS, his colored servant.
JOHN FOXTON, a young married gentleman.
MAJOR PEPPER, U.S.A.
MRS. FOXTON.
MISS ARABELLA PEPPER, a maiden lady.
POLLY, waiting maid at Highland Station.

COSTUMES.

DOWNLEY, gray suit, light overcoat, gray wig, side-whiskers, cap, travelling satchel, gloves.

CLARENCE, light pants, yellow vest, blue coat with brass buttons, hat.

FOXTON, white pants, white vest, black velvet coat, light curly wig, moustache, eye-glasses, gloves, cane.

MAJOR PEPPER, undress uniform.

MRS. FOXTON, Light silk dress, white shawl, white bonnet.

MISS PEPPER, brown silk dress, red shawl, red front with side curls, wrinkled face, spectacles, straw bonnet, green gloves.

POLLY, spotted calico, neat white apron, with pockets.

SCENE. — *Private room in the refreshment department of Highland Station. Table,* C. *Chairs,* R. *and* L. *Door,* C. *Entrances,* R. *and* L. *If no door* C., *all* C. *entrances should be from* R. POLLY *discovered laying table-cloth.*

Polly. (*Sings.*)

"Oh! there's nothing half so sweet in life
As love's young dream," &c.

Now, isn't that touching? But not for me were those beautiful words written. Oh, no! the tender heart of Polly Patten has never felt the ecstatic emotion caused by that dream. And I have so longed for some manly bosom on which to recline my drooping head! Ah, well! I live in hopes. When I took this menial situation, it was with the fond, delusive hope, that, among the manly bosoms that come and go, one might be thrilled by my presence, some penetrating eye might be fastened upon me in admiration, some masculine hand squeeze mine as I passed the coffee. But not an eye, not a squeeze. It's awful to think of. No matrimonial prospect ahead, and my hair getting awful thin on top. Oh if some loving widower, or some rich old bachelor, would only fall in love with me! *Oh*, my! it won't bear thinking of.

(*Cars heard outside, entering the dépôt; whistle, bell, &c., and then a voice, " Thirty minutes for refreshments."*)

The train is here. Now, Polly, keep your eyes open.

Enter CLARENCE, C., *fanning himself with his hat.*

Clar. My golly! Almos' lose my bref. (*Sinks into chair*, R.)

Polly. I declare, it's Mr. Fitts!

Clar. Dat's who 'tis, jes'. Golly, Miss Polly, such a jam! Cars loaded, crammed, stufficated.

Polly. A crowd! Oh, it's an excursion train!

Clar. Yaas, dat's what's de matter. A big jubilum

down dar to York, — down dar. Big fiddles, big trombones, big drums. Golly, what drums! Big as yer head; and all de phusicans a-fifin' and a-blowin', — and such a crowd!

Polly. Was your master, Mr. Downley, on the train?

Clar. Yaas: he dar. Comin' here to eat his dinner: telegraphed for de room. I left him in de hind car, and went into de smoking-car, to have a whiff wid de odder gentlemen. By golly, such fun! Dey made a pos'-office of me, in dar.

Polly. A post-office?

Clar. Yaas, dey did. I'll tell yer all about it. I was in dar, in de smoking-car, and de fust ting I knew, — golly, wa'n't it funny! I'll tell you all about it. De bery first ting, when I was in dat ar' smoking-car, I heard a voice like dis yar: "Mr. Johnsing, would you be so disobliging and so disaccommodating as to do me a very perticklar favor." "Sartain sure," says I; "but my name's not Johnsing. It's Fitts, Clarence Fitts." "I ax yer apology," says de gentleman. "Will you go for to take this year note to de lady what sits in de fourth seat from de furder end, on de right, in de next car?" "Sartainly," says I. So I took de note, and was a jest going out of de door of de smoking-car, when a hossifer tapped me on this year shoulder, and, says he to me, says he, "Mr. Washington, is you going to de next car?" "Yaas," says I, "I'm going to de next car; but my name's not Washington. He's been dead and gone 'bout seventy 'leben years. My name is Fitts, Clarence Fitts." "Misser Fitts," says de milintary man, "oblige me by takin' dis year little note to de lady what sits in de fourth seat from de furder end, on de left." By golly! yer might have knocked me down wid — wid — a crowbar. Two notes, two ladies, two fourth seats in de next car! Did yer ever see sich an infusion of idees? But I took de notes, and gib dem to de ladies. What you s'pose it all mean, hey?

Polly. Oh! the gentlemen were probably unable to be with their ladies, on account of the crowd, and wished to communicate with them.

Clar. Didn't say nuffin' 'bout communion: only said, gib 'em de notes.

Polly. Well, it's all right. But tell me, Mr. Fitts, how is your master?

Clar. Well, he's purty well, and so am I. How's yerself generally?

Polly. Mr. Fitts, is his heart still unaffected?

Clar. Heart! Sound as a cabbage. Got a little rheumatiz, do.

Polly. You don't understand me. Has he formed an attachment for anybody?

Clar. Oh, yis! Oh, yis! He done dat, sartin, sure you born, Miss Polly.

Polly. Indeed! Who is the happy creature?

Clar. It's me, Miss Polly. He berry much attached to me.

Polly. Oh, how stupid you are! I mean, has he been smitten by the charms of any young lady?

Clar. No: he didn't git de mitten ob nobody.

Polly. Tell me, Mr. Fitts, is there any little delicate attention I could bestow that would particularly attract his attention, — that would waken an interest —

Clar. Wall, yis: you jist tread on his corns. Dat's a little delicate attention dat would wake him and de whole neighborhood. You jes' try dat. Hear him swar'. By golly! he jes' take de roof off de house.

Polly. Oh, how stupid you are!

Clar. Wall, I speck I am, Miss Polly. Yer see dat's jest what Massa Downley hired me for. It saves a heap ob trouble, answering questions.

Downley. (*Outside*, C.) No, sir: I want the room all to myself.

Clar. By golly, dar's Massa Downley now.

Enter JOHN DOWNLEY, C.

Downley. "Thirty minutes for refreshments." That's exceedingly pleasant intelligence. I haven't eaten a morsel since breakfast, and my stomach clamors for supplies. Here, Clarence!

Clar. Yaas, Massa Downley.

Downley. Look after the baggage I left in the car.

Clar. Yaas, Massa Downley: I'll fotch him quick. (*Exit*, C.)

Downley. Now then, Sarah.

Polly. Polly, if you please, Mr. Downley.

Downley. Polly? Why, so it is. Well, then, Polly, roast beef, fried potatoes, squash, cucumbers, buckwheat cakes, coffee. Beef rare, potatoes crisp, squash mealy, cucumbers cool, buckwheats well-done, coffee genuine.

Polly. Yes, sir. For how many, sir?

Downley. How many? Polly, how long have you tendered to hungry travellers the solids and liquids intended to answer the calls of appetite?

Polly. About four years.

Downley. And during that long period have you failed to distinguish that happy being, the bachelor, who always dines alone. Polly, I blush for you.

Polly. Yes, I know, Mr. Downley; but I thought perhaps you might have changed your state since you were last here. Men are subject to change. They will marry.

Downley. That is a weakness of human nature of which I shall never be guilty, Polly, — never. I've seen quite enough of it. There were no less than five newly-yoked couples in the cars with me, all going straight to misery.

Polly. Oh, no, sir! they were going to the jubilee at York.

Downley. It's very strange how people can throw their happiness away in this manner. I can't understand it.

Polly. Oh, sir! that's because you have never felt the flutter of a first love. You have never sought among the sex for somebody who would hang upon the words that fell from your lips, — who would listen for your footsteps, — whose heart would beat for you, and you alone —

Downley. I declare, Polly, you are getting sentimental.

Polly. Oh, sir! believe me, there is somebody waiting for you. It may be in an humble position that she is waiting; but she surely is.

Downley. Well, let her wait. In the mean while, my dinner, Polly.

THIRTY MINUTES FOR REFRESHMENTS.

Polly. Good gracious! I forgot all about it. You see, sir, your society is so attractive. (*Exit* R., *singing.*)

"Oh, there's nothing half so sweet in life!" &c.

Downley. "Love's young dream!" That young woman's like all the rest. No sooner do they set their eyes upon a bachelor, than all manner of traps are laid to secure him. Winks, nods, smiles, sighs, sentiment, and nonsense are all employed. But not for Downley. Oh, no! I'm too old a fox to be caught by any of them. Single-blessedness is the apex of human happiness; and I'm not going to descend from my high sphere, to run the risk of being made miserable by a feminine attachment. Now, then, I'll have a wash, and, with clean hands, sit down and enjoy a comfortable repast, while the crowd are pushing and snapping at the counters outside. Luckily I thought to telegraph from the last station for this room; for now I can enjoy a comfortable repast, without fear of interruption. (*Exit*, R.)

Enter POLLY, C., *followed by* MRS. FOXTON.

Polly. This is the room, ma'am; but are you sure there's no mistake?

Mrs. F. Quite sure. Oh, it's all right! I had written instructions to meet a gentleman here in this room.

Polly. (*Aside.*) Well, I never! Oh, these men, these men! Well, ma'am, if you're sure it's all right, — but the room was engaged by a gentleman —

Mrs. F. I understand it all. You need not wait. The gentleman engaged the room, knowing I was to meet him here.

Polly. (*Aside.*) I always thought that Mr. Downley was a sly chap; and now I've found him out. (*Aloud.*) Well, ma'am, you'll find combs and brushes in the next room, if you want to fix up any. (*Exit*, R.)

Mrs. F. Dear John, how I long to meet him! Married only yesterday, and to-day separated; but he couldn't help it, poor fellow. There was but one seat in the car; and, leaving me there, he took refuge in that horrid smoking-car. But he managed to send me a note, telling me to go to room D, immediately on the arrival of the train at Highland Station. How thoughtful of him to secure a private room! I'll brush my hair, or he'll think I'm a horrid fright. The girl said I'd find a brush in that room. Dear John, how anxious I am to see you! (*Exit*, L.)

Enter CLARENCE, C., *with a tray, containing the dinner ordered by* DOWNLEY, *which he arranges upon the table.*

Clar. Wal, I nebber did see, in de 'hole course ob my life, such a permiscuous crowd. By golly! de sandwiches is clean gone, de pies totally vamoused, and de doughnuts, dey ain't nowhere.

Enter DOWNLEY, R.

Downley. Now, then, for dinner.

Clar. Here you is, Massa Downley: ebery ting all ready.

Downley. That's good. I like promptness.

Clar. Does yer? Well, dey ain't got none left. It's all clear gone.

Downley. Now, then, you look out for yourself, outside, at the counters. Make a good, hearty meal, and be lively.

Clar. (*Aside.*) Outside! Yes. Well, I guess dar's a poor show for me. (*Exit*, C.)

Downley. Confound these excursion trains! One is obliged to be so crowded and hustled. I'll be bound they'll not get half enough to eat. (*Sits at table*, C.) This looks inviting. This is one of the comforts only known to a bachelor, — quiet and plenty. (*About to eat.*)

Enter FOXTON, C.

Foxton. So, sir: I've found you, have I?

Downley. It appears that you have. And, now that you have, your business at once.

Foxton. Business! Do you know me, sir?

Downley. (*Gets up and comes down stage.*) Never set eyes upon you before. Who are you?

Foxton. A wronged man.

Downley. Ah, indeed! Well, you're in the wrong place.

Foxton. My name, sir, is Foxton, — John Foxton.

Downley. Well, sir, proceed. My dinner is getting cold.

Foxton. And can you think of dinner at such a time?

Downley. I can, particularly at this time, for I'm very hungry. Look here, Foxton: if you've got any business with me, let's have it at once.

Foxton. Yesterday I took a wife.

Downley. Did you? Well, whose wife did you take?

Foxton. Sir, you are insolent.

Downley. Look here, Foxy, you may be a man of

abstinence: I am not. I want my dinner. Speak or leave!

Foxton. Yesterday I was married to one whom I fully thought the purest and sweetest of her sex.

Downley. And to-day you found out your mistake. Foxton, you have my sympathy. Good-day.

Foxton. Not so fast. You must hear me. I'm very miserable.

Downley. And I'm very hungry.

Foxton. I started with my wife on the train this morning, to enjoy a season of harmony at the jubilee.

Downley. Harmony! You should have started without marrying.

Foxton. The cars were crowded. I could find but one seat. In that seat I placed my adored Angelina, and took my place in the smoking-car. Upon nearing this station, I despatched a note to my wife, telling her to go to room D upon the arrival of the train.

Downley. Well, go on. This but increases my appetite.

Foxton. Upon the arrival of the train, I immediately started to secure this room: it was already engaged.

Downley. Exactly: to me.

Foxton. I immediately returned to the cars to find my wife. Alas, she was gone! but, in the seat which she had vacated, I found this note, dropped by her. Behold the proof of your villany!

Downley. Villany! Look here, Foxton: I can stand being robbed of my dinner; but he who steals my good name —

Foxton. Oblige me by reading that note. (*Hands note.*)

Downley. Oh, certainly! Any thing to oblige; although I must say, Foxy, your manner is any thing but pleasing. (*Reads.*) "On the arrival of the train at Highland Station, go at once to room D. I will be there." Well, what of it?

Foxton. What of it? Can you calmly look me in the face, after reading that note, and say, "What of it?"

Downley. Certainly; and, if it would oblige you, I'll read it again, though I'd rather not. I want my dinner.

Foxton. Sir, I'm getting hot.

Downley. Well, my dinner's getting cold; and that's of more consequence to me. Now, sir, what do you want of me?

Foxton. I want my wife.

Downley. Well, poor fellow, I suppose you do. We're always wanting that which can do us no good. I'm very sorry I can give you no information which might lead to her discovery.

Foxton. This won't do, sir. 'Tis evident to me that you have been tampering with the affections of my wife, that it was you who wrote that note; for I find 'twas you who engaged this room, and here I find you about to sit down to a table evidently prepared for two.

Downley. Look here, Foxy! I'm a man of calm temper. I do detest those who get into a passion: so I tell you, calmly and deliberately, Foxy, you're a goose, — a lunatic, — a booby! Confound it! I never saw your wife, don't want your wife, and know nothing about her.

Foxton. It won't do. This is a calm, deliberate plot to rob me of my wife. Sir, you must first give me my wife, and then make reparation for these insults. You shall be made to pay for this.

Downley. Pay! A case of black-mail. I see it, Foxy. (*Rings bell on table.*) I'll settle with you at once.

Enter CLARENCE, C.

Clar. Ring, Massa Dowuley?

Downley. Yes. Clarence, how is your muscle?

Clar. Golly, massa, dar ain't none in de place. Got some 'ysters, do.

Downley. Pshaw, stupid! Do you see that individual?

Clar. Yaas, sar: I speck I does.

Downley. Remove him immediately from this apartment. No words. Quick! Foxy, it won't do.

Clar. Massa Foxy, dar's de door.

Foxton. I will not leave this apartment without my wife. You have stolen her from me; return her instantly!

Clar. Yaas, sir. Send her right along by express, C. O. D. Going, sir?

Foxton. Keep your black hands off of me!

Clar. Why, Lord bres yer, it won't come off! Dose fast colors. Dar's de door.

Foxton. Very well. Since I can receive no satisfaction from you, the engines of the law shall be set at work. Yes, sir, the engines of the law! Villain, swindler, kidnapper! (*Exit*, C.)

Clar. He's gone, massa, arter de ingine. I'll jes' keep my eye on dat ar feller. He's wanting rubbin' down, I guess. (*Exit*, C.)

Downley. Confound these excursion trains! Isn't it

enough that I have been hunted by all the mothers who have unmarried daughters, without being called upon to hunt up other men's wives? This is some swindling dodge, to get money from me; but it won't do. I'm too old a bird to be caught by such chaff. Ten minutes gone! And I was going to have such a nice, comfortable meal! The meat's cold, the potatoes turning black, and the coffee as dull as dishwater. Confound these excursion trains! (*Sits at table, as before, about to eat, when enter* MISS ARABELLA PEPPER, R.)

Miss P. John. (*Louder.*) John. (*Still louder.*) Dear John.

Downley (*dropping his food*). Now, who the deuce is that? Well, what is it?

Miss P. Did you think I wasn't coming?

Downley. Well, I must say, I hadn't any great expectations of seeing you. (*Aside.*) Oh my dinner!

Miss P. And could you think so meanly of me, after your dear note.

Downley. My dear note? Madam, I'm an unprotected bachelor, alone in this apartment. I'm a little pressed for time, and very hungry. If you'll oblige me with an explanation, I shall be grateful.

Miss P. Bachelor! Yes, indeed: I knew that the minute I set my eyes on you in the cars. Says I to myself, Arabella, there are faces which instantly attract the attention of truly tender-hearted females. Such a face is that which appears above the gray suit in the next seat. I saw your tender glances fixed upon my face. I heard your profound sighs. And says I to myself, Arabella, be brave, be bold; shrink not, for your time has come.

Downley. My tender glances? (*Aside.*) Why, the old fool's mad.

Miss P. I am so sorry to have kept you waiting, dear John. I saw at once you were struck with me, and my tender, susceptible heart responded at once. Oh, this is so romantic, so idealistic!

Downley. (*Aside.*) She calls me John. Who can she be? (*Aloud.*) Madam, will you confide to me —

Miss P. Certainly. Could you suppose for a moment that I would be reticent in the presence of one who has so trustingly, so innocently, so gushingly, so admirably, so discreetly —

Downley. Oh, I shall go mad! Madam, I don't wish to hurry you, but you will oblige me by telling me instantly the cause of this visit.

Miss P. And doesn't my John know?

Downley. Well, I can't answer for your John; but my John doesn't.

Miss P. Have you so soon forgotten your note, John?

Downley. My note?

Miss P. I received it, and immediately on the arrival of the train came here to meet you.

Downley. My note? And will you be kind enough to let me see my note?

Miss P. Certainly, John. Much as I hate to part with this dear token of your devoted love and admiration, you shall have it. Good gracious! where's my reticule? 'Twas in the reticule, and my reticule is gone. Dear me, I must have left it in the cars. I wouldn't lose it for fifty dollars. I won't be gone long, John. Dear John. (*Exit*, R.)

Downley. Is this a lunatic asylum, or an eating-house? What is the matter with that old tabby? Devoted love, — Bah! Admiration for her, — Humbug! This is some new invention of the enemy. But how in the world did she get my name. (*Looks at watch.*) Goodness gracious! how time flies! Twenty minutes gone, and my dinner untouched, when I was going to have a nice, comfortable time! I must gobble it in a hurry. Confound excursion trains! (*Sits, and about to eat.*)

Enter, R., MAJOR PEPPER (*reticule in his hand*).

Major. Fire and fury! Drop that fork! Quick! Do you hear? (*Seizes* DOWNLEY *by the arm, and leads him down*, C.).

Downley. Now what's the matter?

Major. Abduction, — treachery, — blighted affection! That's what's the matter.

Downley. Look here, old fire and fury! I'm a calm, peaceable citizen, unused to gladiatorial contests, unacquainted with feats of broil and battle: but I want my dinner; and, if you don't immediately vacate my apartment, I'll brain you, as sure as my name is John Downley!

Major. John, — John, — John! That's it. There's no mistake. So, sir, I've caught you at your tricks. Where's my sister? Where is she?

Downley. Sister? First, one man demands of me his wife, then another his sister. Is there anybody else about here who's looking for relations? Anybody lost an aunt or a grandmother?

Major. This won't do. Listen to me. I am Major Pepper, of the army. It was my misfortune to have charge of a rather elderly sister on this train. I left her in one car, and seated myself in the smoking-car. Upon the arrival of the train, I hurried off to secure this room. It was engaged. I went back to the cars to get my sister, having previously sent her a short note, telling her to meet me at this room. Sir, she was gone. But she had left her reticule behind her, and in that reticule I found this note. Read it.

Downley. Well, look here, Pepper. I've no objection to reading it; but this thing is getting monotonous. However, here goes. (*Reads.*) "Dearest, — I long to meet you alone, to tell you how fondly I love you, to press you to my loving heart. On the arrival of the train at Highland Station, hasten at once to room D. I will hurry and engage it. Ever yours, JOHN."

Major. Now, sir, what do you say to that?

Downley. What do I say? What in the world do I know about it? (*Aside.*) Good gracious! It must be the elderly female who was here a moment ago.

Major. Now, sir, where's my sister?

Downley. I haven't the least idea. She was here a moment ago.

Major. Oh, she was! Then I am correct in my suspicions. You're a nice man, you are. Travelling about the country, luring respectable females from their protectors with your notes. But you waked the wrong passenger this time. As you're so much in love with my sister, you shall marry her at once.

Downley. Marry her! Look here, Pepper —

Major. Don't Pepper me. The honor of our family imperatively demands reparation for this insult. I don't much admire your taste; but, as you're so much in love with her, why she shall be yours without delay.

Downley. But one moment, major —

Major. No words, sir. I have taken this matter into my own hands. There is a friend of mine, a clergyman, travelling with me. He will perform the ceremony. In five minutes you shall be a married man. (*Exit*, C.)

Downley. Look here, Pepper, you're too hot. It's no use. He's gone. Oh, he must be a lunatic! Marry that old maid? I'd sooner starve. Oh, gracious! My dinner! Only five minutes before the train starts! I wish husbands, wives, brothers, and sisters were at the bottom of the sea. Here I'm swindled out of a capital dinner: only a chance for a bite. Confound excursion trains! (*Sits as before; about to eat.*)

Enter MRS. FOXTON.

Mrs. F. It's about time John arrived, I should say. (*Sees* DOWNLEY. *Screams.*) A man in my room?

Downley. Hallo! What's the matter now? (*Comes down.*) I beg your pardon, madam, did you speak?

Mrs. F. Sir, leave this apartment instantly, before my John sees you.

Downley. Hallo! She's got a John too! I beg your pardon, madam. To what do I owe the pleasure of this visit?

Mrs. F. Don't speak to me. Go at once. You have no right here.

Downley. Oh, yes, I have! I engaged this room.

Mrs. F. Have I made a mistake? Is this room D?

Downley. It certainly is, and I am the rightful possessor of it at the present time.

Mrs. F. What does this mean? Who are you? Where's my John?

Downley. I am the only John here.

Mrs. F. Mercy! I have been betrayed! This is a wicked plot. If you don't leave this room at once, I'll scream for help.

Downley. But, my dear —

Mrs. F. I ain't your dear! You're a wicked wretch.

Downley. (*Aside.*) Well, here's a pleasant predicament. (*Aloud.*) Madam, I assure you this is my room.

Mrs. F. Oh, dear! What shall I do?

Enter MISS PEPPER, R.

Miss P. I can't find hide nor hair of that reticule. Dear me, what a misfortune! I don't know where that note is, John.

Mrs. F. John?

Miss P. Goodness gracious! John, what is the meaning of this? A lady here, after your note to me? Oh, John! How could you?

Mrs. F. Has this gentleman written you a note?

Miss P. Yes, indeed. A sweet epistle.

Mrs. F. Inviting you to meet him here?

Miss P. Exactly so. Room D.

Downley. It's no such thing. It's a mistake.

Mrs. F. I also received a note, telling me to come here. I thought the handwriting was very coarse. Oh, it's very evident that we are the victims of a base, designing man!

Miss P. What! You don't mean it? Didn't I receive a note from this man, full of love and tenderness?

Downley. No: you didn't!

Miss P. Oh, dear! Are all my fond hopes crushed?

Downley. Will you allow me one word?

Mrs. F. Don't let him speak.

Miss P. To think that man could so deceive!

Downley. I tell you, it's all a mistake. I'm a poor bachelor, just sitting down to my solitary repast. I have written no notes; don't know either of you; don't expect company; detest the whole female sex, and wish you were all at the bottom of the sea. Those are my sentiments, and I want my dinner.

Miss P. Abuse our sex! You deceitful man.

Mrs. F. He's a miserable swindler.

Downley. Spare your compliments, and oblige me by vacating my room.

Mrs. F. So that you can make your escape? I shall do nothing of the kind. I insist upon remaining until somebody comes to protect me.

Miss P. And so do I. I'm an unprotected female. Send for the officers of the law.

Downley. Very well: if you won't go, I shall. You are welcome to my dinner. I only hope you may have as much trouble in eating it as I have.

Mrs. F. You shall not go. (*Seizing his right arm.*) Help! Help! Police!

Miss P. (*Seizing his left arm.*) Police! Help! Help!

Downley. Ladies, this is absurd, ridiculous. (*Backs up stage, upsets table, and is seated upon the débris, as enter*, R. *and* C., MAJOR PEPPER, MR. FOXTON, *and* CLARENCE.)

Foxton. Hallo! What's the matter, Angelina?

Mrs. F. My husband!

Major. Arabella, what does this mean?

Miss P. O Elijah! such an escape!

Mrs. F. O John! the monster!

Miss P. O Elijah! the gay deceiver!

Clar. Massa Downley, has yer broke any t'ing?

Downley. Will somebody, male or female, oblige me with an explanation of this ridiculous situation?

Foxton. You scoundrel! You decoyed my wife to this apartment.

Downley. I deny it.

Major. Fire and fury! Didn't you entrap my sister?

Downley. Not a trap. I'm as innocent of guile as the babe unborn. I'm an unfortunate bachelor, and I'm awful hungry.

Foxton. Didn't you send my wife that note?

Downley. No.

Major. Isn't this note written by you?

Downley. No. Look here, Foxes and Peppers! It's my opinion that you are a lot of swindlers, male and female; but you get nothing out of me, either money or marriage.

Major. I want satisfaction.

Foxton. I want reparation.

Downley. And I want my dinner.

Clar. I beg your pardon, gents and ladies. Dere's a little mifstake here, I t'ink. Will you obligate me wid de sight of dat are note, Massa Major?

Major. Certainly. (*Gives note.*)

Clar. And you, Massa Fox?

Foxton. Certainly. (*Gives note.*)

Clar. Now, if you please, I will jes' change dem dis way, and dare you is. (*Gives each a note.*)

Foxton. Why, this is the note I sent my wife!

Clar. Dat what I fought! Dat what I fought!

Major. And this the note I sent my sister.

Clar. Jes' so, massa, jes' so. Yer see, it was all a mistake of dis yer' cullered pusson.

Downley. (*Seizing* CLARENCE *by the throat.*) You scoundrel! Then it's you who made me lose my dinner!

Clar. Don't fool, Massa Downley, don't fool. It was all dem excursioner fellows. Dey crowded de cars so, dat when I was a-going fro dat car, I tumbled over a big foot, and went, ker-sprawl, all in a heap. De notes flew one way, and I flew de odder; and, when I got picked up, we was all mixed togedder. So I did de best I could, and gib de ladies one apiece.

Downley. You stupid blunderhead! I'll fix you for this.

Clar. Don't trouble yourse'f, Massa Downley. I'se all right now.

Major. Well, I'm entirely satisfied.

Foxton. I'm sure I want no better satisfaction.

Mrs. F. Dear me, John, we owe the gentleman an apology.

Miss P. Well, I never! He ought not to be a bachelor.

Downley. Well, I am glad you are satisfied. But I am not. I came here for a nice, quiet meal; instead of which, I have had the most uncomfortable half-hour it has ever been my lot to experience.

(*Voice outside.*) All aboard! All aboard!

Downley. There's the cars, ready to start.

Enter POLLY, R.

Polly. A note for you, Mr. Downley.

Downley. I don't want it. I won't touch it! I've been in deadly peril from notes in the hands of females, and I'll take no more. Polly, order me a fresh dinner. I'll wait until the next train. The room once cleared, it may be possible to obtain a quiet meal. Here's a half-hour lost, spent in this absurd, ridiculous, mixed-up affair, — unless (*to the audience*) you have received some satisfaction from "Thirty Minutes for Refreshment."

SITUATIONS.

R., MR. AND MRS. F., POLLY, DOWNLEY, CLAR., MAJOR, MISS P., L.

"A LITTLE MORE CIDER."

A FARCE.

CHARACTERS

ERASTUS APPLEJACK, the cider-maker.
ZEB APPLEJACK, his son.
DEACON PEACHBLOSSOM.
ISAAC PEACHBLOSSOM, his son.
HANS DRINKER.
MISS PATIENCE APPLEJACK.
POLLY APPLEJACK.
HETTY MASON.

COSTUMES.

ERASTUS and ZEB, old-fashioned Yankee suits.

DEACON, dark modern suit.

ISAAC, genteel modern suit.

HANS DRINKER, rusty-gray suit.

MISS PATIENCE, dark-brown dress, cap, and spectacles.

POLLY, red dress, short sleeves, low-necked; long calico apron; hair drawn back, and twisted into a pug; long ear-rings.

HETTY MASON, calico dress, long apron.

SCENE. — *Room in* FARMER APPLEJACK'S *house. Sofa* C., *back. Small table* L., *at which sits* MISS PATIENCE, *knitting.* POLLY *and* ZEB *seated* R., *he holding, she winding, a skein of yarn.*

Zeb. Gosh all hemlock! Polly, what air yeou a thinkin' on? Thinkin' 'bout some feller, I bet.

Polly. Wa'n't doin' nothin' of the sort. I was thinkin' 'bout my new Sunday bunnet.

Zeb. Well, fashion or fellers, they're all alike. When a gal gits thinkin' 'bout either on 'em, she ain't good for nothin'.

Polly. Precious little you know 'bout either on 'em. I heerd Sally Higgins say that your go-to-meetin' coat looked as though it had been made in the Revolution.

Zeb. Darn Sally Higgins! What does she know 'bout war, any how? Say, Polly, what was Ike Peachblossom sayin' to yeou on the doorsteps last night?

Polly. None'er your business, Zeb Applejack. What were *you* doin' so near Hetty Mason's cheek, deown by the pump, last night?

Zeb. Neow quit, Polly: 'twa'n't nothin'. Ye see, I was a-goin' deown tew the barn, and Hetty, she was a-cumin' up tew the house, and along there by the pump a darned big bumble-bee lit on her, and I was just brushin' it off. That's all.

Polly. That's a likely story. Yeou know pa has forbidden yeou to show any attention to Hetty Mason.

Zeb. Yes; and he's forbidden yeou takin' any from Ike Peachblossom. I guess we're in the same boat.

Polly. Well, yeou stand by me, and I'll stand by yeou.

Miss Patience. Massy sakes! What air yeou young ones quarrelling about?

Polly. Law, Aunt Patience, 'tain't nothin'. Zeb got stung by a bumble-bee last night, and was tellin' about it.

Zeb. That's all, Aunt Patience; but 'twas a bouncer.

Polly. And loaded with honey, wa'n't it, Zeb?

Zeb. Darn it, Polly, don't aggravate a feller.

Miss P. Bumble-bees! Oh, they're deceitful, artful creeters! When Deacon Peachblossom came a-courtin' on me, — afore he married Abigail Spooner, — one arternoon, when we were settin' on the doorsteps, one of them critters lit right on to the end of his nose, — jest as he was a sayin' the sweetest things, tew.

Zeb. Of course. That's what brought him there.

Miss P. I never shall forget how that poor feller did holler. He jest gave one jump, and then went tearin' thro' the village, a-holdin' on to his nose like a madman. It spilt his beauty for a while, I tell yeou; and spilt a match, tew, for he turned right round and went kitin' arter Abigail Spooner from that very day.

Zeb. He's a darned humbug, any how. His nose looks as though the bumble-bees had been a-foul of it lately. He drinks.

Miss P. Why, Zebulon, how can yeou talk so? Isn't he one of the pillers of the temperance movement.

Zeb. He's a darned old humbug. He's talked dad, here, into leavin' eout cider, when dad went down to Gineral Court to legislate last winter.

Miss P. It's a blessed thing that they succeeded in getting it excepted, for what would we have done for our mince-pies.

Polly. I wish cider had never been heard of. Here pa and Isaac Peachblossom must get to quarrelling about it; and the consequence is, that Isaac has been told that his company was not required. I declare, it's real mean! I hate cider!

Miss P. Law, Polly, how can yeou talk so? Why, your father, my Brother Erastus, is making lots er money on it. Well, no wonder, for folks do say that Erastus Applejack's cider beats the world. He's makin' money.

Zeb. Yes; and gitting stuck up, tew. Look at Hetty Mason. There's a gal I set my heart on, and it was all right until this darned cider-bill was passed; and then dad, he up and says I can't marry her, because she's poor.

Miss P. Well, Zebulon, yeou must be patient. Your father knows what's best for yeou.

Zeb. Does he? Well, I know what's best for me, tew; and that's Hetty Mason. And I'm a-goin' to have her, in spite of all the dads in creation.

Enter APPLEJACK, L.

Applejack. Oh, yeou air! air yeou? Well, I rather think I shell have somethin' tew say 'bout that. Zeb Applejack, look me in the eye. Ain't I been a father tew yeou?

Zeb. Well, s'posin' yer hev: 'twa'n't my fault, was it?

Applejack. Haven't I provided yer a liberal edication?

Zeb. Supposin' yer hev: yer took it eout in boardin' the schoolmaster.

Applejack. And neow yeou want ter go and spile all my projects, by marrying Hetty Mason.

Zeb. Well, dad, where'll yer find a smarter gal, or a prettier gal, than Hetty?

Applejack. Waal, Hetty's all very well in her place; but sence I've found eout the way to make the best cider in teown,—and cider's to be the daily and standard drink ov the community, sence the legislatur' has knocked rumselling,—I've made up my mind there's a fortin a-comin' to E. Applejack, and the aforesaid E. Applejack will probably and eventually be the biggest man in teown; and it's high time we held up our heads a bit. Hetty's a poor girl. If yeou must marry, look higher. There's Lawyer Lawson's daughters, five likely gals. Why don't yeou take one of them?

Zeb. I tell yer, dad, it's no use talkin'. Hetty Mason is the gal of my choice. I don't care a darn for yeour high notions. I'm goin' to marry the gal I like, and there she is.

Enter HETTY MASON, L.

Applejack. Yer ain't a goin' ter do nothin' uv ther sort. Hetty Mason, yeou jest pack up yeour band-box, and start eout uv this house at once.

Zeb. Do, Hetty; and I'll pack up a clean shirt, and go right along with yer.

Applejack. Yeou won't do nothin' ov the sort.

Zeb. Yaas, I will. Yeou turn her eout, and yeou turn me eout.

Applejack. Hetty Mason, yeou needn't pack yer band-box jest yet.

Hetty. Well, I declare! I'm getting tired of this. It's the same thing every day. "Pack your band-box, and don't pack your band-box." If you two, father and son, would come to some conclusion regarding my future welfare, it would spare my wardrobe a great deal of tumbling.

Polly. Don't mind them, Hetty. It will come out all right.

Hetty. Well, I hope it will, for I'm getting tired of it.

Applejack. We'll talk this over some other time, when you're cooler. But mind, Zebulon, no sparking round my house. I won't have it.

Enter HANS DRINKER, R.

Hans. Goot tay, mine Friend Applejack: it is varmer dan never vash, and I ish very try. I vould like some trinks.

Applejack. Oh, some of my cider! Hey, Hans?

Hans. Yaw, dat ish goot cider. I have never trinks such goot cider since ven I cooms from Faderland, and dat vash lager bier.

Applejack. Hetty, bring a glass of cider.

Hans. In a mug. Do you hear, my chile? I vill have mine glass of cider in a mug. It ish so mooch better, (*aside*) and so mooch larger. (*Exit* HETTY, L.)

Miss P. Well, Mr. Drinker, what is the news?

Hans. Vell, not mooch. Old Johnson fell into the vater last night, ven he be very trunk. They have not find him. But that ish no matter, 'cause he be not ov mooch use now. Miss Murray, she proke her leg the day pefore to-night. Meester Jones, he failed week pefore next. Meester Smith have a new litter of pigs, and Meester Harris have a new papy at his house. But I ton't think of any news, I pelieve.

Enter HETTY, L., *with mug of cider.*

Applejack (*takes cider, and passes it to* HANS). There, Friend Hans, there is a mug of the best cider ever made.

Hans. Dat ish so. (*Tastes.*) Ah, dat ish goot cider

ash never vash. Vell, I trinks your good health, Meester Applejack. I trinks your goot health, Miss Patience. I trink your goot health, Miss Polly. Py jinks, I trinks all your goot healths. (*Drinks.*) Ah, dat ish goot. Meester Applejack, I shall recommend your cider.

Applejack. Thank yeou, Hans; and, whenever yeou are going by, don't fail to drop in and have a mug of it. Yeou are always welcome.

Hans. Dat ish goot. I shall rememper and call again. By dunder, dat is goot cider. (*Exit*, R.)

Applejack. An honest old fellow, Hans Drinker.

Zeb. Honest. P'r'aps he is; but, if he don't skin yeou out of a barrel of cider afore he gets through, my name's not Zeb Applejack.

Applejack. I'll risk it. But come, Patience, how's this? It's seven o'clock. Deacon Peachblossom speaks on temperance at the vestry at half-past.

Miss P. Massy sakes! So he does! (*Jumps up, rolls up her knitting.*) I declare, I wouldn't miss hearing the deacon for a good deal. I'll be ready in a minute. (*Exit*, L.)

Applejack. Come, Polly, you'd better be getting ready.

Polly. I ain't a-going.

Applejack. Oh, yes, yeou are! S'pose yeou want to stay at home, in hopes that Isaac Peachblossom will happen about here when I'm away. Come, get ready. Yeou, tew, Zeb.

Zeb. Me! I ain't a-goin'.

Applejack. Who's the head ov this here family, I'd like to know? I tell yeou you're both a-going. Now let's have no ifs, ands, or buts about it.

Enter ISAAC PEACHBLOSSOM, R.

Isaac. How are you, Mr. Applejack? How are you Zeb? Ah, Polly, I kiss my hands to you.

Applejack. Well, don't trouble yerself, Isaac Peachblossom. When she wants any kissing done, she won't come to you.

Polly. (*Aside.*) That's a whopper.

Isaac. Well, don't mind me. I dropped in on a little business. You know the legislature last year passed a bill exempting cider from the prohibition law. Of course you do, for we've had many an argument about it, — you contending for cider as a harmless and necessary beverage, I contending that it was an intoxicating drink. My father took sides with you and you triumphed in the legislature, punishing me for my opposition by breaking off the contemplated marriage of your daughter and myself.

Applejack. Well, what in thunder is all this coming to?

Isaac. Listen. In this town, no sooner was it made legal than there appeared to be a determination on the part of everybody to take to drinking cider.

Applejack. Of course. A harmless and necessary beverage.

Isaac. (*Producing letter.*) Well, I don't believe that, you know. But, however, I couldn't understand it. But the matter's all out. A friend of mine, residing in Boston, writes me (*reads*), "I must put you up to a new dodge of your country prohibitionists. Now cider is exempted, we have an unusually large call for empty whiskey-barrels. The parties who make cider buy them to put their cider in, as whiskey gives a particular flavor to the cider. This is bad enough for those who profess to be so temperate; but one old fellow, who lives not a great way from your town, buys regularly six barrels a week, with particular directions to have one-third of the whiskey usually contained in the barrel left in. Pretty sharp practice, hey!"

Zeb. I should think so. Why, it's a downright swindle.

Polly. What rascality!

Applejack. That man — that man — that man — ought to be cut off from respectable society.

Isaac. Of course he had. And I'm determined to find him out and punish him.

Applejack. Well, I hope you will. Where on earth is Patience? We shall be late for lecture. (*Goes* R., *and calls.*) Patience, Patience. (*Exit* R.)

Zeb. (*Crosses to* HETTY, R.) I s'pose I've got to go, Hetty; but I'll be back here in fifteen minutes.

Polly. (*Crosses to* ISAAC, L.) I've got to go to that plaguy lecture; but, just as soon as I've got there, I'm going to sneak out and come right here.

Isaac. A word to the wise is sufficient, Polly. Good-day, Zeb. (*Exit* L.)

Zeb. Good-day, Ike.

Patience. (*Outside.*) Erastus, don't swear so. You're the awfullest man that ever I did see. I can't help it, if I do lose my specs.

Applejack. Well, come along, and hold yeour tongue. (*Enter* APPLEJACK *and* MISS PATIENCE, L., *shawled and bonneted.*) Now, then, Polly, git yeour things; and yeou, Zeb, git yeour hat. It's time we were off. (*Exit* ZEB, L., POLLY, R.)

Patience. So, Deacon Peachblossom's a-goin' to give his idees on temperance. Well, I like the deacon.

Applejack. That's what folks says, Sister Patience. They all think yeou'd be mighty glad to step into the late Mrs. Peachblossom's shoes.

Patience. La, do they? Well, they might say worse things; for, if I do say it as hadn't orter, if there is a livin' woman on the face of this earth, in face, figger, and ability, capable of takin' the place of Abigail Spooner, I'm that woman.

Applejack. Waal, I hope yeou won't be disappinted. But yeou ain't so young as yeou was thirty years ago.

Patience. Erastus!

Applejack. Yer not a tempting morsel to a widower; for they do say they're awful perticular peeple, and gray hair —

Patience. Erastus!

Applejack. Well, I won't let the cat out of the bag, Patience.

Enter ZEB, L., *and* POLLY, R.

Applejack. Neow, then, let's be off to lecture. Here, Zeb, yeou take yer Aunt Patience, and I'll look arter Polly. (ZEB *gives* PATIENCE *his arm*, APPLEJACK *gives his to* POLLY.) Neow, then, forward — march.

Enter HANS DRINKER, L.

Hans. By donder, dat ish de best cider ash never vas.

Applejack. Hallo, Hans, back again?

Hans. Yaw, Meester Applejack. I leave von leetle pit of de cider in de mug; but I coomed pack for it.

Applejack. Ah! Yeou want another mug, yeou rascal. Here, Hetty (*enter* HETTY, L.)! Bring Hans a mug of cider. Make yerself at home, Hans. We must be off to lecture. (*Exit* APPLEJACK *and* POLLY, PATIENCE *and* ZEB, R.)

Hans. Vell, never you mind me. I pe all right. Now, mine chile, you hear vhat de ole man say. I'll take mine mug of cider.

Hetty. Why, you've just drank nearly a quart!

Hans. A quart! No, mine chile, you are meestaken. I have not trink a quart.

Hetty. I'm sure of it.

Hans. By donder, it cannot been. Mine chile, bring me de quart, till I see for mineself. (*Exit* HETTY, L.) By donder, dat ish goot cider. I vish I vas de man vat make dat cider. I vould never get up some more, but vould lay in mine bed all de time, and trink cider.

Enter HETTY, L., *with mug.*

Hetty. There, Mr. Drinker, is the same mug. 'Tis full now, and it holds a quart.

Hans. Ish dat de mug? By donder, I did not think it would held so mooch. A quart. But I did not trink it all. I could not trink it all. I vill show you I could not trink it all. (*Drinks, and turns over mug.*)

Hetty. There, you see it is all gone.

Hans. Mine chile, it has gone. I never did see any ting go so quick in my life.

Hetty. Nor I, either. I should think you had enough to last you a week.

Hans. You do! Vell, so do I; but I have not. By donder, dat is goot cider, mine chile. (*Exit*, R.)

Hetty. Well, I'm glad he's gone. I guess Mr. Applejack will repent of his invitation, for he'll be sure to pester us with his attentions as long as there is any cider about. I'll light a candle, and sit down and wait for Zeb.

Enter ZEB, L.

Zeb. Well, I managed to git Aunt Patience off my hands, without going into the vestry. Who should come along, when we were half-way, but Deacon Peachblossom. The minit Aunt Patience saw him, she began to fidgit. So I managed to get him up on the other side of her, and then I scooted.

Hetty. Very well; and now, Mr. Zeb Applejack, that we are alone once more, will you oblige me with a plain statement of your intentions.

Zeb. (*Sits on sofa with* HETTY.) My intention is to marry you one of these days.

Hetty. Is it? One of these days won't do.

Zeb. Why, Hetty! Don't you know I love you,—that you're the apple of my eye,—that I shall die without you,—that I feel—I feel—I feel—

Hetty. There, don't go to singing that old song: it's played out. I decline entering into any engagement with you in the present unsettled state of affairs. Either your father gives his consent before this time to-morrow, or I leave the house, never to return.

Zeb. But, Hetty, don't be so quick.

Hetty. Zeb, don't be so slow. We have been waiting, waiting, waiting, until I am heartily sick of the delay. You know I love you, or you would never let me be abused — in this — wicked — manner — by — that — ugly — old — man. (*Sobs, and falls into* ZEB'S *arms.*)

Zeb. Neow, Hetty, don't cry. I'll have it settled to-morrow, if I have to lick dad till he gives his consent. I ain't afraid of him. When he comes, I'll jest give him a piece of my mind. (*Noise outside*, R.) Thunder! what's that?

Hetty. Somebody coming back.

Zeb. Oh, law! Suppose it's dad. What shall I do?

Hetty. Why, give him a piece of your mind.

Zeb. But not neow. He's comin' this way, Hetty. I'm sorry to lose your company, but I'm going under the sofa. (*Crawls under sofa, head to* R.)

Hetty. Well, I'm not going to stay here and be found out. (*Exit*, L.)

Zeb. I wonder who on airth that is, anyhow.

Enter ISAAC *and* POLLY, R.

Isaac. Safe inside. Now, Polly, just get a light, for it's dark as pitch.

Polly. No, indeed I sha'n't! I wouldn't get a light for the world. If pa should take it into his head to come home, he'd be sure to make a fuss about it.

Isaac. All right. I'm contented. Here's the sofa. Sit down, and let's have a little quiet chat.

Polly. Of course. But won't you have a glass of cider?

Isaac. No, I thank you. You know I'm opposed to its use.

Polly. Yes, I do know it; but I forgot it at the moment.

Isaac. Polly, do you know I love you very dearly?

Polly. I hope you do, Isaac.

Isaac. And I'm going to marry you Thanksgiving night, if you'll consent to make me happy.

Polly. You know I'll consent. But father —

Isaac. Is not inclined to at present; but I'll find a way to make him, I think. You remember my reading a letter here this afternoon?

Polly. Yes, from a friend of yours in Boston.

Isaac. Telling me that somebody had been ordering whiskey-barrels, with a little whiskey left in.

Polly. Yes, I remember.

Isaac. I did not give you all the information I had, for my friend gave me the name of the party.

Polly. Who was it?

Isaac. Erastus Applejack.

Polly. My father!

Isaac. Your father, who has helped to make a law which he is now breaking by swindling of the meanest description.

Polly. Why, everybody is buying his cider.

Isaac. Scenting the whiskey concealed in it.

Polly. Oh, this is too bad! What will you do?

Isaac. Prove his swindling, and then give him the choice, to relinquish its sale, or public exposure, with a slight condition added.

Polly. Which I can guess. (*Noise outside.*) Who is that? Oh, dear! it must be father returned. What shall we do?

Isaac. I don't want to see him just yet. I'd better go by the back way.

Polly. Well, come quick: this way. (*Exeunt*, L.)

Zeb. What a darned scamp dad is, anyway! I guess I'll git cout, and crawl up stairs. No: there's somebody coming.

Enter HANS DRINKER, R.

Hans. By donder! I never did see such cider. Vhere ish everypody. In der peds, I s'phose. Vell, I vill not trouble dem at all, but vill go to de cellar and gits mine mugs of cider. (*Goes*, L.) By donder, de door ish locked, and ter key stolen mit somepody. (*Noise outside*, R.) Hark! I hear some peeples coom dis way. By donder! vhat vill I do mit myself? Dey vill tink me somepody else, coomed for der money. I vill hide for mineself, till dey pe gone some more. (*Crawls under sofa, head* L.) By donder! dere ish somepody here pefore me.

Zeb. What in thunder do you want here?

Hans. Vhat you vant mit yourself, mine frien'.

Zeb. Clear out, or I'll break every bone in your body.

Hans. Take care mit yourself, mine frien', take care mit yourself.

Zeb. Keep yeour boots out of my mouth.

Hans. By donder! mine frien', you preak your toe mit mine nose.

Zeb. Keep still. There's somebody coming.

Hans. By donder! I yust lose mine cider.

Enter PATIENCE, *followed by* DEACON PEACHBLOSSOM.

Patience. Sh —

Zeb. Sh —

Hans. Sh —

Patience. Don't speak so loud.

Deacon. My friend, I didn't speak at all.

Patience. Then it must have been the echo. Come in quietly.

Deacon. This is very mysterious.

Patience. My brother objects to a light after certain hours, so we are compelled to be very cautious in our movements. You'll find a seat here on the sofa. (DEACON *sits.*) I'm so much obleeged to yeou, deacon, for seein' on me home. Yeour polite attentions are very agreeable. Sha'n't I git yeou something, deacon?

Deacon. Well, now you mention it, a little cider would be very acceptable.

Hans. By donder, dat cider!

Zeb. Sh —! Keep yer hoofs still, Dutchy.

Patience. I'll bring yeou some directly. Excuse me a moment. (*Exit*, L.)

Deacon. Miss Patience is a pleasant body; and if she wasn't quite so old, a little handsomer, and had a little more money, I believe I should be inclined to make her Mrs. Peachblossom, number two. But then there is her brother, making money by his cider. I declare, it's really worth thinking on.

Enter PATIENCE, L., *with mug of cider; draws the table up to sofa and sits.*

Patience. There, deacon, there's a mug of the best cider yeou ever drank. I took it, myself, out of a new barrel that I never saw afore.

Deacon (*taking mug*). Thank you, Pa — Miss Patience. Here's your good health. (*Drinks.*) Splendid!

Splendid! I never tasted such cider before in all my life. (*Hands cider to* PATIENCE, *who sets it on table.*)

Patience. I thought yeou'd like it. Then yeou approve of cider-drinking.

Deacon. Certainly, Miss Patience. It is a healthy and necessary beverage. It is Nature's own brewing for the lips of thirsty travellers in this journey of life. I believe in temperance, Miss Patience; in strict adhesion to total abstinence from all that intoxicates; but cider is a beverage prepared by Nature herself, and to abstain from drinking cold water would be as consistent as to refrain from drinking cider. Both furnished by Nature, both harmless. Miss Patience, a little more cider. (*She passes mug.*)

Hans. By donder! my t'roat ish dry ash never vas.

Zeb. I wish I was eout of this. The Dutchman is crowding me to death.

Deacon. Splendid! Splendid! Never tasted such cider.

Hans. By donder, dat ish true!

Patience. Deacon, don't you find it lonesome at yeour house?

Deacon. Yes, indeed. Now that my beloved Abigail has gone, I do feel lonesome.

Patience. I should think yeou would. I should think that a man of yeour loving disposition would be anxious to fill the place she vacated with some congenial soul —

Deacon. I do, I do. I have cast my eyes about me, and almost decided to take —

Patience. Well, Deacon, disclose yeour feelings —

Deacon. A little more cider, Miss Patience. (*She passes cider.*)

Hans. By donder, dere won't be no cider in de house!

Deacon. Splendid! Splendid! Sp — len — did! That loosens my tongue. Yes, Miss Patience, — dear Miss Patience, — dear Patience, — I do long to clasp to my arms — a little more cider. (*She passes cider.*) Thank you. Here's your jolly good health. (*Drinks.*) Splendid! Splendid! Splendid! That's the nectar (hic) that Jupiter sips (hic). That's glor'us stuff. Yes, dear Miss Cider, — I mean, Miss Patience, — I'm a lonesome man. I'm a dreffal lonesome man. I want somebody at my side (hic) to bathe my throbbing brow (hic), to give me — to give me — a little more cider. (*She gives mug.*) Thank you. Here's your jolly good health. (*Drinks.*) Splendid! Splendid! Splendid!

Patience. (*Aside.*) How strangely he acts! but I believe he is on the brink of a proposal.

Deacon. Yes, I want to take somebody to my heart. Yes, Patience, — dear Patience, — dearest Patience! I want to take you to my heart (hic), this bursting heart — come to these longing arms, and give me — a little more cider.

Patience. Do you ask me to be your wife, Deacon?

Deacon. Splendid! Splendid! Splendid cider! Of course I do! Be my cider, — no, my wife! I love you! I adore you! (hic) I worship you! I want you, and — a little more cider.

Patience. (*Jumping up.*) Good gracious! Deacon! (*Pulls him up.*) Listen! There's a man under the sofa. My foot touched him. We shall be murdered! What shall I do?

Deacon. Come to these arms (hic). Who cares for the man (hic)? let 'em come on (hic)! these arms shall protect you. This manly bosom shall protect you (hic); a little more cider shall protect you (hic).

Patience. (*Screams and throws herself into* DEACON'S *arms.*) A man! A man! Help! Help! Help!

(POLLY, ISAAC, *and* HETTY *appear at door*, R., *with light;* APPLEJACK, L.)

Applejack. Well, well, what's the matter here? Goodness gracious! Sister Patience in a man's arms, and that man Deacon Peachblossom!

Deacon. Tha's wha's the marrer, Flapplejack. She flew to these protecting arms, Flapplejack; and these protecting arms, Flapplejack, clasped her in a warm embrace, Flapplejack; and that's wha's the marrer.

Applejack. Why, Deacon, what brought you to this condition?

Deacon. A little more cider, Flapplejack.

Patience. O Brother Erastus! there's a man under the sofa!

Applejack. Man under the sofa? We'll have him eout, then, quick!

(*Seizes* HANS'S *leg, and pulls him out.* HANS *at the same time seizes* ZEB'S *leg, and they are brought out together.* HANS *sits on floor*, R. ZEB, L.)

Applejack (*between*). Zeb, what on airth are yeou under the sofa for?

Zeb. Well, I don't know; but I s'pect it's the same reason that set the deacon *on* it.

Applejack. What's that?

Zeb. A little more cider.

Applejack. Hans Drinker, what sent you there?

Hans. By donder! Meester Applejack, I never see such wedder pefore for der next five years! I vas so dry ash never vash all de time, and so I coomed here for vat you axed me.

Applejack. What was that?

Hans. A leetle more cider.

Applejack. Will somebody please to explain this?

Deacon. Ov course, Flapplejack. I's all right. I'm goin' to make Miss Patience Mrs. Peachblossom (hic), sure's you live!

Applejack. I'm glad of that.

Isaac. And I'm going to make your daughter Mrs. Peachblossom, Mr. Applejack.

Applejack. No, you're not. I'll never give my consent.

Isaac. I think you will, especially as I've got the name of the party who buys *empty* whiskey-barrels, one-third full.

Applejack. You have, — well, you're a pretty good feller. Take her and make her happy.

Zeb. I'm going to make Miss Hetty Mason Mrs. Applejack to-morrow.

Applejack. No, you're not. I forbid the banns.

Zeb. Too late, dad. I'm posted on all the tricks of the cider-trade; and, if you interfere with my arrangements, I'll expose it all.

Applejack. Well, well, get married to-night if you choose. I don't care. I'm tired of you. I want a change.

Deacon. Then let's have some more cider.

Isaac. Mr. Applejack, there are two interests very dear to my heart: one is the temperance cause, the other is your daughter Polly. Duty to the one demands that I should expose the deceit you have practised on our community. Love for the other equally demands that I should conceal it. I can compromise with duty only through your instrumentality. Promise me to give up the sale of cider entirely, and I am silent. Refuse, and not even my love for Polly shall prevent my exposing the whole transaction.

Applejack. Why, Isaac, there's money in it.

Isaac. Not honest money, Mr. Applejack. You see what a fool one mug of it has made of my father.

Applejack. Well, I know; but Patience must have got at the wrong barrel, and given him the full strength of whiskey.

Isaac. What do you say? Is it a bargain?

Applejack. Well, yes: there is no other course; so I'll e'en make a merit of necessity.

Isaac. You'll never repent of it. The Devil prowls around the earth in many disguises. Don't you help to cover him up, Mr. Applejack.

Deacon. Well, say (hic): a little less talk, and a little more cider, — that's my idea.

Isaac. Not to-night, father. Applejack has shut up shop for the night.

Applejack. Yes, for the night. Call round to-morrow, friends, and you shall see me dispose of it.

Zeb. Well, Hetty, we're going to get married, after all.

Hetty. Yes, Zeb; but I'm not going to have any of that cider round my house.

Deacon. Patience, when shall the wedding come off?

Patience. Law, Deacon, don't ask me afore all these folks.

Isaac. I'll tell you, father. Thanksgiving Day, when Polly and I are made one. Hey, Polly?

Polly. I'm willing, if father is.

Applejack. Well, as you seem to have settled it among yourselves, I don't think my consent is needed.

Hans. By donder, Meester Applejack! dere's one ting you forgot.

Applejack. No, I haven't. It's what you want, but cannot have. No more cider here, Hans. We are going to banish it. I can only hope that our kind friends will go home satisfied that the article least needed here was, — what was it, Deacon?

Deacon. "A little more cider."

Hans. Petter ash never vash, py donder!

DISPOSITION OF CHARACTERS.

L. ZEB AND HETTY, POLLY AND ISAAC, R.

DEACON AND PATIENCE, APPLEJACK, HANS,

NEW BROOMS SWEEP CLEAN.

CHARACTERS.

NOAH TESTY, rich and crusty.
FRED, his nephew.
JACOB TRUSTY, his servant.
TIM REGAN, } new brooms.
ANDREW SWIPES, } new brooms.
JING JIMALONG, } new brooms.

COSTUMES.

TESTY, light pants, white vest, dressing-gown, black wig, black side-whiskers, wrinkled face.

FRED, modern suit.

JACOB, dark suit, gray wig.

TIM, overalls tucked into heavy boots, blue striped shirt, blue coat with brass buttons, red cropped wig, hat.

SWIPES, gray coat, gray vest, gray knee-breeches, top boots, long, white neckerchief, black hat, gilt band, light cropped wig, light side-whiskers.

JING (as a Chinaman), blue blouse, loose yellow pants fastened at the ankles, white stockings, heavy brogans, flesh colored skull-cap (can be made of unbleached cotton like a night-cap, made to fit close to the head: color with flesh ball, cut holes on each side for the ears to appear, and it will be tight), a long black cue, very red face, black about the chin and over the lip to have the appearance of being unshaven.

SCENE. — TESTY'S *Study. Writing-table*, C. *Small book-case with books*, R.C. *Mantel, with plaster bust, vases, and ornaments*, C. *Chair at table. Stool*, R.C. *Chairs*, R. *and* L. *Writing materials, paper, &c., on table.*

Enter FRED, R., *followed by* JACOB.

Fred. You really surprise me, Jacob. After twenty years' service, my uncle turns you adrift in your old age. It's impossible!

Jacob. It's true, sir, I assure you. Turned adrift, after twenty years' service, — and hard service too, — because I took the privilege of an old servant to tell him the truth.

Fred. Ah! what was the truth you told him?

Jacob. That he was making a donkey of himself. He was too old to *transmogrify* himself by putting on a black curly wig and dyeing his whiskers.

Fred. But why did you tell him so?

Jacob. Because I couldn't help it. The idea of that old gentleman trying to deceive the world at his time of life! He's as gray as a badger, and as bald as a new-born baby. Soon he'll have all the young ladies after him.

Fred. Perhaps he wants a wife.

Jacob. Then let him get one honestly. I don't believe in obtaining goods under false pretences.

Fred. Neither do I, Jacob. But he's his own master. I'm sorry for you; but I do not see how I can help you. If he wants to marry, it's none of my business.

Jacob. But, Mr. Fred, I think it is your business.

He's *gallavanting* after a widow. I know that. He's had Mr. Tubbs, the lawyer, here, drawing up a will or a settlement; and I heard him say, "Now, Master Fred, you must take care of yourself."

Fred. Still, I say it's none of my business. If he chooses to marry, let him. I have taken care of myself so far; and, though I might reasonably expect, some time, to have a share of his riches, I can do without.

Jacob. That's very true, Mr. Fred. Still, you shouldn't let your uncle fall a victim to the schemes of such an adventurer as Mrs. Shoddy.

Fred. Mrs. Shoddy! Is that the lady my uncle intends to marry?

Jacob. That's the lady he is *dyeing* for. Yes, sir; *dyeing* by inches. He's commenced with his whiskers.

Fred. She *is* a scheming adventurer; and my uncle must not make a fool of himself.

Jacob. That's what I say, sir; and that's what I made bold to tell him. He took offence, and turned me off.

Fred. But, Jacob, you must not go. I'll see my uncle; and, fortunately, here he is. Don't let him see you.

Jacob. I'll take care of that, Mr. Fred. (*Exit*, L.)

Fred. What a transformation! The old gentleman must be very far gone.

Enter TESTY, R.

Why, Uncle Noah! What a change! Have you "renewed your youth like the eagle"?

Testy. Oh, bother your nonsense! What is it to you?

Fred. Why, uncle—

Testy. Shut up! If I choose to make a change in my personal appearance, is it any of your business? I have had trouble enough with that confounded Jacob Trusty, and I don't want to be bothered by you.

Fred. I beg your pardon, uncle: I meant no offence, I assure you. I am delighted to see you looking so young again. But, uncle, Jacob tells me you have discharged him.

Testy. Yes, I have discharged him; and I have discharged Patrick, and Sally Greaser,—an impudent set, who take advantage of long service to insult me.

Fred. Patrick! you don't mean it, uncle: he's the best servant you ever had. And Sally Greaser too. Why there's not her equal in the city as a cook. Her soft-shell crabs are perfectly splendid.

Testy. Hang her, and her soft-shell crabs! she's an impudent hussy. I've turned her off, and I don't mean to have another woman in the house. I'll have a Chinese cook.

Fred. A Chinese cook! That's a novel idea; but where in the world will you find one?

Testy. That's my business. Fortunately I have friends, sir,—yes, sir, friends, who will see that I do not suffer for servants. I'll teach them better manners than to contradict me. I won't have it. I'll let them know who is master here. I'm going to commence with a new set this very day.

Fred. A new set?

Testy. Yes, a new set. I'm going to turn over a new leaf. "New brooms sweep clean." With a new set recommended to me by a lady who knows something about housekeeping.

Fred. A lady: pray, may I inquire who she is!

Testy. Mrs. Shoddy.

Fred. Mrs. Shoddy? — (*Aside.*) So the schemer is at work. — (*Aloud.*) But, uncle, are you not afraid to give a lot of new servants control of the house?

Testy. Afraid? No, sir. I shall have nobody but whom Mrs. Shoddy recommends. I have the greatest confidence in her; and, whoever she sends, I will employ.

Fred. Ah, uncle! be careful of your "new brooms." They may sweep cleaner than you will like.

Testy. Well, sir, it's none of your business, as long as I like it. You *may* be owner of this property some day, and then you can do as you like with it. While it is mine, I shall exercise the same privilege.

Fred. Certainly, uncle. I've no more to say. Good day. — (*Aside.*) It's too bad. The old gentleman will be swindled by that adventuress. I must know what is going on. Can't I manage to get a "new broom" into the house. There's the Chinese cook. I don't believe Mrs. Shoddy has one to send. At any rate I'll be beforehand. I'll send one myself. 'Twill be a capital joke. He will take any one whom Mrs. Shoddy sends. How shall I get her recommendation? I think I can manage it.

Testy. Well, sir, what are you muttering about in that corner?

Fred. I beg your pardon, uncle. I thought you had gone. I was thinking where I could find you a Chinese cook.

Testy. You needn't trouble yourself. I'll keep my eyes open for one.

Fred. (*Aside.*) And so will I. And I'll keep an eye on these new brooms of his too. (*Exit,* R.)

Testy. (*Sits at table.*) There's another impudent fellow. He'd like to say something saucy, I know; but the fear of the consequences deters him. It's no use, Master Fred: my money goes to Mrs. Testy; for Mrs. Shoddy will not consent to the change on any other conditions. Bewitching widow! I'd sacrifice life itself for her. (*Takes paper from drawer.*) The settlement is all ready. So, Master Fred, your chance for the riches of old Testy are decidedly slim. (*Takes out another paper.*) What's this? My bonds! Good gracious! I forgot to lock them up last night. That's very careless in me, to leave ten thousand dollars of Uncle Sam's indebtedness in this loose manner. (*Knock,* R.) Hallo! Who's that? (*Puts papers in drawer.*) Come in.

Enter JOHN SWIPES, R.

Swipes. Hi beg your pardon, sir. Hi 'ave ha note from Mrs. Shoddy.

Testy. Mrs. Shoddy? Let me have it. (*Reads.*) "MY DEAR MR. TESTY,"—Her *dear* Mr. Testy! Bewitching widow!—"I promised to send you some good servants. The bearer is an excellent coachman, one to be trusted, who never breaks any thing except horses. He will suit you admirably.

"Ever yours, CECILIA SHODDY."

Ever yours! Delicious widow!—So, sir, you are a coachman.

Swipes. Yes, sir; Hi'm ha coachman. 'Ave 'ad hexperience hin the haristocratic families hof the Hold World, hand hi flatter myself hi can drive.

Testy. Well, sir; your name.

Swipes. Swipes, sir; Handrew Swipes, son of Hoscar Swipes hand Hanastasia Swipes; birthplace, Hessex, Hingland; hage —

Testy. Never mind your age. You will suit me exactly. I engage you at once. You don't drink?

Swipes. Never; hexcept hon hextraordinary hoccasions, hand then honly hale.

Testy. You'll find your horses in the stable. As soon as possible, have the carriage at the door: I wish to take a ride.

Swipes. Hi'll do hit hat once. (*Exit*, R.)

Testy. An English coachman. That style will suit Mrs. Shoddy. If he is as fond of his horses as he is of superfluous *h*'s, he will do admirably. (*Knock*, L.) Hallo! Who's that? Come in.

Enter TIM, L.

Well, what do you want?

Tim. If yer plaze, sir, yer honor, I have a letther from Mrs. Shoddy.

Testy. Mrs. Shoddy? Let me have it. (*Reads.*) "MY DEAR, DEAR MR. TESTY," — (Two dears this time! Charming widow! She's dearer than ever!) "I have again the power to serve you. The bearer is a worthy and capable servant, who will admirably suit you. Your devoted CECILIA." My devoted Cecilia! Ravishing widow! Young man, your name.

Tim. Tim Regan, if yer plaze, sir, yer honor.

Testy. You are recommended to me as a worthy and capable servant.

Tim. O sir! yer honor, shpare me modesty.

Testy. What are your particular qualifications?

Tim. Which?

Testy. What can you do?

Tim. Ate, dhrink, and slape, sir, yer honor.

Testy. Ah, humorous, I see.

Tim. Not much. I had the masles once, I think, sir, yer honor.

Testy. Pshaw, man! Can you keep a room tidy?

Tim. I can that, jist; or a pig-sty, eather, sir, yer honor.

Testy. That's all I want. I engage you at once.

Tim. Thank yer, sir, yer honor; and the wages?

Testy. Forty dollars a month.

Tim. Forty —

Testy. You will go to work at once. Get a duster, and brush up my room. I shall expect great things of you, you are so highly recommended by Mrs. Shoddy. Go into the next room, take off that coat, put on a linen duster you'll find there, and come back here.

Tim. To be sure I will, sir, your honor. (*Exit*, R.)

Testy. Well, I must say that Mrs. Shoddy has not been particularly nice as to the outward appearance of the individual she has selected to be my body-guard. He looks more like a hod-carrier than a gentleman's valet. But can I doubt her? — my chosen one; the idol of my soul; the bewitching, beautiful, —

Enter JING JIMALONG, L. *He stands grinning at* TESTY, *with the forefinger of each hand pointing up à la Chinese.*

Who in the deuce is that?

Jing. Muchee purty well? Ki I!

Testy. As I live, it's a real live Chinaman. Oh! I see the beautiful hand of the divine Mrs. Shoddy in this.

Jing. Me muchee big cookie, Ki I!

Testy. Ah, indeed! and who sent you here?

Jing. Muchee fine lady; muchee big bunchee on her back; muchee pig-tail round her head; muchee fine eyes; muchee little feet; muchee fine all over, — Ki I!

Testy. Her description exactly. What an intelligent foreigner! I know I shall like him. So you can cook?

Jing. Ki I!

Testy. Well, I don't want any "Ki I's" cooked here; that may do for your country. Can you cook bread?

Jing. Ki I!

Testy. Meat?

Jing. Ki I! Muchee ebery ting.

Testy. Capital, capital. He'll do. What an angel Mrs. Shoddy is! My friend, you wait here a moment, and I'll find somebody to show you to the kitchen. I'll take you into my service. You shall cook me a Chinese dish at once. I'm going to ride, and I'm always hungry when I return. (*Exit*, R.)

Jing. Be jabers! here's a foine sitivation for an Irishman: rigged up like an owld woman, and jabbering like a Tottenhot. It's all the doings av Mr. Fred. "Pat," says he, — "Anan," says I, — "Would yez be afther kapin' yer sitivation that my uncle took from yez," says he. "To be sure I would," says I. "Then come wid me." And thin he took me to his room; and, bedad, this is the consequince. I'm made a Chinaman widout naturalization intirely. "And thin," says he, "Pat, it's little time

I have to tach the language. Say, 'Muchee,' and 'Ki I!' to all the owld gentleman says, and whativer yer own intilligence may bid yez." But, bedad, it's afraid I am av the owld man: if he finds out the desate, I'm a ruined Chinaman intirely. Muchee, Ki I!

Enter TESTY *with* SWIPES, L.

Testy. Swipes, just show this individual into the kitchen.

Swipes. Certainly hi will. Why, hit's a celestial!

Jing. (*aside.*) A which is it? Begorra! what's that he's calling me?

Testy. Yes, it's my new cook. Take him along.

Swipes. Come this way. What ha cook! What can you cook?

Jing. Ki I! Ki!

Swipes. His that hall? What a blarsted country that China must be! (*Exit,* R.)

Jing. Musha, I'm in for it! (*Exit,* R.)

Testy. What a novelty! I've got the start of my neighbors, thanks to dear Mrs. Shoddy. I've no doubt I shall find something nice on my return.

Enter SWIPES, R. *followed by* TIM.

Swipes. The carriage is at the door, sir. (*Exit,* R.)

Testy. All right. Now, Tim, get my coat and hat in the next room.

Tim. All right, sir, yer honor. (*Exit,* L.)

Testy. (*Takes off his dressing-gown.*) I've got a trio of new servants, and they all *look* smart. That last lot thought I couldn't do without them, did they? There's nothing like a change. "New brooms sweep clean."

Enter Tim *with coat and hat.*

Just help me with this coat. (*Puts on hat and coat.*) Now, Tim, have every thing in order on my return. (*Exit*, R.)

Tim. All right, sir, yer honor. Faith, here's a sthrake av luck. Intirely out av a situation, I dropped in to say me cousin, Biddy O'Honey, who lives wid Mrs. Shoddy. Biddy had a bit iv a shindy wid the lady's own man; and, whin Mrs. Shoddy sinds Biddy to fetch him a note for Mr. Testy, Biddy pops it into my hand, and says, "You go, Tim: he'll niver be the wiser if you give it him, and you'll profit by the place. Shure, it's my duty to look after my own frinds furst." So here I am, ingaged on another man's karacther. It's little I know about the work, for hod-carrying's my perfession. Ah, well, the owld gint said, Have every thing in ordher. Faith, I'll do that same. (*Takes a duster, and fiercely brushes table, sending papers flying in all directions, and upsetting the inkstand.*) Oh, murther! I've upset the ink. There's a black stain on my karacther. (*Takes* Mr. Testy's *handkerchief from the pocket of dressing-gown, and wipes up the ink; puts handkerchief back.*) Jist as good as new. (*Picks up papers.*) The ould gint has covered his papers with pot-hooks and scrawls. They're no good, sure. (*Tears up papers.*) Now for the drawers. (*Takes out will.* "Last will and testament." Sure, that's no good. Here's the last of that. (*Tears up will. Takes out coupons.*) Picters for his ould gint's baby. (*Throws them on table.*) I'll finish my dusting. (*Brushes mantle, knocking off the bust and vases.*) Oh, murther! here's a crash among the fine arts. What will I do? (*Knock*, R.) Who's that? Come in wid yer.

Enter JING, R.

Tim. Och, murther! what's that? It's a cannible, or a — or a — vhat is it?

Jing. Faith, I'd jist like to know what a Chinase dish is, ony how, afore I'd cook it. Bedad! I must scrub up my jography, shure. Faix, thim fellers cook rats and mice and puppies! That's it. Where will I find a puppy? (*Sees* TIM.) Och, murther! if that ain't my own brother Tim. What will I do? He'll find me out, and raise a breeze, sure. Och, murther! Why was I born to die a Chinaman? (*Sits on stool, with head bent down.*)

Tim. By my sowl! that's one av them fellers that come from the bottom av the world. It's a Chinaman. Musha, whist! Vhat's your name, I'd loike to know?

Jing. Ki I!

Tim. Faith! now, is it? And where did yez come from?

Jing. Ki I!

Tim. Vhat's that? Is it a Dutchman yez are, or a Roosian, or a Proosian?

Jing. Ki I!

Tim. I belave yez, honey. Poor owld feller: he's deaf, dumb, and blind. Faix! have yez a small tay-chist about yez, for it's my owld woman that's fond av the wade?

Jing. Ki I!

Tim. Git owt av that, ye dirty blackguard! By my sowl, if yez "Ki I" again, I'll thread on the tail av yer hair. Away wid yez!

Jing. (*Aside.*) Begorra! I'd loike to punch his head for him, the thaif. (*Aloud.*) Ki I! Ki I! (*Exit*, R.)

Tim. By me sowl! that owld chap looks enough like me brither Pat to be his own cousin! Chinaman, is it! Begorra! it's sorry manners he has, onyhow. (*Knock*, L.)

Enter FRED, L., *disguised as an image-vender, with a basket containing images, vases, &c.*

Fred. Imagees! Imagees!

Tim. What's that? Imgees!

Fred. You buy my imagees? Ver sheep; ver sheep.

Tim. Faith, it's not a sheep I want, at all, at all. Have yer a bust of St. Patrick or O'Connell, sure?

Fred. No, no! Ze leetle Nap. See! (*Showing bust of Napoleon.*)

Tim. Faith, it's all the same. How much?

Fred. You buy, eh? Tree dollar: ver sheep.

Tim. Sheep, is it? Three dollars! Faith, it's deer. No, I've niver a cint.

Fred. No moneys! den you no buy.

Tim. Hold on, Parleyvoo! I'll trade wid yer. Begorra! I'll sind off some uv the owld gint's books. He'll niver rade thim all. (*Takes down a book.*) "Paradise Lost." Lost, is it? Faith, it's found once more, thin. Whist! Sh—! This for the little Nap—hey?

Fred. (*Aside.*) My uncle's much-prized Bunyan.

Tim. It's something about bunions. I'm something av a corn-doctor, and I know it's good. Is it a trade?

Fred. For ze leetle Nap? Yes. (*They exchange.*)

Tim. Now for the vases. What will I do fur thim?

Fred. Here's de vases. Ver rich. Two dollar. Ver sheep, ver sheep.

Tim. Will you have some more larnin', Parleyvoo?

Fred. (*Takes up the coupon bonds.*) Sharming picturs! Ver fine!

Tim. Oh! you like them, do you? Faith, give me the vases, and they are yours.

Fred. For ze vases? Too sheep, too sheep. Ver well: you have ze vases. (*They exchange.*) (*Aside.*) Ten thousand dollars! My poor uncle!

Testy. (*Outside,* R.) Oh, murder! Murder! Tim! Tim!

Tim. The owld gint. Begorra, here's a row! Cooming, cooming, sir, yer honor. (*Exit,* R.)

Fred. My uncle! I'll slip away. His new broom has made a clean sweep here. Wonder how he will like it. (*Exit,* L.)

Enter TESTY, R., *his clothes muddy, his hat knocked over his eyes, supported by* TIM.

Testy. O Tim, Tim! That coachman, — he's murdered me!

Tim. And left you spacheless, the dirty blackguard!

Testy. Upset me in front of Mrs. Shoddy's house. Bring me my dressing-gown. (*Puts it on.*) Here's a pretty situation. (*Takes out handkerchief, wipes his face, leaving ink-stains upon it.*) Why, what's this, Tim? (*Looks around room.*) What have you been doing, you villain? My bust ruined! My papers destroyed! Open drawers! The will gone, — and my coupons — (*seizing* TIM). You scoundrel, what have you done with my coupons?

Tim. If you plaze, sir, yer honor, I've been claning up a bit.

Testy. Cleaning up! Cleaning out, you mean. Where's my money?

Tim. Money, is it? How should I know?

Enter SWIPES, R.

Testy. O you villain! back again, are you? You've been drinking.

Swipes. Honly ha little hale.

Testy. Didn't you tell me you didn't drink?

Swipes. Honly hon hextraordinary occasions. This was one, when hi got ha new place. Hi took ha little hale.

Testy. Which upset me as well as you. I'll make another hextraordinary hoccasion for you. Go! I discharge you.

Swipes. Go, without warning? This his han hinsult.

Testy. I give you warning, that, if you are found in this house in five minutes, I'll give you to the police.

Swipes. Hi won't go without my pay. Hit's haudacious! (*Takes off his coat.*)

Tim. True for you, honey: stick to that.

Testy. And you, Tim: I'll hand you over to the police at once. You've robbed me.

Tim. Rob, is it? Begorra! there's an insult to an Irish gintleman. (*Takes off his coat.*)

Testy. What are you about?

Tim. About to have satisfaction, you owld blackguard!

Testy. Come, come; none of this. I'll hand you both over to the police.

Swipes. (*Threateningly.*) Pay hup, hor hover you go!

Tim. (*Shaking his fist.*) Robber, is it?

Testy. Do you dare threaten? (SWIPES *and* TIM *seize* TESTY *and shake him.*) Here! Help! Help!

Enter FRED, R., JACOB, L.

Fred. Hallo, uncle! what's the matter?

Testy. Fred, you are just in time. In a moment I should have fallen a victim to the violence of a drunkard and of a robber.

Fred. Why, these are two of your new servants.

Testy. No, they're not. They're both discharged. One has robbed me, and I want the police. Robbed of ten thousand dollars!

Fred. Which I can restore. Here are your coupons, uncle, safe and sound. I think they have depreciated in value, as Tim gave them to me for a pair of vases.

Tim. Sir, yer honor, I niver set eyes on him bafore.

Fred. Oh, yes, you did! Imagees?

Tim. Begorra! it's the Parleyvoo.

Testy. I've had a narrow escape. Thanks to you, Fred. Jacob, you'll resume your old situation at once; that is, if you have not found a new one.

Jacob. No, sir. I went to see Mrs. Shoddy to ask for a place, but she was in trouble.

Testy. In trouble?

Jacob. Yes. It seems, about a year ago, she ran away from her husband, taking all his money. He's found her out, and this very day arrived to take her home again.

Testy. Her husband? A widow with a husband! Oh, horror! my hair is turning white.

Jacob. I told you, sir, that dye wouldn't stick.

Testy. Fred, I think you'd better come and live with me. I don't believe I shall ever marry. I'm getting too old.

Fred. (*Aside.*) "A hungry fox is passing by." — (*Aloud.*) Thank you, sir; I'll come with pleasure. But what about these new servants? (*A dog heard yelping outside,* L. *Then a crash of crockery.* JING *runs in,* R.)

Jing. Och! murther, murther, murther! It's kilt I am, intirely. (*Shakes his fist off,* L.) Yez murthering thaif av the worrld. Git out av that! Away wid yez!

Testy. What is the meaning of this? It's my new Chinese servant, Fred.

Fred. With a brogue like a wild Irishman.

Testy. You impostor! What does this mean? Speak, quick.

Jing. (*Aside.*) Oh, murther! I've let the cat out av the bag! (*Aloud.*) Ki I! Muchee Ki I!

Testy. That won't do. What is the meaning of that "Ki I" ing down stairs?

Jing. (*Aside.*) Vhat shall I say? (*Aloud.*) Me try cookee bow-wow; bow-wow no likee cookee him. Bow-wow muchee Ki I! me muchee Ki I, too, — bow-wow muchee run into closet: muchee crockery, — bang, — bang, — bang, — muchee pieces, all breakee. Muchee, — muchee, — muchee, — and be jabers! that's what's the matter intirely, or my name's not Pat Regan;

and bother yez blasted Chinese, for it's nearly broke my jaw.

Tim. Pat Regan! be my sowl! I recognize the vice of affection in my bones. (*Seizes* JING'S *pigtail, and pulls off skull-cap.*) It's himsilf intirely. O Pat, Pat! how could yez? Is it yerself that's disgracing owld Ireland by going over to China? Begorra! ye's sowld yer birthright for a mess of broken china. Be my sowl, I'm pale wid blushing for yez.

Jing. Aisy wid yer blarney, Tim, or it's a batin' ye'll git.

Testy. Patrick Regan.

Jing. Sir.

Testy. What is the meaning of this masquerade? Didn't I discharge you this morning?

Fred. Let me speak for him, uncle. I alone am to blame; for I dressed him in the costume, and instructed him in the language of a Chinaman.

Testy. You did, you scamp! and what for, pray?

Fred. To assist you in your endeavors to procure "new brooms," and also to outwit Mrs. Shoddy.

Testy. Well, if that is a specimen of your proficiency in the Chinese language, the sooner you are sent as ambassador to the Celestials the better.

Fred. Uncle, let Pat have his old place: you can't do better. He wont contradict you again, — will you, Pat?

Jing. Faith! Not muchee.

Testy. Shut up! Don't let me hear any of that lingo, or out of this house you'll go: for the present, you may take your old place.

Fred. And what's to be done with the other servants?

Tim. Begorra! that's what I'd like to know.

Swipes. You've crushed my 'opes, hand hi want my money.

Testy. Pay them, and send them off. I'll take back the old ones; for I am convinced, from my unhappy experience of the last half-hour, that, despite the old proverb, *new brooms do not always sweep clean.*

Disposition of Characters.

R., Pat. Fred. Testy. Swipes. Tim. L.,

www.ingramcontent.com/pod-product-compliance
Lightning Source LLC
Chambersburg PA
CBHW020859020726
47497CB00005B/1480

* 9 7 8 3 7 4 4 7 6 8 8 0 1 *